C5

THE MINISTERS

THE MINISTERS

By
Fionn MacColla

SOUVENIR PRESS

First published 1979 by Souvenir Press
(Educational & Academic) Ltd,
43 Great Russell Street, London WC1B 3PA
and simultaneously in Canada

*The publisher acknowledges the
financial assistance of The Scottish Arts Council in the production
of this volume*

ISBN 0 285 62384 2 casebound
ISBN 0 285 62396 6 paperback

Filmset in 'Monophoto' Baskerville 11 on 12½ pt. by
Richard Clay (The Chaucer Press), Ltd, Bungay, Suffolk
and printed in Great Britain by
Fletcher & Son Ltd, Norwich

EDITORIAL NOTE

When Fionn MacColla died in 1975, he had published only two novels. THE ALBANNACH and AND THE COCK CREW. Yet he left three unpublished manuscripts, which one publisher after another had rejected.

THE MINISTERS is the second of these. In editing the manuscript in accordance with the clear instructions of the author just before he died, we are especially grateful for the help and advice of Mr. James B. Caird and Mr John Herdman.

M. MacD
R. McQ
Edinburgh 1977

PART I

I

The sidereal universe: existent, in energy: this moment of time. The planetary order: in motion: the earth tilting over. The northern hemisphere: Europe facing sunwards: the British islands. To their west, at the ocean's edge, the north-west coast of Scotland, rockful, splashed and sun-splintered standing over the waters of the Minch.

He is a consciousness at a window there, in this evasive moment, looking on those fickle waters which choose now to be still, with an effect of brimming-up all over their glassy, sunlit surface. Looking at the shell-white road bursting on the left from behind the house into visibility and sweeping forward over the everywhere dark-brown moor: only to check in front above the cliffs, twist almost right-about and beginning to go steeply downwards run from sight.

Dark brown, bright in the sun at this moment, all the moors and heath-topped rocky islets scattered near the shore in the brimming water. But at certain places here and there in the brown moor away on the left patches of whin were beginning to blaze out yellow and golden where they blazed out yellow and golden every year and he thought it would be possible to smell now the dry, astringent odour that would be carried down the air. And here and there might be detected in more sheltered places, were at any rate known and felt now to exist, dark clumps of green, dwarf, contorted juniper and holly. And everywhere in the open, immense spaces before his eyes, so free and fresh, are scattered bright rocks, thrown down all over, and in the water, perhaps with too prodigal, lavish a hand, but undeniably *with a gesture*. From that gesture no doubt it was that the inhabitants had an *air*; some at least, even in modern countervailing circumstances, yes, even here in this district and even yet: every now and then one would see such a one, bearing about him or her that instantly recognised, authentic air, born unmistakably from the proud, nonchalant and lavish, free and dexterous throwing down of the elements of the landscape, the pique and dash of its arrangement. Yes, even in the modern time . . .

Time is his meditation. The sunlight pouring through the window turns the cuffs of his black jacket sharply silver. Inside the good-quality, well-made clothes he is himself, his body clean-washed and softly glowing, making the air all warm between it and the fabric, to which in every heart-beat it constantly gives up its own warmth, and receives it—seeming warmer—back. The sunlight pours its heat over his hands lightly locked together in front of his breast; even as he looks tiny pinheads of perspiration here and there come through the skin. The sunlight seems a dreamily timeless weight and leaning upon it he can at will and freely in his mind move about through time—though only time past, not what's yet unspun.

Time passing over all ways of life in their several moments is like a revolving beam of light calling each into vision in every solid detail and in the very aspect of permanency—but all the while imperceptibly passing, passing on, so that before its movement can be realised this or the other world-proud, world-conscious culture has already passed backwards into darkness and forgotten-ness: and what in strict accuracy for whole generations of men "could not be thought of" has in fact come about: a way of life, which means a kind of *man* with unique hue of consciousness, never-to-be-repeated potentialities, is gone. And amid that universal unceasing passing-away all individual lives fall unceasingly to oblivion like raindrops endlessly extinguished in a pool.

And my particular raindrop too. *I* shall not escape. Strange that the most necessary, the most urgent, the most salutary thought that could come home to anyone should be regarded as a triteness, as a reflection indicating a sentimental softness, and that anyone who evinces such a reflection should be regarded as a sanctimonious humbug or moraliser.

It is the only certainty in life and therefore the most requiring to be heeded. Not the *idea* that all men are mortal, even the greatest, "the sceptre, learning, physic, must", and so forth. What is necessary to give an absolutely central, fixed point of view is the coming home as it were to every single bodily cell of the realisation that it is mortal, must die and corrupt and disappear, and that soon. And that this solid scene on which I now look, those moors and rocks, and the expanse of water, the deep, sweeping sky ever changing with its movement of clouds will inevitably soon, and—who knows?—perhaps at any minute now, be there in its solidity and reality only for those who are alive after I am gone. I myself will have passed, and for ever, down and out of the whole solid and real thing. This physical eye, which I can now feel moving in its socket, and with which I now observe this solid and real scene, will have become nothing, the socket but an ante-cavity to the vacant chamber which at this moment houses the "I" who feelingly observes all and ponders now upon itself. It is not that the idea of mortality is to be held before the mind; that is not incompatible with a pleasant feeling or unexplicit conviction that one is personally exempt from the fell law of death, as if it were not "I" but "humanity" or "Caesar" who is mortal. No, it is not the idea in the mind of mortality, but the truth of death smiting home in the vital inwardness of consciousness—it is not Caesar who is mortal but I who think on him—it is this which is necessary, and salutary, and imposes on all things the need to show themselves forth divested of everything but their true importance. There would be an end here of short-term views and self-regarding values.

Everyone ought to pause not once but twice or thrice in the course of every day and pose himself at the centre of his own sense of the motion of time, allowing the beam of inward perception to sweep back through the ages, whose solidity after all was composed of nothing either more or less flimsy than this present flickering moment, a rapid conspective view of way of life after way of life, city after city built up with infinite striving and labour, as it were sculptured out of the gross and inert material of life by the mind, the spirit, the consciousness of the mass of persons concerned, and which for a time seemed a structure in which that spirit, that mind might take up permanent habitation, but which none the less passed away along with the mind that had been unable to think such an event. It was now all the same out of the active world, and perhaps even out of the memory let alone the partial apprehension of a later mind. This to be thrown against the notion of the immensity of the stellar space in the midst of whose own energy and continual motion immersed in its own kind of time everything took place—and will take place. Follow with reflections on personal mortality, the shortness of life, the inevitability of death, for instance the metaphor of raindrops falling in the stream—in fact "I" am not even the raindrop or anything so real. The raindrop is the creative will of God active in my regard: "I" am nothing but the momentary disturbance in the stream gone almost sooner than it has time to pit the surface. Finish with an act of the imminence of death present in all one's members. Then go forth with rectified moral vision, fit to judge wisely of human affairs, equipped with a sense of measure penetrating down to the very minutiae of diurnal trivia.

Without such a wide, conspective vision, without the power to reconstruct the fragments of past ages solidly and livingly in the imagination, what basis is there for judgment of the present case? It is knowledge of the past plus that reconstructive imagination that steadies the judgment. But now the world is full of those who have none of the knowledge, for whom all time prior to the day beyond yesterday is shrouded in a dense mistiness, impenetrable except that here and there in its depths loom a few distorted forms of past events—and a good few looming shapes that never were events at all but myths, which serve many in place of events for they look as solid as anything else in the general gloom of impenetrable ignorance. Equally, merely factual knowledge, dry-as-dust, statistical, without the imagination, is of little worth for judgment forming, for it is without life and therefore reality, relevance, significance for *us*. Perhaps worst of all is imagination without knowledge, imagination to picture solidly, as if it had been real, a false version of the past, thence to derive sanction for lines of action that can only carry the interior judgment that accompanies unrealism in action.

2

Beyond the sweeping foreground of these ideas, bodily figures outside the window had for a little time been moving; he had been too idle to move his eyes to focus on them. Some time before a grey bulk had appeared in the part of the garden just below and had been moving about with a creeping motion since. He did not need to lower his eyes: he recognised the shape, colour and characteristic movements of the only man who was likely, or had any business, to be there. Old Bando, gardener and handyman in general. Little, spry Bando, whom one never saw without simultaneously a little bubbling of amusement, a little trickle of nervous irritation, and a little haunting of apprehension. Pottering down there, encased in a sense of proprietorship of the whole material surrounding neighbourhood, a stranger all his life to self-questioning or any form of backward-turning thought. Satisfied with himself once and for all and never questioning his rôle, which he conceived as general moral overseer and censor, local estimator-in-chief of capacities and adequacy of performance, and, when occasion arose and with the utmost readiness, theological oracle. It was the superb disproportion of this assurance, among other things, that made one smile faintly, while at the same time the massive, immovable concrete of that same assurance commanded a certain respect—which he had locally—and his utter lack of prudence or reticence in speech and his loud pertinacity and senseless aggressiveness and want of tact in following up anything he conceived to be a "scent"—his implicit invitation of all within hearing to join in the chase—rendered him formidable even to the most innocent and accounted for the faint apprehension his appearance occasioned and the general tendency to respect and placate him. If one's first reaction on coming in company with Bando was a slightly amused, patronising smile at his mobile, monkey-like face, this was followed very soon by a sudden return to sobriety and a quick enquiring glance mingled with apprehension. Even if one had the best conscience in the world that faint apprehension would be there, the feeling that one never knew what might in the end be dragged into the public gaze, if once one were unlucky enough to attract his noticing eye.

No one was immune, he reflected. Not even oneself, his employer and as it were superior. It was clear Bando regarded himself as of the two the more secure, permanent and fixed in his position, and that even where the spiritual functions and as it were magistracy were concerned—if the notion were permissible to-day—his, Bando's, was the supervisionary office and intelligence. Indeed, the impression came not infrequently that one's performance gave doubtful satisfaction, falling far below others' in unspecified respects. He had a certain eloquently suggestive way of enunciatiating, "Your predecessor, Mr Matheson"—here he would smack his lips with unction and conviction, and gazing into the distance, continue in Gaelic—"*a man of God!*"

He smiled a little, his eyes the while resting on his hands still with entwined fingers clasped lightly in front of his breast, noting absently how the silver cuffs seemed to be extending farther up the sleeves of his black jacket, as if he must have moved forward or the sun have moved somewhat down the sky. Chiefly what had made him smile was the recollection of the mistake he always made in a matter of Bando's appearance. He always in thinking of him apportioned him a beard. Even when speaking to him, looking at him, he often had the impression that he had a beard. A short, square chin-beard, iron-grey, which jerked up and down, jutting out, and wagged continuously with great emphasis—and the utmost effect of moral censure. The little warrior Bando lacked that small touch of art to complete the correspondence of his outward man with his active nature; to express especially his pertinacity and quickness on the "scent". Even at this moment, still without looking at him, one was aware of him down below in the garden there straightening up every now and then to glance about for anything that might be stirring. That was his way: the moment anyone came in sight to aim a stream of screaming talk at him, whether he was within earshot or not; then, without interrupting the scream, to advance across country. But even when standing beside you his talk was a deafening stream. Nor was it any use to attempt to draw away, for in that case he simply came forward, left foot after right foot, after you. Holding you with his eye, which never yielded contact.

Yes . . . and that eye. What you eventually noticed was that his eyes, under their shaggy, overhanging, dirty-white brows, held no expression at all, except alertness—simple bright alertness. That unvaryingly. Similarly his face, though of a twitching mobility, was an expressionless mask.

He smiled, standing inside the window that looked on the bright brown moors and, beyond, blue spaces of sea and sky: indeed laughed inwardly. That monkey-like mobility of Bando's visage was in great part an effect produced by his tobacco-chewing. He was in the habit of shooting incessantly streams of mingled tobacco juice and saliva at the ground as he worked, or, more correctly, pottered about; and with an even greater rapidity and vigour when in talk and excited—

which was his invariable condition when in talk. There was a constant apprehension lest he get his impulses confused and send a yellow stream of liquid in one's direction in place of a stream of screaming speech, and when talking to him one endeavoured to be mentally prepared for what was possibly coming.

He raised his eyes to the immense sky and looking at it was aware that two other figures had appeared away in front, and under his line of vision were approaching, slowly, along the white road. After a slight struggle in him between the opposed pull of contemplation and curiosity, or rather mere irritation of the optic nerve, he abandoned a high moral position, lowered his eyes, and there saw two stout figures of middle-aged-looking women walking on the road. Planting their feet very deliberately and firmly while advancing with great slowness and a sort of pacing dignity. The reason for their quasi-liturgical gait and dignity was at once obvious, it was that they were deep—but *deep*—in conversation together. He recognised the one on the near side of the road by her motion and outline: his housekeeper, Bando's sole daughter, Mina Bhando as they called her; the other who was about the same middle height and much more than middle bulk he did not recognise as yet, though from the direction in which she was facing she ought to be a woman from the township of Aird, on the borders of the parish. But the walk was utterly characteristic, that slow, hesitant, pacing walk. They were *drunk* in gossip. Even as the recognition moved in him they had halted altogether, and now stood turned, almost facing each other. He could see now that each was holding what must be a grocery bag or basket in front of her with both hands, and there they stood like a pair of stout, elderly, female praying mantises, their heads nodding slowly. He could imagine their voices—their topic, more likely than not, the moral state of the population. Now they resumed their pacing, stepping, unconscious advance down the middle of the white road. Mina Bhando's expression, from long familiarity, he could *see*. The concentration of all her thinking soul in her eyes—those eyes that were wont to rummage furiously among your clothes the while she was speaking to you, feeling the stuff of them, searching for any brand tags or marks denoting quality. (People walked away from her unconsciously adjusting their clothes about them as if they had been physically and not only morally rummaged and disarranged.) She and her old Daddy, Bando, were both given to stepping well back from you in the midst of a conversation and, while continuing it, examining your lower parts in a thorough and business-like fashion. Or they might let the conversation lapse on their falling into a speculative trance or abstraction and resume it when they had at their leisure concluded their discourse with themselves—head speculatively aside—anent your trousers or boots. He could at this minute see Mina Bhando's expression, therefore, hear her low-set voice, though she was far out of earshot and her face shadowed by the sun which was over her head and slightly behind her.

The two figures were getting slowly bulkier, stepping as if in slow hypnotic dance, leaning somewhat with an intermittent turning towards each other and formal bowing or slow nodding of the head. He almost thought that in spite of the distance and the shadow over her face he could make out Mina Bhando's teeth. If that was so she was in what he had come to know as the latter stage of her intoxication and highest degree of her inspiration. In the earliest stage, in the moment when her interest was first caught and curiosity first aroused, her eyes seemed to come forward and protrude themselves and she drew her upper lip down till it covered her teeth. But only just, and with a stretch. She possessed a double set of regular but particularly large and yellowish teeth—all her own. Ordinarily her lips covered them, or at any rate almost covered them; at best you were always conscious of a formidably bulky something filling her mouth. But when she was "at gaze", having seen "something", her more intense degree of excitement showed when her eyes narrowed every moment in their increasingly intent and steady fixation while her head was drawn back in a series of small, intense jerks, in time with which the lips were drawn back from the teeth: until during the orgasm—yes, the satisfaction of her curiosity was with her a sort of sensual orgasm—when interest and curiosity completely satisfied and fulfilled themselves, her teeth were all formidably exposed, back to the pale gums under which the whitish shapes of their large roots could be detected bulging. At such moments she might be said to "look" with her teeth, with her full endowment or complement, her eyes having become almost invisible points in her back-drawn head. She was rigid then and, one felt, very little if at all conscious of anything in the world except her "object".

Her high, thinnish, slightly hooked nose was raised at such moments, immobile. That nose which always gave the impression of being slightly obstructed, so that her contralto voice was pronouncedly nasal—unlike Bando's high, clear, screaming falsetto. Mina's nasal alto could on occasion resound, none the less.

The two stout, stepping women in their slow promenade, their measured walk like some pavane or other antique, stately, formal dance that brought them along the white road in the sun, reached the point where the wall across the west side of the garden, built against gales, gave place to the fence running right past the front of the house. Thus they were now visible to Bando and almost immediately a falsetto scream announced that he had caught sight of them walking along beyond the fence wires running all shining and new between their whitish concrete posts. He had been walking towards the back of the garden, his jacket thrown with a jaunty air over his shoulder. He had a little bit of a croft near by—part-payment for his job of handyman—and whenever prompted by inclination he would leave what he was doing, which consisted for the most part of a sort of impeccable pottering with an utterly indispensable air, and go off, over the steps he had had constructed for his convenience in the back garden-wall. This time he had caught sight of the two women before he reached it and with a scream of recognition turned and cut diagonally across the garden towards them, under such a head of steam that his jacket fell from his shoulder and he either did not notice or felt he had not time to pick it up, so continued in the sleeves of his grey, red-striped flannel shirt which were rolled up above wrinkled sexagenarian elbows. The housekeeper Mina stopped and wheeled at the edge of the road; the unknown of equal bulk swung round over the extra distance in mincing steps and drew up at her right hand again. And there was the little man facing the two larger, stouter women, stretching his neck, his chest even, up towards them over the top strand of the fence. There was a rapid moment when words flew like pebbles from all three and seemed to collide in the air all about them. For a moment Mina Bhando appeared to be holding the subject with her teeth while the other two worried it. The unknown woman seemed to be fit and mettlesome at any rate for she kept moving her feet and her bulky body was borne up with ease on their small elastic steps. The three voices were quite audible, Bando's high up, the housekeeper's low, the unknown woman's between the two, although he could make out no words.

To other ears also something had been audible. There in the garden, right below the window, standing at gaze, "pointing" towards the group by the fence, drawn forth by the sound of voices . . . Peigi Snoovie, the maid, aged 15: now crossing towards the group as if irresistibly, drawn without her own volition, her spindle arms already crossed before her thin and narrow bosom in right gossip-maker's posture, not even noticing where she was putting her long, pointed feet. In the business of observing, noting and reporting, to say nothing of embroidering, Peigi Snoovie was the housekeeper's capable understudy, lieutenant, and . . . but why beat about the bush? Precocious and unnatural though it might seem, this young female was Mina Bhando's superior in the art, had her beaten hollow—like an arrow from a bow where the older woman was only a hound from the leash in pursuit of every particle of gossip. Now she was up beside the group, joining in, the tallest of the four on her thin as knitting-needle legs, standing at Bando's side with a forefinger hooking a detached strand of her limp, greasy-looking black hair away from her mouth, completing the group of busy figures underlined by the white road running straight along the edge of the spreading bright brown moors, rock-spattered. His feeling of discomfort became conscious and he realised it was what he always experienced on seeing, or thinking of, that hair of Peigi Snoovie's . . . Although, of course, one could not be sure. And of course one could not *say* anything . . . or even hint. One had to be so careful . . .

so careful. (He smiled inwardly at the recollection of the man over at Aird about the time he first came to the district who had *tiptoed* round the corner of his house to point out to him the house he was looking for—half a mile away!—speaking in a whisper and pointing from the hip!) There was the group, the two stout, the thin-tall and the thin-small, as he knew them, thus engaged in the face of the immense sky, the wide, smiling sea, the air of the bright landscape; in face of the infinity of stellar space, of those aeons of the past—which, one wondered, derived significance from which? The conversation was going on, with dramatic nods, with animation. Peigi Snoovie put up her skeletal arm above her head—still talking—and (he felt he could see it) agitated her long middle finger among her hair.

3

He turned away into the room. His back now to the window. The temperature changing on his hands now they were out of the sun made him conscious of them; he thrust them into his trousers and, raising himself and letting himself down on his heels, looked about this way and that. White book-shelves, breast high, occupied the whole wall on his left as he stood now, the north wall, and also the length of the inner wall opposite him, as far as the door; and the bright splashes of the book backs in many different shades of red and blue and green and yellow were the only colours in the room to break the uniform wash of cream-pale walls, except the dark green of the long hanging window curtains almost touching each shoulder as he stood now; and also on either side of the other window, in the south or front wall, over on his right. Elsewhere all was without colour and blank, no object whatever breaking the pale spaces. He would have had it so, the clean austere. Every object hung on the walls detracts from the significance of all the rest, and diminishes its own. Therefore have them bare, clean, bringing a sense of space, imparting sweep to the mind by the exclusion of thought-breaking detail. Or reserve their space for one single object so precious, so significant, that it might be worthy to draw to itself the indicative force of their total bareness. Some object of so deep and wide symbolic relevance that its presence would raise and elevate no matter what train of thought and could never be out of relation with any . . .

He went across the room to the door in the wall opposite. First he touched it gently, tentatively, as if to make certain it was really closed, then, again very gently, pressed on it with the forefinger of his left hand while with his right he softly, noiselessly, turned the key in the lock. Something slightly surreptitious had crept into his movements—and was more marked when he crossed the room again for another glance through the west window. The group out there had broken up the instant before. Only Mina Bhando, the housekeeper, was coming in a brisk walk along the road approaching the house, without doubt some domestic task in mind to be instantly set about. The unknown woman was floating above her feet whose elastic steps seemed to indicate a disposition soon to move away, but she was still there submitting to have her ideas energetically dusted by the imaginary short beard on Bando's athletic chin. Peigi Snoovie had just left them and was stepping across the garden towards the house, her pale face under the lank hair blank in expression, her arms folded high on her problematical bosom in the attitude of a veteran returning from the conversational wars.

He had only just glanced out, as if to see what the position was. Now with an air of even greater secrecy he went across to the large flat-topped desk which stood in the middle of the floor and sat down behind it, facing the south window, through which, far in the blue, certain rather opulent-looking clouds that had formed seemed to be wallowing majestically, borne up in an infinite pillow of sun-warmed air. His back to the mind-constricting or concentrating bookshelf shapes with the audacious colour conjunctions of their backs and wrappers, his face entirely towards the suggestion of depth and light. Not surprising that his colleague, old Mr Norman Maclennan of Drum, on the only occasion when he was in the room, after looking all round said, "You have a leaning towards the austere, I see." Although that sort of austerity might easily be a subtle form of sensuality—the freeing oneself from everything complicating and burdensome; a refined sensual indulgence, with no merit of abnegation in it. One cannot judge by external appearance. Look at Tolstoy whose "austere" peasant garments were of the very softest and freest at a time when the garments of the pampered and indulgent were at a height of constraint and discomfort. His action therefore could have been a device—an immensely credit-earning device—for *escaping* discomfort, for indulging himself.

But he was not to expand in any more of his contemplations just at present. Something was obviously making him feel expectant, as he sat in the midst of the room looking round. Not without another furtive-seeming glance towards the door—and even up towards the windows, although nothing could look in on him there save the slow, fleecy, elongated clouds—he extracted a small key from a little pocket of his black waistcoat and turned it in the lock of the wide shallow drawer right in front of him and just under the lip of the desk-top. He drew this wide towards him with both hands, and with both hands lifted out a broad, album-like flat book that was lying in it and placed it on the desk. Pushing the drawer back in he drew his chair slightly forward. Then—with just another half-glance at door and window, and almost seeming to betray some eagerness now—he drew the flat album-like book towards him till its lower edge rested across his black-clad thighs. There was a flicker of colour as he opened it at random; and immediately he had stilled, looking at what he saw therein.

The silence grew, till there was a hint of presence. But he sat in it . . . he might have been anywhere. Every now and then a broad page turned, seeming to flash between his black clothes and the whitish light, but scarcely a flicker disturbed the stillness in his features on which a light seemed to be reflected up from the looked-at page.

But this contemplative stillness was ruffled by some change within. The eyes with an effect of loudness rose over the broad pages' top and became fixed on distance, filled with an expression both passive and intense; he seemed to be both present and far away, gave the impression of being drawn away and held rather than, as in the matter of the album, following some impulse of his own will. Once or twice as if pulling himself away he brought his eyes down again to the page, but the next minute they had moved upwards again and become fixed as on some non-spatial category of distance, where they rested finally, and their depths filled with a light both sombre and radiant. This light spread from his eyes, till his features became smooth-set and luminous. His breathing changed . . .

After a moment to consolidate occupation and re-establish control and contact he turned his head to the left and looked fixedly straight at the keyhole, which was right in line with the desk where he sat, in the middle of the floor. Then he looked round the room again, over his shoulder where the books stood in their ranks. Finally he closed the broad flat album and laid it on the desk, drew the top drawer towards him, and having deposited the book in the bottom of it slid it shut. Locked it and got to his feet slipping the little key back again into his lower waistcoat pocket.

His movements in the bathroom were still slightly habitual, the face that emerged from the towel smoothed by abstraction, the eyes looking at but not seeming particularly to distinguish the knuckles of the hands that twisted agitatedly in the towel, that flicked it aside. In the bedroom in the mirror he looked not at himself but—his arms over his head, frowning and concentrating—at his hair, his brown, short hair which he brushed vigorously with brusque movements, as if he might have had a distaste for it. Only when he had put down the brushes did he deliberately look at himself: the face looking back at him was a pleasant, fresh, young-looking, clean-shaven example of the "five-pointed" type. The jaws square, with accentuated cheek-muscles, coming forward to the point of the chin. The complexion, wholesome and clean as if made pure by constant washings with warm soft rain, was cream- rather than milk-white, the faint colour in the cheeks fainter under a light coating of sunburn. The eyes, grey, giving an impression of steadiness rather than force, looked at this face with neither favour nor disfavour, not as if in any way concerned with it, but with a sort of firm, impersonal attentiveness, as it were simply noting it. And the black-clad breast and shoulders, and the round, glossy-white collar under the pointed chin.

He fastened the black jacket, pulling it down all round, making his trim, middle-sized figure still trimmer, then went out and down the stairs with a cantering briskness; to the front door, facing south again. He closed the inner door behind him—it could not be done quietly, especially when there was wind—the inner door with its silvery opaque design all over its large glass panel, and as he turned in the small porch some hesitation seemed to come over him again. Standing on the red-brown tiles with their designs in off-yellow, in the small porch now partially filled and lit up by the sun's transverse beams, whose warmth he could feel especially in his eyes though he had not yet approached it, he was hesitant again . . . if indeed there was not something slightly furtive in his air and movements. The two half-doors facing him were opened back, the one on the right green-dark, the other pale and bright in the sun, showing its surface here and there the worse for weather. The silence was almost a hum: as if one had stolen up when the warm, golden light was splashing down all over the world.

Forward he stepped, plunging, all of him, into the sun sweeping the front door-stone. Standing there, eyes contracted in the light, he looked this way and that again . . . one would almost have said as if seeking a way of escape in this bright landscape without a single human being in sight within its glorious sweep from which stirred and rose as always an aromatic freshness. At length he stepped back into the porch, passed a dark grey hat from the row of hooks on to his head, but at the same time was manifestly giving more of his mind to a tentative, questioning patting of his right-hand jacket pocket. Therewith he stepped with decision straight forward and immediately from his feet rose a cascading and splashing of gravel. He turned left along the front of the house with unavoidably loud, deliberate-looking, splurging steps in the gravel and turning the corner took half a dozen loosened strides across the grass and disappeared in the deep shade of bushes and a blue-looking fir tree. To reappear an instant later going up the slight grassy slope towards the stone box of the grey rectangular church, and passing along its side under one, two, three plain glass windows with the white lines of their moulding breaking the pale grey sweep of the glass. When he reached the end he put his right hand into his jacket pocket and drew out the key whose presence he had ascertained by that questioning pat, and slipping it into the green door of a small, still more box-like structure with its own slated roof, leaning against the gable of the church, opened it and going in closed it after him.

4

Peigi Snoovie in a pale blue apron at once left the bushes and spindle-legged it back over the grass to the back door, her small mouth drawn in almost to invisibility, her large, long hands drooping from her wrists which were slightly raised in front of her in a characteristic posture and moving slightly in time to her steps.

In the kitchen she was short-breathed. "He's inside the church."

Mina Bhando, more solid and formidable-looking at close range than out on the highroad, was standing in her kitchen holding up a white dish in her left hand while she polished it with her right with a blue-and-white checked dishcloth. She put both down promptly in front of her on the table, the white dish and blue-and-white cloth together on the table cover of large dark-red and buff checks. Her own narrow apron was bright yellow from her neck all down the front of her brown dress of serviceable, hard-wearing material and was tightly stretched where the tapes were tied at the decidely though not yet emphatically bulging waist.

At the first word her eyes had sprung wide and her lips come together in a thin line over her bulky teeth. Now her head went back, chin in, with a jerk that narrowed her eyes to concentrated dots fixed speculatively on nothing. The light in here coming from east and north windows was uniformly clear and grey, the bunch of spoons and knives lying farther along the table gleamed with a dull, even metallicity, as except for a few small bright points of light did the taps above the white sinks under the north window, and the polished edgings of the range fireplace behind her back. Her narrowed eyes continued fixed on nothing with a venomous speculation. The edges of her bulky teeth were beginning to appear. Peigi Snoovie in her pale blue apron stood just inside the door, as the recoil had left her when she discharged her explosion. Her pale small face was somewhat pinched-looking between the lank black hair hanging to below her ears, a face that for its size seemed high above the ground. It was hunger and suffering that filled the grey and suppliant eyes fixed on the stout housekeeper, the while she moved the first two long fingers of her bony right hand up and down on the breast of her pale blue apron as if twanging some sort of guitar in her large expectancy in the grey, even light.

"What would he be wanting in the church on a Monday?" she ventured in a twittering voice, more than anything to nudge the situation along, since Mina remained immersed in her contemplations.

"*Umm*," emitted the housekeeper through her high, thin nose, and looked at the maid. And in the look some idea passed from one to the other, or else sprang to both minds simultaneously, for with one movement the two of them turned and scuttled out through the door, the housekeeper having reverted from her needle-like expression to a more normal one.

And as it happened Bando had just that minute come back into the garden to retrieve his jacket. With eyes closed and head judicially aside he listened to them.

He gave, inside his mouth, a sort of scream . . . "*Im-phm!*"—and bent a severe look on a distant portion of the sky. "*Im-phm!*"

The two women drew back with gasps, placing their hands across their mouths. Bando was walking away along the back of the house with so purposive and decided an air that as their eyes followed him they could not help knowing they had flushed some horror that had to be dealt with. Bando's silence seemed terrible, portentous.

He crossed the little space of grass at the far end of the house, passed under the dark fir tree among the bushes and at once reappeared climbing the little slope to the box-like church building. With hardly a slackening of his hand and shoulder swinging strut he passed along its grey side and going round its end came to the little slated box-like porch where he stopped, to look with head bent at the key protruding from the lock. Then he went this way and that with a sort of sniffing movement of his sharp, reddish-pointed nose. Bending himself down—which there was no need to do—and on tiptoe he passed inside.

At that moment a pale yellow and a pale blue apron appeared at the far corner of the church, next the house, fluttering side by side. The pale blue particularly agitated since Peigi Snoovie had, when excited, the habit of scooping up her apron and appearing to dry her hands on it.

Bando's energy and purpose had not survived his finding himself inside the building. Very carefully—one would have said nervously—he set about opening the inner door, and even, when it gave out a loud, ecclesiastical-sounding creak, stepped back a pace and stood a while, biting the ends of his moustache. No smallest sound coming from within, he went forward again, leaving the door open behind.

There was no one in here, in the vestry. And moreover silence beyond the other door, in the whole building. Bando's nose "pointed" at a shabby grey hat thrown down on the long table and lying where it had alighted. Cautiously he moved on tiptoe towards the church. At the last minute he remembered with a sweeping, backward movement of his left hand to slip his cap off sideways, exposing his shallow, bald skull at the very moment he quietly passed inside.

No one here either it appeared. Quite still he stood inside the door, looking round; rather impressed one would have said, and reluctant to move, not knowing where to move next. There was something peculiar about there being no sign of anyone here, if there was someone here, which there was bound to be; there was not a thing in the utterly bare, cold-looking building except rows of seats facing him, and beside him the square box of the pulpit which he could look into, and which was empty. It was too early in the year for the humming of flies in the sunny south windows. In such a stillness, after a little even ordinary breathing might have been audible. But he heard nothing—and he was extremely good at hearing. Simply nothing. Or what was that? No, that was a sound outside. Footsteps—he did not need to wonder whose—advancing with hesitations, along the grass by the side of the church.

The sound gave him a visible impulsion forward, although his feet had some appearance of still clinging to the floor. His shoulders went forward and his neck stretched out, while his eyes moved wide and tentative on this side and that.

And then he gave a little silent gasp, and his body jerked and remained a moment stiff and immobile before the pushed-forward portions of it were, with an air of great caution, retracted, and he remained standing irresolute and excited, out of sight of the "something" that had smitten him to this state. Perhaps even the thought of retreat visited him—the ragged ends of his moustache were being subjected to a violent series of snapping bites and chewing motions and his feet were loose on the floor—but a distinct though faint sound behind him at the outside entrance had the effect of stiffening him again at once, either with resolution or the encouragement of impending moral support. Even so he drew back a little first until he had shaken down his shoulders and firmly composed his features in an expression of elaborate casualness before, with a "*h'm-h'm*" behind a forefinger crooked across his moustache, he stepped forward and round the square corner of the pulpit.

He lost even his summoned-up courage, however, when there was no movement responsive to the disturbance of his audible approach. The figure was kneeling at the other side of the pulpit. On the bare floor; the medium-sized, well-knit, familiar, black-clad figure. Not facing the wall or away from the wall . . . as if it had dropped simply to its knees. The arms were hanging down in front—one hand clasped over the back of the other. The face, now he could see it, was very slightly raised, the eyes closed. And on the features rested a familiar expression: such a serenity as may be seen on the face of a composed and "beautiful" corpse. There was indeed an unearthly suggestion of a corpse about the kneeling figure. It appeared rigid, and seemed to convey an impression of coldness. Nor was there sign of breathing. His disconcerting impression was that the man within was "not there", he was "away", or at any rate he was more "away" than he was "there".

But the furtive sounds that he could now hear starting up in the vestry gave him a renewed impulse of encouragement. When the sounds—though still furtive—became open and amplified in the church itself, about the vestry door, Bando took fresh heart to approach closer, right up beside the figure in fact, and his little eyes, their fixed expression augmented with porcine unrestraint, fed greedily at will and at closest range, his head tilted down and his thin nose appearing to be shaken sideways, all over the well-knit, medium-sized, black-clad figure, from the impeccable parting in his brown hair down to the heels of his shoes behind, and the soles, the right one of which was "going" in the middle, and back to the place where the round, glossy collar was fastened with a brass stud at the back of the recently barbered healthily pinkish neck. His zeal became impious, he let his eyes fall upon and pass wanderingly, both with voluptuousness and tightness of scrutiny, over the unconscious features so close to him, in front of and just below the level of his eyes, as if mentally tearing off mouthfuls and gobbling them down. What a dish! And utterly defenceless, to be enjoyed at ease, nakedly and without subterfuge!

The mere lack of barriers to his satisfaction, the running too free of his impulses (he looked as if he would have savaged the defenceless form before him, his fingers twitching by his side) gave him pause. Having hesitated he became double-minded, cast sideways an uncertain look. The sight that met his eyes ought, even in the circumstances, to have moved him to laughter, had humour been in his nature. A stout, middle-aged woman with a yellow apron tied on her front, and a tall thin girl with a pale blue apron hanging down her length, standing side by side at nervous attention in the church, well in from the vestry door—and each with her right hand raised above her head, the elbow squarely out and the flat of her hand resting posed on her crown . . . a pair of odd-looking ancient Egyptians who would none the less have broken into an angular dance had their limbs not been shackled by the ecstasy looking out of their eyes. Bando merely saw that they were covering their heads as was proper for women in the house of prayer, and that he had an audience whose enthusiasm outran his own.

He would have liked to proceed to the next stage but hesitation troubled him. He mumbled "*h'm-h'm-h'm*" once or twice in an attempt to affect assurance, swinging his shoulder a little, but the fact was he now felt the figure was a little too near to him; he would have liked to step back a pace. But there were the waiting women. Yet when he would have put forward his hand it twice slipped behind his back, the fingers flickering. At length he fell back on speech, though the first words were confused, mumbled. "Was you . . . *h'm*—was you wanting something . . . Maighstir MacRury?" There was no reply. Bando worked on his jaws moistly, with a flicker of his eyes towards the women.

But he had spoken. Action brings energy, courage. He said, "Maighstir MacRury!" with insistence. But when he went the length of tapping the figure on the shoulder he drew back with a jolt and even recoiled bodily against the foremost pews. The glances he involuntarily cast at the women contained confusion and even pleading. With antique and angular immobility they gave him no outgoing but, with eyes alight under palms pressed on heads and tense with increasing excitement, seemed to prod him on with invisible nods. Accordingly he turned back, though for the moment mutilated in his enthusiasm, having lost both face and stomach in the business. A brace of important clearings of the throat put him in some heart again and though the words became glutinously involved and failed to leave his mouth he lifted his hand and successfully tapped on the black-clad shoulder just in front of him. This time he did not recoil, though he stepped briskly back when there were signs of returning life.

Then it came in on him that with the return of life queerness was gone and his curiosity again came relentlessly forward in the situation, his alert eyes glued on the figure so as to miss nothing of what might happen now. Even so they were elsewhere, running up and down, when the eyes opened. He was somewhat shocked to find them so but then immediately noticing they had not the look of sight he left his place and scuttled back towards the vestry door, through which a pair of skirts fluttered ahead of him and disappeared. Bando wheeled about just inside the vestry and with a couple of hitchings-up to his lapels and three or four energetic and determined shakings of his shoulders into position stepped nonchalantly back into the church swinging his arms as if only now arriving. At that very minute he was aware of four actively moving feet carrying the weight of two female bodies rapidly away along the outside of the building, with a suggestion of rustling whether of clothes or grass or both; the next minute he came face to face with the young clerical-collared figure inside the building. And again there was a moment of check since he found himself confronted with a young man of the most natural and even casual bearing and firm and pink with health, instead of . . . what had he expected? . . . something quite different.

"O Bhando," he said, stopping. "Did you want me?"

Bando wondered at his air, in which there was not a trace of vagueness, though there might have been a degree of reserved calm, combined however with an alert and recreated freshness, a poise and suggestion of inner glow, characteristic—though Bando could not have recognised this—of someone coming from a warm, invigorating bath. To complete the startling impression of naturalness the minister raised one knee after the other, looked at it, and openly brushed some dust from the black cloth.

"No, no," exclaimed Bando, who was as near embarrassment as he ever could be. "No, no, Maighstir MacRury. I . . . it was just a seat that I . . . that I thought yesterday . . . needed a nail . . ." Feeling how empty his hands were he slipped them out of sight behind him.

They were standing in the empty shell of the slightly echoing church, between pulpit and vestry, the minister of middle height and well-knit in his black, larger than Bando who was scruffy and nondescript in his workaday grey, his bald, flat skull a dull, unshining white above bushy overhanging eyebrows and weather-tanned cheeks.

"That's good, then, a Bhando," Mr MacRury said in a gentle, casual way, a breath of equal benevolence and indifference, and passed on into the vestry.

Bando, however, was not to be left behind. He was "on to" something now that things were normal again. He followed into the vestry, snatched up his cap where he had thrown it down and was slipping it on to his head and emerging through the door of the porch even as he seemed to see—though part-blinded in the sudden bright sunlight—the minister's black form vanish round the corner of the church. And indeed by the time he himself got round the corner there was the minister—with the addition of his shabby hat—making his way not ten yards ahead along the side of the building. The next minute Bando stopped dead, then bounded forward . . . He had seen the trim figure ahead suddenly halt—in a strange way—and stand there, half turned towards the wall.

Bando almost ran round to the front of the minister, to peer up into his face.

He could hardly believe in his good fortune. This was like "it" coming on. He could not pull his eyes away, even crept nearer . . . the same inexpressible peace overpassing the features, and the stillness over the whole person . . . Bando, drinking it all in, even dropped his head on one side, edging nearer.

But he was to have the cup of delectation and power dashed from his lips. Almost at once the young minister with a little negative shaking of himself—as if he had internally said "no" to something—opened his eyes and moved forward . . . all but colliding with Bando who, having his faculties concentrated for a period of uninterrupted gloating, was quite unable at one and the same instant to adjust the expression of his face and take the necessary backward steps out of the way.

He need not have been embarrassed. Mr MacRury with an unsurprised glance noted his presence in his path, interrupted his step and then walked forward along with him, nearer the wall than Bando and too much at ease apparently even to need to speak. The limitless air breathed about them, and the church. Away to their left, beyond the solitary dark yew-tree mid-placed in the thin-growing lawn between them and the white road, swept the broad vista of brown undulating moors bright in the sun.

"*Heh-heh* . . . It's fine weather just now, Maighstir MacRury!" Bando hastened to say in a little scream: the moment must not be allowed to pass unimproved.

"It is that, a Bhando."

"*Heh* . . . I'm just wondering if it won't be too fine . . . for the time of the year, I mean. I haven't been feeling altogether well these days that went past. *Heh*—it's in my head it takes me, you know . . . sort of queer"—with a darting glance—"*eh, eh* . . . dizzy, you know. Do you think it could be the weather?"

But he had nothing for his pains. Mr MacRury seemed to be barely conscious of him, walking by his side. "Yes, I suppose it might be the weather. Sorry you're not feeling well . . ." Saying which, abstractedly, he passed before Bando, under the blue-looking pine tree, and through the bushes: then straight along the back of the house where it was cool suddenly, and where a cluster of grey-looking pipes coming out of the wall ran down near the kitchen and into the ground.

5

Bando marched into the kitchen swinging his shoulders.

"Well!" he announced in an emphatic scream, "Well! no doubt of it . . . we've got something on our hands here!"—with a sort of bitter twist under the straggling moustache: other people were a responsibility one would have gathered.

"*Cooshtl*" came in a warning whisper from stout Mina, standing in long yellow apron over brown dress behind her dark-red-and-buff-check-covered table. A commanding position, from which she had seen the minister pass the window: not long enough ago, in her impression. Bando had consoled himself with a large chew from his bolt of tobacco as he followed the minister under the blue pine and through the bushes and had been systematically masticating it into shape ever since. He stepped straight across the floor and—*puh!*—sent a mouthful of yellow fluid straight at the fire in the range, which snarled loudly and coughed back at him a cupful of ash which reached mid-air before suddenly stopping then unfolding and slowly floating upwards and part falling downwards. "*Tit-tit-tit-tit!*" said the housekeeper intensely, reprovingly, "a Bhando!" then turned away to her more important listening even as Bando turned towards her his dripping moustache. Peigi Snoovie's lank, black hair flicked at her ears as she went back to her looking out the window. She had her shoulders pressed back flat against the pale wall, her right cheek likewise, straining to see past the window's edge over the tops of the sinks.

Then, "*Tsst!*" said Mina more intensely still, casting up her head in a high listening attitude. She gave a sudden, stout-womanly leftward plunge, swiftly set wide the door into the hall of the house, and was back in her place behind the table. She placed one hand on top of the other above her stomach, squared and settled her shoulders and with chin held high and lips coming together over the bulkiness of her teeth slowly narrowed her eyes.

The others also held their breath . . . Through the hall, from outside the front of the house, came rhythmically a faint, emphatic, hissing sound . . . the housekeeper's eyes widened . . . "his" footsteps in the gravel. The housekeeper's eyes began to narrow again, and her teeth to show. The footsteps all at once sounded out quite loud, and flat and muffled or hollow . . . "he" was in the porch, the buff-patterned, red-tiled porch beyond the inner door of glass design. Almost immediately the porch was full of emptiness again, and they knew that he had gone. Outside, the renewed scrunch and hiss rapidly decreased to nothing. There came a distant and very faint click. Then the light near-clang of the light-metal gate that stood by the road. With one intent the three in the kitchen plunged out through the door into the house.

In a moment . . . "There's no sign of him! No, there's no sign of him!" The two women were reporting from the landing at the top of the stairs, between the minister's study and bedroom, where they were craning at the window.

"Depend on it he's taken his bicycle!" Bando screamed up to them from where he stood in the hall. He had not ventured to go farther in his working, outdoor clothes: Mina would not have tolerated his boots on the stair-carpet. He was standing in the hall looking up at the figures at the window on the landing, their shoulders moving and re-moving across the light. He had taken off his cap again and held it in his hand: he was allowed to wear it in Mina's kitchen, but not in the interior of the house. "If he hasn't gone to Aird you'll be seeing him coming into sight again above Aultnaharrie," he called up. "You've only to wait."

The shoulders moved against the light.

"There he is!" cried Peigi Snoovie. "Yes, there he is! He's got his fawn coat on. And his grey hat."

"Well, he hasn't gone to Aird," Bando called up, moving and champing his jaws. "So he must be going to Strath!"

"If not further afield . . . if not farther afield! . . ." it was the housekeeper's adenoid contralto, in a sort of nasal croak. But they all three stiffened and looked at each other, with startled expressions and in some dismay. It had been as if someone else had spoken, in her voice. Mina had spoken even before she realised the intention; some impulse . . .

Bando cleared his throat and turned away into the kitchen. Immediately after, Mina with a sort of squeak pushed past Peigi Snoovie and made an agitated flopping plunge down the stairs.

That left Peigi alone on the landing. After a time during which she gazed away out of the window with a faraway, sleepy look in her grey eyes under her black brows, during which also Bando shut the back door and silence fell below, she moved quietly to her right until her right hand fell on and grasped the handle of the study door. When she had turned it, and the door silently opened, she went quickly in, though still without looking, still moving sideways.

She went straight to the top drawer of the desk and laying hold of the two little knobs pulled quietly and gently, with a listening look on her intent face. The drawer was locked, and would not budge. She gave it at length a sharp little irritated rattle and, removing her hands, crossed them large and bony on top of the back of the chair which sat behind the desk, the seat pushed mostly under it, between the side-tiers of little drawers.

There she stood gazing through the south window in

front of her away into the distance. Nothing was out there save mile upon mile of sky looking in at her, and some fluffy clouds floating lazily, almost motionless. With a movement like a sleepwalker she raised her thin arm above her head and, dreamy and absent, agitated the long middle finger in her top hair.

6

At that time the Rev. Mr MacRury on his bicycle had passed Aultnaharrie and was flying down the two miles and more of brae below it with coat-ends madly flickering, the brim of his hat alternately held flat against his brow and standing up from it, his fingers spread ready beside the brake handles in case of sudden need, and with an "expensive" ticking mounting frantically in his rear hub. He had never stopped indulging himself with this sensation in spite of the certain amount of risk involved—since the surface here was not as even and hard as in the immediate vicinity of his own place, Mellonudrigill. Then as well as speed he had the sensation of plunging straight into the base of the mountains, their enormous unbroken mass in the east seeming to rise higher each instant as he swept like a chip in a torrent flowing downstream, tossed occasionally and jarred by unevennesses only sufficiently to enhance his sense of speed and increase his exhilaration.

The country was changing its character. No longer the high, bare countryside round Mellonudrigill manse, hanging above the sea and the west. Lower lying. On his right stretched still the bright brown moors, though there was the sense now that the sea was not far away on that side. Also the ridge rising on his left had its shoulder into the west thus giving the whole

Strath protection and one had a sense of warmth or greater mildness even in the air flowing fresh and cool past one's ears.

His speed decreased when the road levelled out at near sea level. Now there were trees flowing up the slope, the wonderful light spring-green of larch and spruce seeming to gather all the sunlight in masses. Then, simultaneously, he had sea-shore on his right, crofts everywhere on his left. Another mile and he was going past the dozen or so of mostly two-storeyed and slated houses whose straggling intermittent line made up the main township of Strath, with the sound and sense of other movements than his own around him and feeling himself in his usual dilemma here—whether to watch his front wheel for the holes in the road surface and in case of some child running out incautious from the houses, or to turn his head and take recognising note of the heads he was aware of turning on his left as he passed—or to look at the sea, or rather the loch, on his right, whose boulder-strewn edge formed the veritable other side of the street.

But the houses were behind, and the sea. There was a slight rise, tall elms on either hand, fields shining beyond their trunks. Then on his left a high railing of an ancient dusty brown rising from a foot-high wall, and he dismounted, for here the slope told more strongly anyway, walking the twenty or so paces farther to a tall ornamental iron gate set well in from the roadway. He was to have propped his bicycle up here, but on second thoughts took it with him inside the gate which he closed before putting down the bicycle out of sight of the road.

The driveway he was now walking along was bordered by strips of green lawn, their outer verges on both sides lined with tall elms and sycamores, all of them covered from waving tip to lowest branches with bursting buds, and under the trees and over the strips of green lawn, blazing in masses, bloomed what looked like thousands of yellow daffodils. The rather large three-storey house he was approaching, its grey stone front covered for the most part with a reddish creeper, must have faced slightly east of south since it stood completely neutral and unilluminated by the sun's beams striking down from high above on his left.

Just as he was coming up to the door it opened and a minister came out. A taller man than his visitor, in rather shabby indoor blacks, a common grey cloth cap tilted high on the back of his head and forward over his nose. Mr MacRury had the feeling this comer from inside knew he was there an appreciable instant before he raised his head and looked at him with heavy green eyes under the cap snout.

"Oh, it's you!" he said with marked want of enthusiasm in tone and eye. "Come in, come in"—and going back inside began leisurely climbing the stairs.

7

Mr MacRury climbing the stairs behind him—he had been left to close the outside door—could not help feeling deep down the beginning of laughter. That was the effect of the man slowly and with reluctance and stiffness going before him.

The Reverend Aulay MacAulay, minister of Strath, was not at sixty-seven an old man, despite that hint of rheumatic stiffness. He was above the middle height and of medium build, or rather spare, inside his rusty blacks. His long, solemn, horse-face—his acquaintance felt that he had trained it to keep more solemn than it was by nature: and he had not enough vanity or was too indifferent to have cared had he overheard it called "horse"—was surmounted by a generously proportioned skull completely bald except for some tufts of brindled red-brown hair at the sides and a very narrow fringe of the same low down at the back. He was, as to his exterior, a dry, rusty, crusty man, a sarcastic bookish fellow who when he did move abroad never smiled (the nearest he came to it was a lightening of the solemnity of his face), would never be caught going out of his way to interest himself in anyone, and was gruff and abrupt without distinction unless it was to older persons, especially his clerical colleagues; women he would never come near or hold any converse with if he could avoid it: when they could not be avoided he would treat the older ones with a sort of stiff, either offhand or standoffish courtesy. Yet he was regarded by great numbers for miles around as a sort of absolute perfection.

For one thing, of course, he was a native of the district, one of "our own" which gave him a head-start in their regard and claim on their indulgence—even the defects and weaknesses of "our own", so long as they are of the common sort, tend to be endearing. But then his integrity was wonderfully attested down the years, as his discretion was known to be absolute. He was regarded as an extremely shrewd and at the same time extremely close man. He was a tower of confidence in the whole countryside in that everyone knew his name and business were safe with him; he didn't "talk", and at the first hint of gossip starting up he would give a snort expressive of disdainful impatience and simply get up and leave. His exterior and mannerisms in fact were continuously felt as manifestations of a strongly-individual, idiosyncratically gifted and beyond question attractive personality. People actually liked being flicked by his quiet, sarcastic tongue because of the light, deft way he had of administering the stroke, and because there was never felt to be any personal feeling in it. Indeed as soon as he appeared—approaching at his not-to-be-hurried pace, with his sour-looking, long visage—people became lighter-hearted in anticipation of some wry, quirky cut deriving its originality, its striking quality, from its background in a mental world of more individual, idiosyncratic association than any they knew, and they were not the less on tiptoe of expectancy in that the victims of the cut might be themselves. In general his neighbours "attended" to what he said, with lightened, expectant looks. He never gave the slightest sign that he knew how he was regarded, his attitude one of unvarying dry indifference. He almost never looked at the person he was speaking to—although it was universally understood that he "didn't miss much". But if his habitual attitude appeared lightly or slightly contemptuous it was still a pleasure and an amusing experience to be in his company. You felt you were regarded as pretty "light" and of small account but that did not depress you personally since it was understood you were only so as part of, as involved in, a whole rather trivial system—that being, one presumed, everything in which Mr MacAulay had no interest.

But if most found it pleasant and amusing, a change from the usual, to be in his company, no one would ever have dreamed of intruding upon him. It was recognised that his nature was solitary, and above all that he was not the sort of person one took liberties with . . .

Mr MacRury, climbing the stairs behind him, made no attempt to repress the sensation of rising laughter:

the old man was so droll and attractive. And how the smell of this manse, old, and overfurnished with ancient furniture, took you back in time and instantly set you to wondering what sort of life was filling it, going on in it and round about it—what persons and what concerns—say, eighty years ago.

8

The study, on the first floor, was a darkish room. It faced the front, which by noon-time was slightly turned away from the sun. The wallpaper was faded, carrying a pattern of large dark-purple blotches. Curtains of heavy plush were dark at the window, subtracting light from the room. Then one was conscious of the heavy trees outside along the drive.

"Sit you down," said Mr MacAulay.

He had indicated a small leather armchair by the side of the fire and Mr MacRury went and sat down in it, looking now, as he sat, across the fireplace towards the window, which in turn looked down the drive. He found the light wonderfully cold, dark grey and strange after having been in light suffused with sunshine from morning until now. From the interior of this south-south-east-looking box the sunny light looked removed, active indifferently; one saw it through the window, swimming with golden motes in the blue of the profound sky, and caught among the very tops of the tall trees adown the drive, setting multitudes of half-burst-open buds swaying and trembling like tiny lights or flames.

It was obviously not Mr MacAulay's own chair. That was it sitting directly in front of the fireplace where a small bright fire had been lighted despite the mildness of the afternoon. This chair of Mr MacAulay's—a little cane-topped table stood between Mr MacRury's and it, and on the table, within comfortable reach of Mr MacAulay's left hand, in an arrangement of heavy-looking tomes, "Garvie on Exodus" and "McCrie on the Ephesians"—this obviously favourite chair of Mr MacAulay's, directly facing the fire (the faded hearthrug was worn in an oval patch in front of it, where his feet had rested countless times), was an ancient, roomy armchair, tapestry covered, with high back and semi-circular side headrests: the tapestry here and there smooth-worn and dark where Mr MacAulay's earthly casket had so often rested. Many and many must have been the warm summer afternoons, with the bees humming outside—or the winter afternoons and evenings with the gale howling and pushing at door and window and the peat fire, glowing and flaming, puffing out intermittently its aromatic fumes—he had passed a-snooze in that; his legs crossed comfortably, his bald head ensconced against one or other of the headrests, until "Garvie on Exodus" or "McCrie on the Ephesians" slipped from his knee to land with a thud on the rug.

Mr MacAulay himself had been at his leisure taking off his grey cloth cap and laying it on the top of a desk near the window, and his bald head was now glimmering gloriously in the neutral light of the room as he approached. But when he had only begun to sit down there was a noise outside of what sounded like a decrepit car drawing up at the gate. Then a rasping of gears and the vehicle seemed to be reversing off the road. Mr MacAulay, bent forward in the act of descending into the chair, his hands behind him on the handrests, held himself there while fixing a solemn, both listening and speculative look on the fire. A small, slamming noise came up from the car. The iron gate opened. With something resembling a groan Mr MacAulay straightened himself and took three steps forward towards the window. Presumably he could see the gate and part of the drive from where he now stood. He said, "Let's hope he shuts the gate," as if merely thinking aloud and without much real hope.

There was the noise of the heavy iron gate shutting. Mr MacAulay was standing, stretching his head a little to look down through the window, his large dry hands hanging by his side, the palms turned backwards as if holding themselves in readiness for as quick a return as possible to their duty of grasping the handrests while their possessor lowered himself into his comfortable chair. Footsteps could now be heard, brisk in the drive.

"Well, well," said Mr MacAulay (he had a mannerism which was all his own and altogether expressive of him, and which sped his quirkish remarks home with laugh-provoking force: this was—at psychological instants—a dry sipping in of the air at the right-hand corner of his mouth). "Well, well," he said, "if it isn't our energetic colleague—*sip*—from our—*sip*, *sip*—industrial parish of Kinloch-Melfort! The Reverend David—*sip*—Macpherson Bain!"

Mr MacRury was smiling openly. Mr MacAulay walked back to his chair and really let himself down into it, but relaxing backwards in its ample depths, hands on the handrests, as if the chair and he clasped each other in a close accustomed embrace. He did not stir when the bell buzzed imperiously downstairs. Muttering, "The woman will let him in," he crossed his legs.

There was a sudden outburst of high, excited female speech at the foot of the stairs mingled at once with a light, male voice. The two came up the stairs, seeming at every word to interrupt each other—Mr MacAulay shook his head commiseratingly—the voices continuously rising higher as if striving to get above each other. Mr MacAulay retained in his chair a martyr-like immobility and silence, an air eloquent of suffering and protest. Mr MacRury's appreciation broke in a smile. The door opened and the male voice was of a sudden very loud, saying, above the other, "Thank you! . . . thank you! . . . yes! . . . yes! . . . thank you very much! . . . thank you! . . . yes!"

The door closed. In the suddenly fallen silence with tremendous rhetorical effect a light soft voice said quietly, "Good afternoon."

Mr MacAulay came to life in his chair. He turned his long face up over his right shoulder and, tilting back his head so as to throw his voice above the high chair-back, said, "Have you young men no parishes?"

The owner of the voice, apparently only then catching sight of Mr MacRury, shouted, "Ewen, by Jove! . . . it's you, is it? . . . *ha-ha-ha*"—bursting into a loud, jolly laugh which gave the impression of being almost entirely genuine. Mr MacAulay contracted his left cheek as with a prolonged twinge of neuralgia. He said drily—he had not yet turned towards the newcomer—"Take a chair."

Up the room towards them at the hearth had meantime come floating—so elastic was its step—a shortish, rounded form in light-coloured clothes. Now halted between Mr MacAulay and the window facing on the drive a rotund or chubby young man of under middle height and beamed down, snub-nosed and boyish, through glasses which every other instant were turned by a slight movement into two grey, opaque though gleaming discs. His hair was fair, cut short and brushed straight back from a good brow.

"Well, well!" he exclaimed in his sweetish tenor voice, slightly unctuous and hearty, and looked round for the chair he was to "take". In all his movements and manner he was the modern, out-of-door parson, clerical collar abandoned, in eye-catching open-air tweeds—that type. Had "plus-fours" still been in fashion he would, one felt, have had on a very sporty pair and a bag of golf-clubs behind his shoulder. The chair was beside him, cane-bottomed and cane-backed, the narrow frame and slender legs and whorled arms strong enough looking, however. He drew it towards him and sat down, across the hearth from Mr MacRury although not so near the fire, his back to the window.

"Well, well, lovely day; what brings you here today, Ewen?"

"I suppose partly the day," said Mr MacRury, looking black in the brown armchair, blacker than rusty Mr MacAulay, "although"—crossing his legs—"as a matter of fact I *had* something I meant to ask Mr MacAulay, as an elder colleague."

Mr MacAulay gave him just one glance from his eyes, which were a greenish hazel under their sandy brows, a glance sufficient to tell him the "something" was not of a really grave nature, whatever it was.

"I've only just got here, you know."

"Oh!" exclaimed the newcomer, the (not ostensibly) Rev. Macpherson Bain, concerned immediately and getting ready to get up, "have I interrupted? . . . am I intruding?"—looking solemnly and with pleading from one to the other.

"No, no," said Mr MacRury deprecatingly with a soft laugh, "it was a very small matter really . . ."

"Oh," said Mr Macpherson Bain, short, while Mr MacAulay *almost* looked at Mr MacRury again.

"Yes . . . you know . . ."—he eased his glossy collar with a forefinger—"a short time ago I had to start holding an evening service in English . . . every second Sunday. There was a tendency for the young people not to turn out, and I was given to understand that the trouble was they had difficulty following the Gaelic . . . Which might well be true enough, of course; a good many of the younger people seem to have slipped their connection with the language . . . can't, or won't, return your greeting on the road . . . The trouble is a good part of the congregation want to stick to the familiar order of things in these services. I don't gather there is any opposition to the English services as such. What they object to is the standing for the hymns and sitting for the prayers. They persist in standing for the prayers and sitting for the hymns, as they have always done in the Gaelic service. It's not because they are in any sort of confusion about it: I have explained it to them more than once. They're very independent, lots of the older people especially . . ." He pushed himself up in the chair, by his elbows. "Of course . . . if the question had come up in the time of my predecessor, Mr Matheson,"—Bando's voice, very unctuous, said "*a man of God*" so distinctly in his ear he almost turned to look behind him—"possibly the situation might not have arisen. He had grown old among them, and they were accustomed to accept him as a guide. I fear—and feel—they look on me simply as a young man interfering with the old ways, and are inclined to question my authority . . . I sympathise with them, of course: it can't seem reverent to the older people to sit down when prayer is being offered . . . And there was nothing of this till *I* came . . . a mere infant. But on the other hand there's unseemliness . . . You see, they don't *all* ignore the new rule. Yesterday evening, for instance, about half were standing when the others were sitting. I even think I intercepted some looks of challenge passing between members of the two parties. I believe there *has* been some contention, and I am anxious of course that it should not go to the length of war, even if only a war in Lilliput—you know, the 'down-sitters' against the 'up-standers'. I don't want to seem to 'throw my weight about'. That wouldn't look well in a comparatively young man and a quite recent incomer; and besides it might have the opposite effect to the one desired. At the same time . . . I thought perhaps . . . *umm*, did *you* have any trouble of this kind, Mr MacAulay? You introduced English services here, did you not?"

Mr MacAulay had remained limp and withdrawn, without any evidence of attention, lying back in his tapestry-covered chair with his legs stretched towards the fire, on which his eyes rested absently while idly he plucked at a tuft of reddish hair at the side of his bald skull or down-twisted the top of a large ear. But as soon as he spoke it was evident he had been attending closely. His tone was different. As invariably when matters of the church came up all flavour of waggishness left his conversation. He gave the impression of grave candour.

"Yes . . . I started services in English here. Or rather I should say it was in my time that they were started, for of course it was no wish of mine that they should start. The situation here then—this is a few years ago—was the same as you have described it in your more remote parish *now*. The younger people losing, or abandoning, the language and so on . . . But I had no trouble of your sort. There may have been—I rather think I remember—some slight confusion on the first occasion or two . . . old people absentmindedly getting up at the wrong time. But that merely called for another word of explanation . . . No, I had none of the trouble you're having . . . Of course, as you say, I had the advantage of being a native of the district . . ."

He left off turning down the top of an ear and thrust himself more upright in the chair, drawing his legs back and crossing them. "You know"—he gave Mr MacRury one straight clear glance from his greenish eyes under their sandy brows—"have you considered the possibility that they may be trying to see how far they can go with you . . . a young minister, and an incomer as you say? Of course the Mellonudrigill people have always been looked on by us here as both stiff-necked and 'tricky' . . . the Mellonudrigill people and the Aird people . . . especially the Aird people, all in your parish. We in Strath look on ourselves as more civilised, more supple altogether . . . And if you've got a few of the 'lawyers' at work . . ." He pondered . . . "What about that chap Snoovie, in the Aird . . . is *he* mixed up in it, do you know?"

"I'm afraid I don't. I haven't heard his name mentioned. But of course I'm quite in the dark."

"It's hardly possible he isn't. Like Saul, he's been a 'man of war from his youth up'. I need say no more. And of those MacMillans of Aird: I need say no more. And then there's your own Bando, a theologian of no great modesty . . . where is he standing in the matter?"

"Again, I have no means of knowing."

"At your evening service yesterday when the side-taking seems to have crystallised or come to a head, was Bando among the standers or the sitters?"

"Neither, as it happened. He wasn't there. A sore throat, I understand."

"*Hm* . . . a diplomatic sore throat possibly. It allowed

him to keep his attitude undeclared at any rate . . ." He sat up straighter. "Well anyway . . . I'd be inclined to give you Paul's advice to Timothy: 'Let no man despise thy youth.' Not that you're so very young at . . . what is it?"

"Thirty-six."

"Young enough to their way of thinking, I suppose . . . Well—*sip*—I'd be inclined to advise you to try taking a firm line. If the people I suspect are at the bottom of it, they're only doing it out of love of trouble, and to see how far you'll let them go. Snoovie, and your own man and one or two others . . . they've been well known down the years for turbulence. Theologians in the strongest line of succession from the apostle, Jenny Geddes." ("*Ho-ho-ho*, that's a good one," went Mr Macpherson Bain.) "If they see," said Mr MacAulay, not appearing to notice the interruption, "if they see you firm, and not put about, they won't think it worth their while."

Mr Macpherson Bain, except for that one outburst of laughter, had all the time, with an air of deferential attentiveness, pointed his snub nose first at one speaker then the other in turn, the thickish lips as always when he was serious placed together with a look of preciseness, the gold bridge and legs of his glasses emitting a glint of light and the cane chair creaking under him each time he turned. (It was incredible really that he was not wearing sporty plus-fours and bright flashes on clocked stockings on those plump, short, widely-planted legs.) Judging the conversation was at an end he now said, showing his good teeth, "Thank God I have none of that sort of trouble. My parish is mostly industrial. People from the south. Mostly employed at the colossidium factory." One could detect the modest pride in all this. The teeth showed more widely . . . "I avoid your difficulty with English services by having no Gaelic services."

Mr MacAulay had not yet looked at him. He seemed to have suddenly dropped half asleep, his head against the side head-rest of his chair. His voice was at its driest.

"Sounds rather like—*sip*—governing wisely by having no subjects."

Mr Macpherson Bain was quick to sense an implication.

"I've had no complaints," he promptly said, smiling a little painfully, giving the impression that he was blushing. "No one has ever *asked* for a Gaelic service."

"Quite so—*sip*—never asked."

Mr Macpherson Bain seemed puzzled, and troubled.

"But you're a Gaelic man yourself, Davie," protested Mr MacRury across the hearth.

The tweed-clad minister responded with relief. "Born and brought up in it!" he declared, now with some pride. "But you've got to face facts, you know. Gaelic's dead. It's no good being romantic . . . going about in a mist looking for Bonnie Prince Charlie!"

"He's dead too!" commented Mr MacAulay in a musing murmur.

"Yes," said Mr Macpherson Bain looking aside at him but not catching his meaning, or perhaps even his words, and not noticing Mr MacRury's grin. He was serious, solemn, corrugating the brows in his rather boyish face surmounting his light-coloured tweeds. "You've got to look at the fact that this is an industrial age we're living in—machines and factories and turbines instead of sails and oars and rowing songs and sheilings and the songs that went with them."

It was noticeable that in some subtle way he had absorbed into his voice an echo of the intonations, the uninhibited vowels, the gutturals, of his parishioners from the industrial south (whom he professed himself "thrilled" to have address him familiarly as "Davie": he felt in that case that he had begun to do them some good). And proportionately the Gaelic flavour was subtly going out of his speech. Whereas the origins of the other two were at once and all the time evident even though only in a certain aeratedness in their speech and a gentleness in the way the syllables left the tongue, in his case it was already sometimes doubtful what his background was . . .

"By Jove, you know"—he slapped his plump knee and for some reason turned and glanced out the window behind him—"it's extraordinary when you think of it, what these fellows did, marching and fighting and losing everything, just for the sake of the bright eyes of a Frenchified foreigner frisking about in yellow hair and a kilt." (He paused a perceptible instant with stilled concentration, regarding that inwardly—he lectured to social clubs.) "And there they were: they lost everything because they didn't know on what side their bread was buttered."

Mr MacRury leant back in his brown leather armchair. "You know, Davie, I have never found the theory of the romantic motives of the Jacobites finally convincing. I grant that, viewed from the standpoint of the present day and going on the assumption that the ideals of our age, if they can be dignified by the name, have a universal and exclusive validity, the Jacobite Risings have the look of picturesque irruptions from some region of the irrelevant. To me, though, the manifest poetry in the whole movement of the thing, foreign as it is to the feeling of the present age, would suggest not that it was a flourish of the superficial but that on the contrary it arose where all the sustained poetry in human life must arise, in the permanent and universal depths of the human spirit. But—that apart—the romantic motive is too flimsy, it simply isn't solid enough, in a rational man's world, to support the weight of the Jacobite action. The very fact that the whole thing bears so romantic an aspect to *us*, from the point of view of our age and time, ought probably to make us suspect that it wasn't so in fact, and to the persons concerned, that the true motives must have been compellingly real . . . the difference being that we have no longer an apprehension of that reality or of its compulsive authority. After all, Davie, men just simply don't act from such motives as are commonly attributed to the Jacobite Highlanders—great masses of them risking all they possess, and life itself, in an arduous and hazardous enterprise, simply because a young man has yellow hair and looks 'fetching' in a kilt. To me that has never made sense. It looks a trivial, nonsensical kind of motive. And it has this unfortunate—and improbable—implication that the highland parts of Scotland in the eighteenth century were populated by fatuous, somewhat weak-minded persons . . . who were, moreover, all feeble and fatuous in the same way . . ."

"Och, well . . . it would be their officers that pulled them out. The authority of the chief, you know . . ." Davie flourished an easy hand.

"I know that the chief had authority, although I doubt if he had the power to call out the clan simply for a whim: as far as I have apprehended it, there would have had to be general agreement as to the legitimacy of the objective. But, that apart, why should the chiefs have been more romantically inclined than the clansmen? They should really have been less so, should they not? They had more to lose, and they were in a better position to assess the risks: many of them were of continental training and outlook, and very much of the political world of their day, and it was not a day of romance in politics. But the positive evidence is that the rank and file were not behind their leaders, in fact were in advance of them, in devotion and enthusiasm. For instance, in the '15 (and remember it was the '15 that was the really large and formidable Rising, and there was not a single romantic figure in its leadership) the abandonment of the campaign after Sheriffmuir turned the Highland army half mutinous. It took Mar two whole days to get them dragged back from Perth to Dundee. Hundreds deserted on the way, and those that did reach Dundee mutinied openly and ran about insulting the officers in the streets for having betrayed them. Mar had to send the French ships out of the Tay and on up the coast to Montrose in case the men might suspect they were intended to embark and carry off the royal party, and he even took the precaution of having a Lowland regiment for a headquarters guard for fear the infuriated Highlanders might try to kidnap the King and carry him off to the Highlands as a means of ensuring the continuance of the campaign."

"Is that really so, Ewen?" said Mr Macpherson Bain in a tenor voice higher by his surprise, his lenses giving him an appearance of goggling as he sat forward with a plump hand on each plump knee.

"So I understand, Davie . . . I don't honestly think you stand any chance of making out a case for the reluctance of the rank-and-file participants in the Risings."

"Well, what do you think brought them out, Ewen, if it wasn't a romantic impulse? It must have been something pretty strong."

Mr MacRury shifted in his brown armchair.

"We-ell. Yes, I think it was." He sat more upright, and took hold of his leg under the knee. "We know the Gaelic people . . . even today . . . they're the same stock . . ." He looked aside at the grey smoke spiralling out of the heart of the little fire. "Even if they're not as a rule very energetic in the circumstances given in their homeland, I don't think they could ever be accused of not having a shrewd eye to their material advantage."

"You're telling me! *Ha-ha-ha*," burst out Mr Macpherson Bain.

"They're not in general people likely to forego a concrete material advantage for the sake of some piece of sentimentalism."

"I'd jolly well say not . . . *ha-ha*."

"There's only this . . ." Mr MacRury looked straight across at Mr Macpherson Bain, pulling his body once or twice jerkily forward with his hands clasped side by side on his right shin. "That if they become convinced that religious truth is involved in such and such a course of action they'll follow it at no matter what cost materially."

"By Jove!" exclaimed Mr Macpherson Bain falling serious instantly and leaning forward in some tension, "that's true! They *are* like that!"

"Yes," went on Mr MacRury, "we may sometimes indulge a sneer at the narrowness of some of our brethren, especially of the smaller sects . . . and of course a lot of pride and arrogance can be mixed up in these bickerings too . . . but, allowing for all that, I don't think we'd find it easy to imagine that many of the individuals we know, if it ever came to a plain issue, would not adhere to the apprehended truth and let slip the material advantage."

"By Jove, Ewen," said Mr Macpherson Bain with illumination and enthusiasm, "you're right! you're right!" He tensed a little, forward; the opaque greyness coming over the discs giving him again a goggling look. "Do I understand, then, that you think it was a question of religion with them?"

"Not exactly, Davie. What I do think is that the Highland people then simply had a burning, compelling sense of 'right' where the royal house was concerned. That is my reading of the facts, and I think it is the only one that explains them rationally, gives the Jacobite Risings a rational motivation. The people were brought out not by romance, but quite simply by a sense of the 'right' involved. I don't believe many of them even pondered the matter. The thing was simply right, and they did it, without thought of consequence or reward, as a man does who knows he must one day come to his Judgment and therefore has no choice but do the right thing or lose out in the end. My reading is that this was the universal attitude throughout the population at the time. It was not in fact a case of some chiefs dragging their people 'out', though it was a case of some chiefs keeping their people 'in'. You see, I think the people who have tried to understand the Risings have been falling into the cardinal sin in historical thinking—the projection of their own age into the past. They have been trying to explain the Risings in terms of the only motives they could imagine making people take such action in *their* day, and a very unconvincing job they made of it with their supposed romantic motive . . . although of course when you repeat a thing often enough people come to believe it, no matter how improbable it may be on examination. But you and I who are of the stock that participated, and for whom moreover as Gaelic-speaking men the contemporary evidence, the songs etc., are accessible, and in which romance doesn't appear, are in a position to know better . . . that the motives of Gaelic Jacobitism were not romantic but *real*, that is, they arose out of the moral realities involved in the contemporary situation as the people then saw them . . . I don't know if you recollect the dying speech of MacDonald of Tirnadris."

"No, Ewen, I can't say that I do. MacDonald of . . .?"

"Of Tirnadris. He was a Jacobite of the '45 who was captured and executed. In his dying speech, which in my view represents the attitude of the whole mass of Jacobites, he declared that it was 'principle and a thorough conviction of its being his duty to God, his injured King and oppressed country' which engaged him to take up arms. I think I remember the actual words; he went on: 'It was always my strongest inclination as to wordly concerns to have our ancient and only rightful royal family restored, and even, if God would, to lose my life cheerfully in promoting the same.'" Mr MacRury looked up at the ceiling, recalling . . . "'I solemnly declare I had no by-views in drawing my sword in that just and honourable cause, but the restoration of my king and prince to the throne, and the recovery of our liberties to this unhappy island which has been so long loaded with usurption, corruption, treachery and bribery; being sensible that nothing but the King's restoration could make our country flourish and all ranks and degrees of men happy.' I think we have no course but to believe these words, spoken on the threshold of the next world. They're not the words of a romantic, Davie . . . I think you'll agree."

"I quite agree," said Mr Macpherson Bain though still with the smallest trace of hesitation or unconviction. "There seems to have been a tremendous unanimity of misunderstanding, though . . ."

"Yes . . . Of course there's this consideration too,

which ought perhaps to be kept in mind, for what it's worth . . . If you get people to accept a false view of the facts, by getting them accustomed to see them as the outcome of romantic motives, you may thereby prevent them from looking for and taking heed of the real motives, and perhaps pondering their validity, then and even for later times."

Mr Macpherson Bain seemed quite puzzled for a moment, considering that. Then he pointed an accusing forefinger. "*Ha!*" he laughed. "*Now* we are getting admissions! You wouldn't be a Jacobite yourself all the time?"

Mr MacRury shrugged. "I'd have to have notice of that question. I'm not an advocate for anything, but I mean everything I say quite seriously."

"Yes, yes, I know, Ewen," said Mr Macpherson Bain, serious again, with some return of his puzzled expression. "*Eh* . . . and you don't think there was self-interest mixed up in it, in the Jacobite Risings?"

"Self-interest is liable to be mixed up in some degree or other in every human enterprise. But in the Jacobite Risings the hazards were great, and they were risking everything. In any case, what was the self-interested aim? What could any Gaelic Jacobite have hoped to gain for himself in a self-interested sense? A few positions about the Court perhaps for one or two of the greater chiefs, assuming they were interested in being persons of little account at Court in place of persons of the highest consequence at home in the Highlands? There's nothing I can see in the thing to appeal to self-interest . . . Besides, if you want to push the charge of self-interest now, won't you have to drop the charge of romanticism?"

"Yes, you probably have me there, Ewen," said Davie Macpherson Bain, his cane chair squeaking, taking it very matter-of-factly. "I suppose their main motive could hardly at the same time have been romantic and self-interested." He paused, drew an audible breath, the chair squeaking again. "I suppose I'm just prejudiced against the Prince Charlie boys: to me there's something in the whole affair that seems skittish and away off the point, and I'm simply looking for something like a reason to justify my feeling about it. But then"—pointing a rhetorical plump finger—"*you* are probably prejudiced on the other side. A man from the Isles! And a MacRury, next thing to a MacDonald! Your people were probably 'out'!"

Mr MacRury smiled in candid appreciation of the rhetorical, accusing accents and gestures. "Quite possibly they were, and quite possibly, as you say, my feelings lean to the Jacobite side rather than the other. But that after all is beside the question, since your feelings or mine can have had no influence on the coming 'out' or staying in of the clans, which is the point at issue . . . the motives of those who came out in the Jacobite Risings remain whatever they actually were at the time, unaffected by your feelings or mine about the things, in our very different age." Mr MacRury's features, ordinarily only pleasing and youthful, became distinguished by a light that sprang up in them when his soft baritone voice took a note of warmth or enthusiasm. This happened easily, at a touch; for the most part in his case the body seemed a pretty transparent envelope; it was fascinating to perceive through it the flame of the spirit rise or fall at the touch of interest, from the very moment when his faculties were engaged. Just now, as if feeling he had sounded slightly too enthusiastic, to the point perhaps of being didactic or dogmatic—he was even leaning forward when he finished speaking—he smiled swiftly;

a candid, warm smile with the needed hint of deprecation.

"True, Ewen, true," said the stocky Mr Macpherson Bain . . . "Well"—for some reason he made the motion again of turning and looking over his shoulder out through the window behind him—"whatever their motives were they didn't know on what side their bread was buttered."

His note of some contempt or implied patronage remained hanging a little in a disembodied echo of his tenor voice in one of those silences that tumble down on conversations. They remained quiet, Mr MacRury leaning back in his chair, Mr MacAulay reclining in his. The moment was deep between them. By contrast with the emptiness of the room the outside, beyond the window, appeared crowded and noisy, full of activity, the same faintly apricot-tinted clouds wallowing in the blue sky, the upmost tops of the trees dipping.

Soundlessly through the room, between them, came marching a regiment of those dead ghosts. Mud-stained and their tartans tattered from the campaign. Coming from their deeds and advancing with urgency upon their fate. The light was clear on their accoutrements and antique panoply, a surge in all their motions, but their expression "inward", averted and inscrutable; nothing they gave away of the thought in every mind that made their faces "set", and poured over all their forms that air of resolution. A long minute they kept passing . . . not an army, some detached portion, all of the same badge and tartan . . . till the last stragglers passed through the fireside wall and away, their backs and swinging tartans and bonnet-covered heads darkening, contracting to a point, becoming nothing. Soundlessly . . . what they knew they had taken with them.

"You know, Davie"—with a quick conviction Mr MacRury sat up, leant forward—"you're *wrong* there ... You *must* be! Look ... 'By their fruits shall ye know them.' Since the '45, since Culloden, the forces the Jacobites were opposed to have had a clear field, without opposition, to run things their own way. Therefore what has happened since the '45 in the Highlands, and the present state of Gaeldom, are the result of the nature and Will of that which the Jacobites were fighting against. Agreed? And what *is* the present state of Gaeldom? You know as well as I do what it is. The life is gone out of it; as a separate culture, an integral way of life, an element of the creative riches of God conferred on His favourite creature, Man, it's a corpse ... dead ... The glens that were the homeland of our race, a race in those days so virile that a handful of them were able to shake an empire, these glens are a gaping desert. Seek for the descendant of the Gael now, mingled with other strains in every city, and in nearly every country overseas, already oblivious of his heritage or daily more and more forgetful of it, in any circumstances not in a position to preserve it. While we here are a mere sprinkling, a dwindling remnant; and every day another portion of our language and heritage slips from our mind, from our grasp. Any day now is bound to see the last of everything that has a continuity with the life-experience and consciousness of the Jacobite Gael, and even the disappearance in time, and from the world, of his physical progeny. It's as clear a case of ... what's the word they're using nowadays? ... genocide as anything in history. The murder of a whole race, a people."

"We-ell ... That's putting it pretty extremely, I would think ... but ... substantially ... ye-es, I suppose ..."

"Well now, surely it's no stretch of romantic imagination to credit the Gael in Jacobite times with some appreciation, some apprehension of this. I don't mean that they had second-sight and could look into the future. But it would be strange if none of them had sensed or assessed the degree of malice that was opposed to them and that threatened their way of life and their children and the very soil of their homeland . . . They had after all plenty experience of it, at Glencoe for instance, to mention only that. And if so, if they had any apprehension of the essential spirit that animated the other side in their regard, conveying to them the slightest idea of what awaited them, then obviously the throwing of their support into the Jacobite attempt was the most sensible, practical, down-to-earth thing they could have done—apart altogether from the intrinsic justice and moral rightness they attached to the Cause."

Both young ministers stopped and looked round when they sensed that Mr MacAulay was about to speak. But that did not hurry him. Idly he plucked with his finger tips at the reddish wisps flanking his gleaming head, and a quirk came at the corner of his rather long mouth . . . "Perhaps they knew, after all, on which side—*sip*—their bread was *bittered*."

After a puzzled instant Mr Macpherson Bain threw himself back, to the main danger of his thin protesting chair, and stamped his whole foot on the floor. "Oh!" he roared, with undergraduate abandon, pretending to be in pain . . . "Dreadful! dreadful! *Ho-ho-ho!*" he went on laughing with wholehearted goodwill and quite a deal of real amusement.

Mr MacAulay had slipped his little *mot* in with so dry a dexterity, however, that it could never have been interpreted as his taking sides. And one would still have hesitated to ask for his opinion.

The episode had enlivened Mr Macpherson Bain again, however, and with renewed unction he declaimed, lifting his musical tenor voice, "But they are coming back, Ewen!"—looking across at Mr MacRury—"The people are coming back! Look at my parish! Look at Kinloch-Melfort!"—triumphantly.

The amused smile on Mr MacRury's face became sad simply; he shook his head . . .

"No, they are not coming back, Davie. They will never come back. Other people are coming in to take their place. *Other* people, with different background and mind and language. *That's* the profound significance of Kinloch-Melfort . . . They may be as worthy people, they may be as socially valuable, of equal or greater usefulness in every sense to the world—you can argue all that—but they are indisputably *different* people, and the effect of their coming in will be to complete the extirpation of the remnants of the Gael and the Gaelic way of life in their own homeland . . . to make an end of *us* . . . This is no restoration of the Gael. Now I must give you your own advice, not to be romantic. Take a realist view of the situation, taking every element in it into consideration, the nature and power of everything opposed to our survival, including the factors within ourselves, in our minds and spirits . . . We Gaelic people have had our day, such as it was . . ."

Mr Macpherson Bain looked steadily at Mr MacRury with an arrested, frustrated look; an expression containing all at once misery, surprise, bewilderment and hurt.

9

"We were drawn up in the street in Kinloch-Melfort"—Mr Aulay MacAulay had changed again within, they could sense it a candid, kind mind was in him, and the younger men felt warm towards him, sensing that he had "come in" to the conversation with them, as one of them—"one evening a little while ago . . ." He left off plucking at his fringe of rusty hair and sat up a little, rearranging his rusty black-trousered legs. "Our venerable colleague, Mr Maclennan of Drum, and myself . . ."—he stroked the point of his chin a number of times with his dry, long fingers—"Some mechanical defect developed in our hired car . . . The window was open and there came in to us a . . . a kind of stench, a kind of warm stench that got tepid and then hung cold in the air. Something sharp and rancid in it too. 'What on earth's that?' I said, 'that smell!' Mr Maclennan was far more wordly-wise than I. 'The Feeshancheeps,' he said, quite calmly." (The two young ministers gave quick and perceptive smiles at the exactly "true" suggestion of the Rev. Mr Maclennan of Drum's accent: he was, in actual fact, perhaps because of his greater age, several degrees more "Highland spoken" than Mr MacAulay.) "I suppose then that 'the feeshancheeps' would be the substance a good number of people standing about on the street outside were lifting up to their mouths out of yellow papers or bags which they held under their noses. The stench at least seemed to be coming out of those papers . . . if not also from the people's mouths, which I observed most of them while chewing kept generously open . . . as indeed the eyes of most were too, in a ruminative sort of way . . .

"The car moved on, but had only gone a few yards

when it stopped again. This time our open window was right opposite the place, a kind of shop, where they seemed to be getting 'the feeshancheeps', since those going in had no yellow papers and those coming out all had. I looked into this shop or devotorium because just then there was a loud and startling metallic crash in its interior accompanied by what sounded like a hoarse prolonged shout, and was just in time to see a cloud of steam ascending to the ceiling, in which there were lamps already lit, giving a peculiar garish or livid light. The steam dissipating I caught a glimpse of a young man standing under the livid light of the lamps—at least I think it was a young man, though he looked rather like a young woman—with an unhealthily pale, shining face and waves in his long black or—as it more appeared—blue hair, which was hanging down like a small mat beside one side of his head; and not far from him was a stout woman, who, but for the same sort of blue-looking hair coiled on the top of her head, might have been a man, for she had a well-defined—and indeed I almost think shining—black moustache. Peculiar looking people. I never saw anybody like them before. These two seemed to be presiding. They were in white clothes and facing the crowd of dark heads and the mass of bodies, and from the fact that they both gave the impression of doing something exceedingly energetic with their hands, stepping back and forth, leaning this way and that, every other moment seeming to lift up an arm and stretch it into the crowd, I gathered that these were the dispensers of the—*sip*—aromatic goods. I had no time to verify the supposition, however, for the car moved on—just as there was another loud metallic crash from inside; from which I took it that this was a normal feature of the function of some piece of mechanism connected with the preparation and distribution to the public of 'the feeshan-cheeps'." He seemed about to stop; then—"Oh, yes ... *hm* ... and as we moved off a head appeared at the car window and a yellow ball of crushed paper was tossed in, together with an uncomplimentary remark ... The fellow must have had some beer in his stomach too ... I gathered we were some—*sip*—sort of parsons." He paused, with his lips together, raising his eyebrows a moment on the fire. "When later on I picked the paper up to throw it out, it was saturated with grease ... It was quite a time too before the stench cleared away from the inside of the car." He wrinkled his nose, as if at that minute he smelt the sharp odour of "feeshan-cheeps" contending with the fragrant fume wafted intermittently upon them from the glowing peat.

After a moment he said, "You seem to be quite right, Mr MacRury ..."—stroking his long, sardonic jaw—"I hardly recognised my native place."

His speaking had shaken them all looser to the subject. The concluding of his remarks left the other two smiling slightly in a detached way, and for a moment all three sat quite quiet in that room into which—contrary to all custom—the past had intruded with its faded stir, imparting a quivering, self-turning motion to time going past in its diurnal groove.

"You were no doubt wanting to ask me about something yourself, Mr Macpherson Bain"—Mr MacAulay's tone, the careful enunciation of the double name, showed him returned to his dry satirical humour.

Mr Macpherson Bain turned his snub-nosed face towards him. "Yes." To Mr MacRury his spectacles were again twin grey discs joined by a golden bridge, one golden leg reaching back to a rather small, round ear. His visible in-drawing of a breath aerated the dregs of the recent topic, which had grown stale: the expiration rid him, gratefully, of it. He was himself again, brisk and with unction in the actual minute.

For some time he had been thinking of a plan to do something for the youth of the area. For those in his own parish of Kinloch-Melfort he already had a number of activities organised of course, suited to the different ages, and he was glad to say that a number, yes, quite a number of young people who were not members of his church, or even . . . as yet . . . actual goers to any church had been drawn to take part, and he dared to hope that in time . . . But besides those apostolic and in a sense missionary activities in his own parish and district he had been thinking that if they put their heads together, all the clergy of the neighbourhood, they might organise something of the same kind for the whole area. He had no doubt they would agree with him—he was very glad to see "Ewen" there today—that this would be of great benefit, a fine thing for the youth. What he had in mind was that they might make a start in a small way, say, with junior and youth football, a team or teams centred on each of the churches. They would have inter-church matches, a local league perhaps; perhaps they might even rise to a Cup. In time their best teams or players might even travel outside the district. Then as to winter activities when the season came round again there was the whole range of indoor sports and games from badminton to dominoes, as well as more cultural activities such as debating. There again they might be able, though beginning in a local way, to expand to county and even ultimately national level.

His idea was that the whole of this should be run by a youth committee attached to each church, in each of which youth committees, of course, the young people would themselves be largely represented. They would, in fact, largely run the "show", the minister and other adults only acting in an advisory capacity. He thought this very important—that the young should largely run everything themselves. After all, it was their own "show", and soon they would be running the national concern. It was not too early to start acquiring the "know-how"—one couldn't in a democracy begin too early; didn't they think? And it was really remarkable how they took to it, the young people. Why, in his parish debating and public-speaking club, before it closed down lately for the season, he had had them—boys and girls in their early "teens" even—getting up without embarrassment and speaking with the utmost readiness on the great questions of the day, such as, for example, foreign affairs and the place of the church in the community. The ideas they had on that were worth the Elders of the community listening to: they would make you think. And the conduct of the whole meeting was in their own hands: one of themselves in the chair and himself, the minister, speaking simply as an ordinary member, from the floor. He felt this was all so important that he would like to see it extended throughout the region . . . He was so earnest that from time to time his eyelids behind the glasses flickered rapidly with sincerity and his eyes closed, his tenor voice took a note from the earnest enthusiasm that filled his throat, he was fervid as he turned from one to the other; while he spoke of the expanding of the work he set his arms wide and made little upward wavings with his plump hands and fingers, while he "placed" his lips together with formal precision. A certain dignity sat throughout on his person and boyish snub-nosed face, a dignity as from a dedicated will to carry manfully an appointed and apportioned weight of responsibility that was really too great for him or for one flesh-and-blood man . . . What did they think?

Mr MacAulay cleared his throat roughly.

At last . . . "*Sip*, *sip*—I think you must make up your mind whether you are—*sip*—a minister of the Gospel, or—*sip*—a Youth Education Officer."

Mr Macpherson Bain recoiled, stricken, with round-spectacled dismay. The atmosphere was uncomfortable. His brows knotted in the middle above his nose.

"But *surely*, Mr MacAulay, you realise the value of it, the nourishing of responsibility, the . . . the pre-training in citizenship."

Mr MacAulay had not altered his position or expression. He looked taut inside his rusty blacks in his worn tapestry-covered chair.

"I realise nothing of the sort." He raised his eyes from the fire to some damp-stains on the wall above it. "I don't see how you think you are going to make good citizens by teaching young and ignorant persons to rely on their uninformed judgment on things of most moment. There's more than good-will needed . . . The world has gone on for a very long time, you know. And all that time the best minds, and some of them of almost more than human power and sweep, have addressed themselves to the great questions of human life, and addressed themselves with humility and patience—and you ask us to applaud or receive with reverent awe the views of some apprentice in his teens, any shock-headed apprentice with grease behind his ears out of your thingumbobbium factory, who has neither the means of knowledge nor the capacity for reflection, who has no experience of life unless it is from A half-way to B, and is more than innocent of the first pre-requisite for judgment-forming on any subject, which is some knowledge of what has already been thought or said about it. *You* on the other hand would encourage the very generally held and dangerous view that there is no truth save in opinion—with the corollary that the more ignorant and crude the opinion the more valuable it is, the more practical, the more inspired, the more requiring awed respect, whereas the voices of the past all speak folly and any contemporary judgment is invalid and even contemptible that comes out of knowledge and learning, piety and refinement. That's the wrong-headed and fatuous idea that's rising to the ascendant all over the place today so far as I can gather—I believe some call it democracy, when it's only the deification of crudity and ignorance—and it's so dangerous an idea that it's capable, of itself, without impact of external pressures, of bringing down our entire civilisation, which was built up on the contrary belief and the opposed scale of preferences, the belief namely that a judgment was worth consideration in proportion as it was the outcome of learning and experience, of patient and pious submission to the 'fact' and the objective truth of the case involved.

"And so you see my reason for thinking that what you're giving in your debating society is not a pre-training in citizenship but, unless you're careful, early preparation for a part in the destruction of our society itself. That's what you do if you train young citizens in a habit of relying confidently on the first ignorant notion that comes flying into their heads as if it were a final guide on grave matters of civic principle . . . or even policy. However . . . what I *do* realise . . ."—there were some very large brown freckles under the dry skin of the long hand he put up to relieve the pressure of the rather frayed clerical collar under his chin, and his voice had suddenly taken a note of magisterial severity—"what I do realise is the complete unfittingness of a minister of the Gospel sitting among children and submitting, presumably, his judgment to theirs on the question of the Church's place in the community—or on any other question concerning either the Church *or* the community. He is understood to be a pastor—*pastor pastoris—sip*—a shepherd. And a shepherd is excluded by definition from being one of his own sheep. It's shameful. It's absurd, Mr Macpherson Bain."

Mr Macpherson Bain flushed. His bearing, however, had remained perfectly restrained and correct. His voice now was even and reasonable.

"But that was merely by way of the mechanism of debate."

Mr MacAulay was dry . . . "You may have intended it so."

"Well, but," urged Mr Macpherson Bain persuasively, his spectacles owlish on Mr MacAulay, "if the young people are not to learn to discuss and ponder those questions *now*, when and how else are they to be introduced to them?"

Mr MacAulay's eyes seemed for a moment as if they would have turned towards Mr Macpherson Bain. "Questions of the Church and the community?" The eyes *almost* turned towards him.

"Yes. *Particularly* those."

Mr MacAulay drew himself more upright in a leisurely way in the roomy, tapestry-covered chair. He stretched out his legs in front of him and crossed one ankle upon the other.

"It's a question of this . . . Has the Church a message, a definite message in the form of a series of propositions or creed which it has been given authority and a mandate to deliver? Which it is its business to deliver?"

Mr Macpherson Bain made a sideways bite at his lip

and sat chewing it with a large motion, looking aside at the floor. Mr MacAulay raised his eyes to the ceiling long enough to say with a quirk of his mouth, "I mean that question to be taken rhetorically."

Mr Ewen MacRury in the leather armchair had started forward, and now sat with the edge of a forefinger stroking one side of an imaginary moustache, looking at Mr MacAulay and wearing a slight, anticipatory smile.

"What I mean is this," went on Mr MacAulay with even more of dry precision, and still that faintly ironic air. "If the Church has a message given it from on high, has the minister any other duty than to deliver it to the people? . . . or is it perhaps the people's duty to deliver the Church's message to the minister?" He had been sliding down in his chair and now drew himself up again, and shook off his ironic air. "If the Church has a doctrine, a message, a theology, there must, so far as questions at large are concerned, be principles to be drawn from that theology governing in both the civic and personal moral sphere, governing both the public life of the nation and the private life of its component citizens, and it should therefore, one would think, be the business of the Church's ordained ministers to draw out those dependent principles and to enunciate them from the pulpit, in and out of season, for the guidance of the nation and the individual—'they that have ears to hear, let them hear'. The function of a minister is before everything else to *teach* . . ."

"To exhort? . . ." said Mr Macpherson Bain turning on him his glasses and raising his eyebrows.

"Yes, to exhort," agreed Mr MacAulay without looking round, letting his long chin fall down towards his breast and looking at the fire now from somewhat under his tufted reddish brows. "But to exhort to what?

You can't simply exhort for the sake of exhorting. To exhort to the observance of what has been delivered, to exhort to correspondence with the principles that have been laid down and *taught* . . ."

His voice ceased unexpectedly, and the topic might have seemed to drop dead. Mr Macpherson Bain with a hand on each plump knee sat half-turned towards him, the dull flush still on his neck and face, his thickish lips "placed" together in attentive deference. The Rev. Ewen MacRury sat not quite relaxed in the other chair, his grey-blue eyes—fixed somewhat sideways on Mr MacAulay—bright with a light not easily read, as if the spirit behind the eyes had been enlivened but remained poised and uncommitted as to direction of flow.

Mr MacAulay stirred, raised his greenish eyes as high as the damp-stains on the wall and lowered them again. "If on the other hand the Church has no theology, then it has no principles that can be drawn from its theology—*it has nothing to teach.* In that case it has no longer any reason to exist and it would be better for it to get itself gone, to hie itself hence; it is only cumbering the ground. The duly appointed and paid officers of the public education service can easily enough organise all the debating societies that are wanted . . . Though in that case they would be as well not to waste their time debating the function of a non-existent entity in the life of the community."

Though his words implied a great definiteness of view he spoke with a dry detachment, without heat or "feeling", just like an elder person making something simple in itself clear to some rather obtuse juniors.

"That's the whole question and I come back to it. Has the Church a theology, a creed? If so it has a message from God and it has no other business than to deliver it. If not . . ."—he shrugged and moved his hand.

The silence remained more tense than before, till Mr MacAulay broke it again.

"As for the spacious and edifying prospect of inter-parish football matches and inter-congregational dominoes . . ."—he again fell to plucking with the ends of his long fingers the rusty tufts that edged the sweep and expanse of his baldness. "*Sip*—I'm not opposed to bodily exercise, but I can foresee no advantage to religion from turning the church porch into a skittle alley."

"But, but surely . . ." Mr Macpherson Bain was vexed and at the same time prompt to seize the opportunity of breaking free of his silence. "How else can we . . . And in any case haven't we the highest injunction, aren't we positively instructed to 'go out into the highways and hedges and compel them to come in'?" With instinctive pulpit manner he had set wide his arms, making waving-on movements with his plump hands falling open from his wrists, although Mr MacAulay was not looking at him.

"Compel them to come in, yes—*sip*—but not to a football match. You, it seems to me, are ready to 'compass heaven and earth to find one proselyte'. But when you have found him what have you converted him to? Football, and dart-throwing and card-games?"

"But those are only means, surely?"

"If the means go no farther then they become ends. You may get a person in by handing him a set of darts, but when you have got him the most likely thing is you'll find you haven't got a communicant but only a dart-thrower. Go out into the highways and hedges by all means, but offering the message of your faith, not darts."

"That's open-air meetings again. I wonder how much success you would have with that method at the present day. You yourself, Mr MacAulay, have you tried, or do you try the method of carrying the message into the highway?"

Mr MacAulay stirred, and something like a shadow seemed to pass across his long face, leaving it heavier. "*Sip*—I might plead, of course, that I am an old man, and entitled to regard myself as past those active phases. However . . . I engaged to proclaim the Gospel in this particular parish, and I do that, and there my particular responsibility ends. You see, the whole of *this* parish *does* come to church . . . *sip*—I agree your situation is quite different."

As no reply came from Mr Macpherson Bain who was staring at him and manifesting again the tendency to gnaw the corner of his lip, Mr MacAulay went on in a tone that fell on the air with less of an effect of dryness. "No . . . the Church—*any* church—joins to itself the people to whom its message is directed only on condition that it enunciates its message and in no uncertain voice . . . on condition that it propagates the truths of God, of theology, of religion, of which it conceives itself the depository . . . Amid the incense of acceptable truth—not the aroma of fish and chips—the Church must proclaim its message, and be 'instant in season and out of season' in doing it, so that all be compelled to hear. And if they will not have it, then—'behold ye despisers and wonder and perish'."

Mr Macpherson Bain sounded despondent for the first time, with a touch of resentment, blinking behind his spectacles . . . "In that case the present generation, as they cannot be brought to feel that theology is *real*, will perish."

"Very well, then—*sip*," said Mr MacAulay, the

lights for the first time shifting really massively on his bald skull as he turned his head, stretching his arm towards "Garvie on Exodus".

The suggestion was unmistakable. The two young ministers got simultaneously to their feet.

"Are ye away?" said Mr MacAulay as if surprised, making to get out of his chair.

10

Mr MacAulay had not once looked squarely at Mr Macpherson Bain during the whole visit—and only twice at Mr MacRury. Now—standing in his doorway, the flat bonnet on his head again, and tilted well forward above his long face—he let his greenish eyes rest on them from under the down-tilted snout; just a momentary glance while they both were still facing towards him but moving backwards away.

"Well," he said, "*sip*—goodbye!"

"Goodbye," they murmured, smiling as bound in duty, Mr Macpherson Bain showing his good, rather widely spaced teeth; and turned about together: and together commenced walking down the drive. They had for some time felt themselves to be walking away from a closed door when a small, shatteringly distinct voice seemed to say "Thanks!" from behind them. They wheeled round, startled. Only to see, or seem to see, the door in act of quietly closing.

Immediately they resumed their walk, nothing said. Mr MacRury appeared to be having difficulty in restraining a strong disposition to laugh outright. Mr Macpherson Bain held forward, with just perhaps a slightly heightened colour.

They were walking now in an area of quiet, and the

trees stood back from the drive. In the enclosed, disengaged air their feet sounded unpreventably crisp and full.

The sun above their right hand was lying farther down, but its light still drenching nearly the whole of the wall of tall trees on their left. All through the branches the uncountable bursting buds were as if lighted up in the dulcet beams. The buds on the right, though scarcely any were touched by the sun, seemed almost equally bright against the darkness of the wall of shadowed trees. Walking down between, one saw and felt the bursting buds like a great shower of large snowflakes halted in mid-descent, suspended in mid-air, among the branches. Just for a moment there was a sense of a world tumbling to pieces beyond the silent wall of this visible, illuminated world.

"That's wonderful, isn't it?" Mr MacRury said with inclinations of his head this way and that towards the daffodils; stricken by the depth of their golden flame, the intensity of their great unmoving masses seeming alive and watching by the path, under the trees.

Mr Macpherson Bain, at his left side, did not seem to have heard. He was bareheaded, his fair hair, cut close, brushed straight back. He looked straight forward through the thick gold-legged glasses sitting astride the bridge of his snub nose which pointed bluntly ahead, his rather broad lips "placed" together with an appearance of preciseness.

He suddenly dropped out, "*Eh?* What did you say, Ewen?" without turning his eyes.

"Wonderful place, this," said Ewen again, nodding his head this way and that, but without quite the same degree of conviction now that the flat impersonality of his companion's tone threw into self-conscious relief the intensity in his own voice, speaking of the daffodils.

The other glanced here and there up at the tall elms and sycamores standing so still, their heads barely moving.

"Diabolical racket when there's a storm, I believe."

He threw off the words with a sort of snapping movement of his thickish, hard-looking lips. The ground colour of his fine tweed suit was a very pale green, with thin nigger-brown and light brown lines criss-crossing in large fashion all over it. It fitted well on his plump shoulders as they moved slightly with his somewhat bouncing walk.

Inside the gate Mr MacRury went and drew his bicycle out from among the bushes and, while Mr Macpherson Bain, looking anything but a minister, held back the tall half-gate he had opened, passed through on to the edge of the road. He set his bicycle with a handlebar resting against the tall dusty brown railings while he put about him the fawn raincoat he had been carrying over his arm from where it had hung inside the door of the house all the time of his visit. The while Mr Macpherson Bain closed the gate with a low clang and came up beside him.

"Well, well," said the latter, with an air of "cutting his losses".

His bespectacled glances this way and that up and down the empty road—not at him—spoke so appealingly of a severe blow and dignified reserve and resignation that Mr MacRury had said before he realised it, "Well, I'll speak to the teachers about your ideas, Davie. I don't see why something couldn't be done . . . About the football idea at any rate," he added somewhat hastily.

But enthusiasm at once having returned, Davie gave, in his delicate pale green, brown criss-cross suit, a dancing or re-enlivened step backwards on the road.

"Splendid! . . . Well, let me know what comes of it, what they're prepared to do, and we'll make contact . . . I'm very glad to know you're with me, Ewen." His snub nose was now turned directly on Mr MacRury: his teeth had appeared widely. He glowed with reassurance. "I knew you would be, though."

This was too sweeping, taking things too much for granted: Mr MacRury felt impelled to say: "Oh, well, I'm in favour of everything that's for the benefit of the young people, Davie . . . especially those that are at that unprovided-for stage, just left school. But of course" —with a small deprecating laugh—"I wouldn't be prepared to say in advance that my ideas would be identical with yours in all respects." He seemed to feel he had to say this.

"No-no-no-no, of course, of course not," said Davie at once, eager not to lose the new reassurance and at-one-ness by any lack of supple promptitude in conceding and modifying, "but"—with happy relief at falling upon a "safe" line or formula—"we do at any rate agree in this, that we must move with the times . . . take heed of the fact of Progress. *Eh?*"—taken suddenly aback and with face-falling—"what are you laughing at? What's the joke?"

Mr MacRury's chest moved still, inside the fawn raincoat, with the laugh that had risen in him involuntarily, although he had suppressed it to all but an invincible smile in the upper regions. It was still in his baritone voice, however, full and alive.

"It's that word! . . ." he got out. (Also there was the sudden completeness with which a very sincere effort towards mutuality had been blown sky-high.) "You were unlucky. It's my very private and favourite aversion."

"What? . . . *Progress*, Ewen?"

Ewen had to suppress the laugh deep in him again—the way in which his own definiteness in assertion and Davie's incredulity showed them to be in two completely different worlds while standing on the same spot on the surface of a third. "Yes," he said, his mouth quirking, "'*Progress*'. I simply don't recognise the thing."

"*What!!*" Davie Macpherson Bain stood in front of him on the road facing him squarely in his pale sporty tweeds. But he had resource to signal up some show of humour to save what was left of the situation.

"*Et tu, Brute!*" he said in mock-tragic accents of reproach. "Crikey! What a day!"

But there was a sadness in his air: he looked, in spite of "gameness", forsaken or betrayed, standing in his light sporty clothes by himself. Also there was considerable real puzzlement in the eyes that screwed themselves up and blinked a number of times behind the thick glasses and looked intently—it had to be a little up—at Ewen with reflection and enquiry simultaneously. Where they were standing the air moved cool though languid about them. The sun did not reach just there because of the trees. They had, in that shade, paler and larger impressions of each other. Mr Macpherson Bain's roundish snub-nosed face swam in stillness above his rigidity, the hardish lips held "placed" together, the features smoothed and tense with inward preoccupation. His eyes, crinkled, were fixed reflectively on Ewen with only partial sight . . . He stirred.

"Let's sit in the car!" he said suddenly, and his heel scraped on the road.

II

It was entirely in line with the character he assumed or cultivated, or coveted, for himself—of careless and nonchalant detachment—that his little car should have been of an ostentatious decrepitude. A sour and surly green where it appeared through the grey coating of concreted and impacted dust, having an air of sagging between its wheels, its canvas hood dark with age and darker in streaks that suggested decomposition: yet retaining enough tension between its ribs to knock off the Rev. Mr MacRury's hat as he stooped—but, though not a tall man, did not stoop low enough—in getting in.

Inside, it was a tight fit. It was a question whether the car doors could be shut on the both of them side by side, though neither was large, and Davie Macpherson Bain was chubby rather than stout. At last, by leaning across, pressing hard on Mr MacRury with a "Watch yourself, Ewen!" and slamming the door with violence, Mr Macpherson Bain managed to close it and get it to stay closed.

"Now," he said, crossing his hands on the driving wheel in front of his breast, "let's have this out . . . It's important to me!"—he turned to Ewen as far as there was room. "Do I understand you to maintain that there is no such thing as Progress . . . that we are not living in an age of Progress?"

"I would really need to see that question in writing, Davie. It all depends on whether you're spelling the word with a small or a capital 'p'. If with a small 'p'—certainly there is progress to be observed from time to time in one direction or another in human affairs, and certainly ours is—strikingly, I should say—an age of that kind of progress in a number of directions, chiefly in the direction of technical means: though it is equally an age of no progress in other directions. But I understood you to be using the word with a capital 'P'—in the sense of 'Progress', total, continuous, inevitable . . . a sort of impersonal Law presiding over the whole of history."

"But certainly, Ewen. Of course that's how I meant it. And surely one *must* believe in Progress in that sense. Surely it's the great fact of human life and history. Why, man, it's the saving and sustaining Hope! What would we fall back on if we lost the conviction that in spite of everything man was slowly but surely advancing, conquering fresh ground? And in our day too . . . among all those things that apparently threaten and mean world destruction."

"Yes . . . I was afraid that was what you meant . . ." Mr MacRury was sitting with his head very near the disreputable-looking canvas of the roof, his arms lightly encircling his hat which rested on his lap. His grey-blue eyes regarded the slope of bare earth that formed the other side of the road, surmounted by a layer of grass out of which could be seen protruding the lower parts of wooden paling-posts—the whole rather indistinctly seen through the long uncleaned part of the windscreen in front of him. "Today is always and in every way better than yesterday," he said quietly, meditating almost dreamily to himself, "and yesterday has always been in every way better than the day before, and so through inevitable degrees back to the altogether primitive and, in the bad sense, simple beginnings . . . and how very flattering to us it is too. And then again on, and on, to better and better things, through an endless stream of tomorrows improving on an endless series of improved todays, till an inevitably perfect state of human happiness is reached, as distant and vague in content as it is desirable . . . It was the true religion of the last century . . . and so fatuous an idea that nothing less solid than the incredible expansion of last century could have given it apparent substance . . ." He woke up and turned his head. "But why bring this thing up if the idea means so much to you? Wouldn't you be better . . ."

"No, no, Ewen . . ." said Davie. "I admit I cherish the idea, because it's an idea that gives meaning to my life and activities . . . to feel oneself an agent, however humble, in advancing the great beneficent tide sweeping through history, sweeping man on and on to better and yet better things . . . It's an idea I'd not like to give up, and I'll admit I feel uneasy even to hear it called in question . . ." He was in fact perceptibly restless behind his driving-wheel: the springs proclaimed it. "But if your contention is that it won't stand the test of reality, let's hear what you have to say; whatever happens. I'm no ostrich to stick my head in the sand—which by the way I understand they never do—or . . . or shut myself up in an ivory tower, or to be more up-to-date a steel and concrete tower, or . . ."

"Shoot off in a private rocket perhaps . . ."

"Exactly, and become a one-man satellite in space . . . No, no, let's have it . . . the gen of all this, so long as it's pukka. What are your grounds for denying the operation of a Force in history, shall I put it? Guiding or leading mankind along all the time towards better and better things, and bound in course of the fulfilment of time to sweep him on to a happy state on earth, his natural beatitude?"

"That's very simple. My reason for denying the evident presence of such a Force in history is its manifest absence."

"What do you mean?"

"I mean that one cannot find in history any slightest sign of an inclination to follow a course of uninterrupted, unilinear progress. If Progress so conceived—universal, impersonal, continuous, inevitable—were a reality, if there were a Force continuously leading man on to a better and better state of life, and that independently of him, in spite of his tendency individually and in the mass to error, to misdirection of effort, to inertia, at times to destruction and mania and outright evil, then the graph of history would describe one continuous upward line: it couldn't be otherwise."

"And what *does* the graph of history describe then, Ewen? You draw it, and let it be hung on every wall in the country, say I, for the education of us all. I mean that seriously. What could be more important?"

Ewen had that quirk in his mouth that he had when he spoke while smiling. "I doubt if you'd care to have it hanging on your wall. It's a bit of a mess. If it resembled anything at all it would be rather like a ton of knitting wool tangled by regiments of puppies or kittens.

"Seriously, Davie . . . in the first place the sum total of what all historians know about history is only a fragment of it; and even if historical scholarship and research should yet add much to our knowledge, it will still only be a knowledge of a fragment of history, a mere fraction of human time. That of necessity; whole eras have gone for ever without leaving decipherable trace. Now, if history has a meaning, that meaning must extend to the *whole* of history: it must require that the graph of the whole of history come under our eyes so that its course and shape may appear and hence its meaning. The fact therefore that great areas of history—we do not know how great—are not within our knowledge means that the full graph of history can never possibly come under the observation of any observer, and therefore that the meaning of history, assuming that it has one, can never be grasped by anyone anywhere at any point within the temporal stream. Similarly the future is a part of history just as much as the past, and equally requiring to be shown in the complete graph that is to exhibit the course of history and in legible handwriting state its meaning. And the future is closed to us, since it has no existence as yet. So there you have it: the history we know is simply a partially lighted middle belt or area between two areas of darkness of unknown and unknowable content and extent—known history: a mere moment of some six thousand years, the early parts even of that overhung by an obscurity of our yet undispelled ignorance, the contemporary part equally obscured by too much knowledge of detail of as yet unknown significance—and the whole, in fact, to some extent or other distorted by the condition of every observer's immersion in his own age and for that matter his own constitution and temperament, which will in spite of his best precautions affect his vision and apprehension of what he perceives. In these circumstances who is to discern the meaning of history?" He smiled aside at Davie Macpherson Bain. "You will see why I respectfully declined the task of chart-maker."

David Macpherson Bain did not smile back: he was too serious. "Yes, I see the force of all that, and maybe I *was* too sanguine, too optimistic. But look here . . . Could it not be if the line of history emerges into the light of our knowledge going in a certain way and keeps on going in that way right across the territory of what we know of history, and is still pointing that way when it, so to speak, passes into the future—would we not be justified in taking it that that has been its course all along and will continue to be its course in the future, and basing our chart or graph that is to yield up the meaning of history on that?"

"You're forgetting the kittens and the ton of knitting wool, Davie. A great number of trends of different nature and different force moving men in different directions and at different rates simultaneously—an involved and tangled skein impossible for a merely human or finite intelligence to disentangle—that's the real graph of history through the whole of its visible course. Admittedly you will find lines of clear progress in it, but only here and there and from time to time, over a limited course, and you will find at least as many examples of retrogression and decay. At times you will find very long lines continuing on the same level, going neither up nor down, where a culture has arrived at a sort of equilibrium of its internal elements and the elements of its material environment. There doesn't seem to be any reason why these should not continue for ever on a horizontal line if only they don't suffer an impact from outside them. There is, of course, the possibility of their being overwhelmed by a cataclysm, in which case the line representing them would simply come to a dead stop on your chart. But there are lines of all sorts jumbled together and superimposed one on the other: some rising slowly and declining slowly, or rising steeply and declining steeply: too many instances of lines starting very definitely upward, sometimes going up very rapidly, only to be overwhelmed by inferior elements before they had time to rise to any distance, and this totally without any visible or conceivable sense or usefulness in the business, just simply an absolute loss of culture potential. Well, there you have it—the graph of history, Davie. It's not a single line, going in any direction, or describing any sort of shape or pattern, but an indefinite number of lines all going in different directions at different rates; and as for seeing a pattern in the whole, it would take a million lives for one intelligence to plot them all, let alone contemplate the resulting pattern, if any, and read its meaning."

12

There was a moment of pregnant silence. Then Mr Macpherson Bain with a dramatic flourish brought down his thumb solemnly on the button above the steering column and a long dismal hoot blared vulgarly under the disreputable car bonnet out in front. Immediately the little car was filled with their laughter, in different voices from those in which they had carried on all conversation up to now, fresh, student voices much younger—a decade younger—than their present years. "*Ha-ha-ha* . . . well, well . . ." went on Mr Macpherson Bain, trying to regain the power of articulation, "I hope you feel you've more room now that you've eliminated me! What a squelch!" Then immediately, "Good heavens!" he exclaimed in concern, trying to turn round and look behind. "What if Mr MacAulay heard that! He'd think we were more irresponsible than ever!"

After a pause to recover his sobriety—"History is inscrutable then, Ewen?"

"You've got the right word for it, Davie—inscrutable. All the attempts to read its ultimate meaning are as presumptuous and doomed to failure as they have frequently been pious in intention. I'm afraid it must be said that those who have claimed to draw the true graph of history—whether they drew it in a continuous upward line that denoted Progress, or in whorls and spirals, or with a cyclic or dialectic motion—have all been imposing on the facts of history a pattern preconceived in their own minds, very often traceable to nothing more historical than their own temperament or the contemporary emotional and intellectual climate to which they have attempted to force the facts to conform. A closer acquaintance with the facts won't sustain the theory of any of their all-explaining schemes and formulae. History continues to follow a course that cannot be plotted out beforehand and to move towards an end which no one can anticipate . . . short, of course, of mere guess-work; that's open to us all. In actual fact theories of history are interesting not from the point of view of history but of psychology—why did precisely those johnnies hit on just those notions? That's the real significance of these theories and as you can see it's not a matter of history at all."

There was the same tense silence in the car. Then . . . "You astound me, Ewen. Really you astound me, laddie. Of course you know I always thought you were 'cracked' on your ancient history, even when we were students. Remember how we used to rag you in the digs about your Amenhoteps and Thutmoses and Allthebadhats? D'you remember how Colin Gunn used to tease you about that romance he made up, King Hammurabi the Badhat running away with Queen Atishoo?"

"Hatasu, Davie," corrected Mr MacRury earnestly, "Hatasu or Hatshepsut!"—before they were simultaneously in the midst of another burst of that laughter which they had in common and which sounded so much younger than their present years and station. An unexpected touch had switched them back in consciousness to their student days and released a burst of lighthearted, undergraduate laughter.

It died away strangely soon, and left them in the present again, with the Rev. Mr Aulay MacAulay not far away behind the back of their heads, reading his books, and the afternoon sun all round them except where they were, and in the front of consciousness again "the questions"—the nostalgia, the gnawing thirst, after the truth in and beyond the grave, inescapable matters and situations co-existent with themselves. And it was in the former tone of maturity and earnest, rather anxious preoccupation that Mr Macpherson Bain's tenor shortly said . . . "Of course, mind you, your immersion in your historical studies never reached the point where your superior knowledge was any burden to me personally. Nothing like that. That was because I absolved you from any disposition to 'come it' over anybody by means of superior knowledge . . . in fact I quite appreciated even then that it was a something that made you strain after truth, even as the hart panteth after the water-brooks . . ."

After quite a pause—"But what's the profit of the thing now, when it's brought you to a radical scepticism about the ultimate meaning of it all? Your view would pretty well knock the feet from all our programmes of practical action and betterment, wouldn't it? Did it do you so much good to fight your way through to this truth if it removes the main incentive to a positive use of life—the consciousness of participating in, and being an agent of, something greater than oneself?"

"That's the incentive of all fanatics and destructive 'actives', Davie—a highly dangerous incentive. My view does a good thing if it destroys *that* incentive to action. In a person naturally mild and humane like yourself, it may emerge in a life programme of practical good works, but in a cold and unfeeling or a passionate and unbalanced personality it lies as a conviction behind all the greatest cruelties and tyrannies and outrages against humanity, all the great periods of suffering for the sake of some 'truth' imposed on masses of actual men and women by those who conceived themselves its servants-in-chief . . . But why should you need any such incentive? If a man knows his duty to God and his neighbour he has all the incentive he needs to a good and useful life without invoking a quite imaginary, impersonal Force in history and bowing down to it—or, and I think in most cases this is the deepest psychology of the thing, invoking an impersonal historical Force as justification for the uninhibited expression of his impulses, often primitive enough." With a sigh—"Well, there it is, Davie . . . history itself says that as an interpretation of history Progress is 'out'."

"Yes, but can one be as sure as all that, Ewen? I mean . . . you have the knowledge of course and I don't . . . but can't facts be made to say more or less anything? To be frank, your incentive of 'duty' sounds a bit dull and discouraging . . ."

Mr MacRury laughed quietly. "You feel you'd float along more agreeably buoyed up with the sense of destiny!"

"You have the most devastating knack of handing one's phrases back, deflated, Ewen," said Davie in mock reproachful tones. "I confess I hate to let Progress go altogether. Although I can't confute you, of course. I wish I had a little more knowledge of the facts."

"Console yourself, Davie," Mr MacRury smiled gently. "I believe I can show you the doctrine of Progress is untenable without recourse to the facts of history."

"Without recourse to the facts? . . . That's a curious claim to make! How do you propose to show that?"

"From first principles," said Mr MacRury, "in the nature of the case, on *a priori* grounds."

"Go on!"

"Well then . . . The first thing to note is that the doctrine of Progress, and the theory of the cyclic or seasonal development of cultures—spring, summer, autumn, winter; you know the idea—and the theory of the dialectical or side-to-side plus upward movement of cultural development, all the cut-and-dried pattern-theories of history, have this in common, that they presuppose *necessity*, they every one of them assume that the course of events is *predetermined* to accord with the pattern or chart in question. Think it over and you will see it is so; they all assume that there is a course which human events *must* follow. By so doing they all rule themselves out of court as valid interpretations of history.

"Because in order to make out their case they ignore, set aside and implicitly deny the only fact about which there can be no dispute, namely that history is about *Man*. History is the record of what *Man* has done and said and thought—and not what man has done and said and thought while acting as an uncomprehending puppet of some impersonal Force dragging him this way and that according to some predetermined pattern, but in its highest sense what man has done and said and thought while acting *as Man*, while acting in his capacity and according to his proper nature as Man. And man's proper nature is to possess reason and free will. Don't let's argue about how free man is; that's old games and we could be here for a week. We know we are free and in what way. I am free to get out of this car this minute and go and pluck daffodils in Mr MacAulay's garden. And however trivial an act that may be it would none the less become a constituent event in history, along with all the multitude of other events equally trivial, more trivial and not so trivial. *That's* history, and history is nothing else but that. We all create it, with everything we do. And let me point out this:

"My action in getting out of here and going and plucking some daffodils may be trivial enough in itself, but even so it has the effect of to some extent dragging down or bending downwards the line of history, since it involves a consciously wrong action, the taking of what belongs to another. Such an action is bad for me, leaves its effect on my conscience and will—on my soul, if you like—it's bad for you, who witness it, it's bad for Mr MacAulay who may have to suffer the physical and spiritual consequences of indignation, which are bad at his age, it's bad for any casual witness—of whom, as you know these parts, there are bound to be at least one or two—who will have been given not only a bad example, but also cause to think less of ministers and thence probably of the Church and religion and to take less seriously their own responsibility to their conscience and their duty to God. Take all those consequences in all the persons concerned and carry them forward into all the actions and circumstances they are to be involved in in the ever-extending future—adding of course their effect in their to some extent spoiled state upon all those who are to meet and be influenced by them—and you can see that the ultimate consequence of this outwardly trivial act which I am perfectly free to make this minute are quite capable of being catastrophic for someone or even for whole numbers of persons. You only need to imagine someone—say, a young person or schoolboy at present—influenced by having witnessed my bad action, or by having heard of it, later on being in a position of public trust and at a certain moment requiring to make a decision depending on the utmost integrity, unable to rise to the required standard because he had lowered his own standards thanks to having once seen me lower mine . . . It is many times the case that the welfare of whole nations hangs upon a moral thread no thicker than one man's integrity. Actually there is nothing fantastic or intrinsically absurd in the supposition of a national catastrophe as the ultimate event of a quite trivial act which I am free to do *now*, such being the mysterious economy in the moral world of man."

" 'See how great a matter a little fire kindleth', eh?" quoted Mr Macpherson Bain appreciatively and in agreement.

"Yes. Well, that's how history is made . . . history is nothing but the totality of the acts of men, in, of course, their various relationships. Known history is the inconsiderable proportion of the acts of men that we have knowledge of, in their various relationships and significance, in so far as our impressions of that aspect of events are valid or worthwhile. History in its highest sense is truly *human* history, that is, the record of man's acts when he acted *rationally* and *freely*. In any case as the whole of history is made up of man's acts—from the most irrational, instinctive, impulsive or compulsive to the most rational, deliberate and willed—there is no room left anywhere in it for impersonal Forces and so forth. Least of all could there possibly be any room for 'impersonal Forces' in the highest movement of history which is by definition, as I have just defined it, the area of events resulting from acts rationally conceived and freely willed: manifestly anything not rational, not freely willed, and not of man, is specifically excluded here from the category of human history in the highest and truest sense."

"So you exclude from history everything but man and his acts?"

"Directly, yes. Of course, these human acts that make historical events don't take place in a vacuum: there are the forces of nature—climate, soils, etc.—which fall to be taken into account, but only so far as they create the conditions in which man acts, only so far as man has had to take them into account in acting. In themselves and directly physical laws and the material world do not enter into history. History only begins when man is on the scene."

"Yes . . . well, there are still a few things . . . First I want to ask this . . . Those chaps that made the theories—Progress, the dialectical movement theory, the cyclic or season theory, and so on—how did they manage to convince either themselves or a great section of the public if there is nothing in history to correspond with the theories?"

"Ah, I don't say there is nothing in history to correspond with the theories. The trouble is there's enough in history to correspond with a whole heap of theories. No, I don't deny for a moment that those theorists and system-makers had perceived a movement which really *is* in things and events. Such movements can all be seen, or something very like them, in various parts of history. Where catastrophe entered was when they went on to lay it down that the particular movement they perceived was the sole movement, was *that which alone moved* throughout history, and then—going further—that it was *that which moved history*. The movement was not only in history, it was itself the cause of history. Presided over by such a Force, the whole of history, future mark you as well as past, was now seen as one necessary, predetermined process. It goes without saying that men who had spent years in 'seeing' their own notion illustrated by the course of history had first a great admiration for the finished structure and then a firm and even fervent belief in it. Such was precisely the type of man who, in the name of 'enlightenment' and 'scientific thinking', would pour scorn on the men of distant antiquity for their personification and divinising of the forces of Nature; yet in reality they were themselves guilty of something still more superstitious when they, in effect, personified and divinised a mere movement in the historical process to which their own minds alone had accorded an identity and objective essence. All our contemporaries have become infected with this superstitious mystagoguery and myth-mongery; it's the New Astrology: the men of distant antiquity and the culture-primitives of our own day in divinising the powers of nature at least divinised something *real*.

"No, no, the absolute predictability of history is strictly ruled out by the nature of its main ingredient or active principle, Man; his possession of reason and free will ensures that history is created as it goes along, cannot be determined in advance. That is, while history may be seen to tend to conform, within limited contexts, to certain patterns, it is never under the external necessity of doing so; there is no moment in the course of *any* trend or movement of events when the minds of the people of that age, the actors of the drama, are not open to receive fresh ideas, and when by choosing to attach their wills to altered ideals or objectives, they cannot turn history out of the line of the pattern it has partially traced and set events off on a different course and with a different tempo, thus avoiding or evading what may have seemed till then a predetermined or inevitable end awaiting their original course. That's the whole thing; if man possesses the freedom to *will*, his actions and therefore his history cannot be determined in advance or from the outside . . ."

"But look here, laddie . . . with your 'History is nothing but Man' aren't you just a little bit dispensing with Divine Providence? Surely you're not going to deny That in history?"

Mr MacRury laughed. "Not in the least—unless by Divine Providence you're simply reintroducing your old idea of 'Progress' under a more imposing title and with theological sanctions attached! No, I don't deny that Divine Providence is in history. But I don't profess to be able to recognise Its workings with certainty and assurance. Providence doesn't act by descending into the region of human affairs and obviously pushing and shoving events this way and that. Providence is in history as by Its usual operation by first being in human minds and wills and acting on them—so it's still *human* history, you see, and my definition of history as man's acts holds perfectly, taking into consideration all the ordinary workings of Providence. What I do want to deny is the idea that God through His Providence rules events in the sense that He directly Wills whatever happens. The effect of that would be to cancel out Providence altogether. And it would also have the unfortunate effect of making God responsible for evil."

"Ye-es, I see the bit about making God responsible for evil: that's an old difficulty. An old dilemma—either God is Good, in which case He cannot be Omnipotent, since He tolerates evil in the world; or He is Omnipotent, in which case He cannot be Good, for the same reason. I see that. But I don't quite see how making Providence directly responsible for history is the same thing as abolishing Providence *from* history, if that's what you meant. *Expliquez-moi ça!*"

"I haven't ever seen any difficulty here . . . and the explanation is at the same time also the way of escape from your ancient dilemma which sets God's Omnipotence against His Goodness. It's simply this . . . Providence can only operate by preserving creatures according to the constitution of their being, according to their proper nature. Now, the proper nature of man is to possess among other things free will; that's the structure of his being. If he ceased to have free will he would cease to be man. Do you agree so far? It follows then that God's Providence operates by preserving man in being in possession of his free will; that is to say, along with the possibility—the certainty, rather—that he will often act contrary to the highest ends to which Providence ordained him, and to which he could conform himself if he so used his free will. That seems to be the fairly clear solution to the question that troubles so many people—and especially troubles their faith in a time of great catastrophe, as for instance a war—why does God permit such evil and suffering and injustice? The answer surely is that God *could* halt the evil that men do—but only by halting the men that do it, only by taking back from man His gift of free will, only in effect by withdrawing humanity from His creation, that is, destroying the whole moral structure of human nature. And of course as mankind, whether we like it or not, is One, it is in the nature of the case—and we all recognise it is in the nature of the case—that the innocent should suffer for, or along with, the guilty . . . Providence shows itself in the preservation of man with his free will, then. And if so it follows that very few human acts are ever according to the will of Providence, for there can be very few human acts that are entirely conformed to the Providential Will. In that sense it is understating it to say that most of the acts of all of us, and all the acts of most of us, are *not* according to the Will of Providence. And history is the record of those acts. Whatever history shows, it shows what the design of Providence was *not*; and that is because man, imperfect man, and not Providence must take the responsibility for it. Providence cannot be the Force that controls the shape of events, because the rôle of Providence is something quite different, the preservation of man in full liberty to act like a man and that in general is imperfectly. And that is what makes history—man's imperfect acts, and their natural consequences."

Mr Macpherson Bain had his plump thumb in the air poised ready, and a dramatic moment after Mr MacRury had ceased to speak brought it down on the button in front of his chest. This time, for fear of Mr MacAulay, only a faint apologetic "peep" came from out of the bonnet in front. They were both laughing again, as heartily as before, to which the uneasy movements of the car bore witness. A boy whose legs looked long in his short trousers, strolling up the sunlit road from Strath village, going south, saw Mr Macpherson Bain rather like a pale green fish sitting upright in a small tank of muddy water, and made out Mr MacRury a larger black shape beside him. His passing was seen but unnoticed by the two who from the front were but two sets of teeth smiling side by side in the car and who missed even the sharp throwing of his head sideways over his shoulder for a last glance in the moment just before he passed from sight.

"Och, yes, but Ewen," Mr Macpherson Bain said at last more seriously. He pulled off his spectacles and held them out forward with both hands, squinting through them or at them with his head somewhat aside, then replaced them on his nose and slipped the legs over his ears. "But you almost seem to be taking Providence out of history yourself."

"That's not how I conceive it at all. I see Providence as active in every moment of history, in every moment of every life. Every act of life means in some fashion a co-operation with its inspirations or a rejection of them. No matter how much or how often the design of Providence is defaced by man's acts, Providence is still continuously *there*, to bring, with man's consent, good for him out of however soiled a situation. In that way Providence can turn every situation to man's good. But that is very far from the position that everything that happens is in itself good and part of the design of Providence. Such a belief would at once have the effect of making man's free will an illusion: it would mean that he is not, after all, the architect of his own fate. And he is. It is his splendour and his misery that he is. Every act of every man—and I include thoughts, of course—has either a positive or a negative effect on the content of history. That is how the line of history is bent up, or down—by every act of every man. We all in fact are making history with every breath we draw. Whether we know it, or like it, or consent to it, or not. Man cannot evade his responsibility, or shuffle it on to 'Providence' or an imaginary impersonal 'Force'—call it 'Progress' or anything else. We are fully responsible for history, for our human destiny; Providence has chosen to make itself our assistant. But man is the one who does it, and as I say, he is doing it with every breath he draws."

"Gad, Ewen, you frighten me. That's a terrible weight of responsibility to lay on every poor fellow's shoulders."

"I agree, Davie, that it makes everything a lot less easy than simply leaving everything to 'Progress', or

'Rise-and-Fall', or even Divine Providence, and oneself drifting along with the tide, indulging one's inclinations in detachment. Nevertheless that is where the responsibility rests: and if that 'poor fellow' drops that burden of responsibility he makes the line of history turn downwards, were it by ever so little: and if enough of these poor fellows drop their responsibility, or alternatively use it to engage on wrong or negative courses, they can bring down their whole age in ruin—providing some cyclic or seasonal historical theorist of the future with the 'proof' that the time of the autumn and winter of their culture had arrived . . . On the other hand it is in the power of these fellows, or a sufficient number of them, to impart such a positive character to their acts that their present, by reason of being so charged with a positive content, will rise and impart an upward line to the graph of history."

"Well, Ewen . . . but . . . This is all too devastating . . . I must think of something . . . Oh, yes . . . What about the Devil, and demons? Some people believe there are forces of personal evil active among men. How do they fit into your scheme?"

For answer Mr MacRury said, "Look, Davie, do you mind if we have this door open for a while?"—his right hand fumbling, unsuccessfully, round behind his left elbow.

"Certainly, certainly, Ewen," instantly returned the other with that immediate, simple and direct response which was his undoubted charm. He lunged across Mr MacRury's front, crushing him backwards, and, after some violent manipulations the mystery of which was his private secret, freed the door and set it to swing somewhat open.

Fresh, mild air immediately spilled through the interior, enlivening them where they sat. "Yes," said

Mr Macpherson Bain, "it *was* getting stuffy in here.

"Well, now, let's have it, Ewen. How do the forces of evil fit into your scheme?"

"As before, Davie . . . it is still *man's* history. In so far as influences of personal evil have an effect in the human world they do it only through man; they don't descend in person into the arena and actively push events about—the Devil never stands for parliament in person." (An explosive sound from Davie ending in "*ha-ha-ha*"—though one still detected preoccupation.) "They can only act by being first in men's mind and will; it is still exclusively men who do the acts of which history is composed. Men are free to resist demons if they are importuned by them. As the Scripture says: 'Resist the Devil and he will flee from you.' To show what I have been meaning—just think of the difference, historically considered, between the character and effects of an act done after resisting the Devil and one done after not resisting him. I think you will see how right it is to place the responsibility for history right in the act of the individual personality."

Mr Macpherson Bain was silent, his breathing beside him declaring some straining or exasperation. "Yes, but Ewen, we're away into theology. Simply as a matter of . . . of *fact*, would you not have to admit that the present age can knock spots off any other?"

The springs screeched as Mr MacRury moved in his seat a little outwards to his left and crossed his legs so that his right foot dangled in the space of the opened door. Looking round at Davie at his right shoulder, and away again, taking a minute as if to get down from the level of the argument, he said, "Not unless the assumption is first made that all the things that distinguish our age from others are also in themselves the things of most value to man . . . no, I wouldn't admit anything of the kind. Regarding human nature most comprehensively, taking into consideration the hierarchy of *all* the elements in it that can find satisfaction in the life of culture and society, my own opinion would be that there have been lots of historical moments far more essentially humane than this."

"Och, but that's this *laudator temporis acti* business. You're just sentimental about the past. Hullo, where are you off to?" seeing Mr MacRury had turned, and his shoulders in the doorway. "Oh, I see. Good idea. Hold on and I'll be with you!"

13

A tall thin crofter in a dark-grey flannel shirt without a collar and open at the chest, with the sleeves rolled up above his elbows, was cycling to Strath for a pint of medicine for a sick cow. His shapeless-kneed trousers were of the same yellowish brown as the rust on the machine. At every turn of the wheels the bicycle cried out "*caw-caw*", and shuddered. The crofter although making no great speed was pressing hard on the pedals.

Just as he came abreast of the manse garden a voice, a light baritone voice, stated in the English language with the clearest possible articulation: "Our own century and civilisation is like a man without one of his senses in that it has lost the consciousness of the Eternal."

Startled by this announcement which seemed to come to him out of the sky, he looked to his right, and was further startled to see quite close to him, facing directly towards him, the head and shoulders of a young minister appearing above a bush inside the brown iron railings of the manse garden. The figure was clothed in a fawn-coloured coat and old-looking grey hat and although facing directly towards him was not seeing him but, smiling, looking away right over his head. Then immediately as the bicycle carried him past he caught sight of another head a little distance from the first. This time only a head, uncovered, with short fair hair, spectacles and a snub nose, turned directly towards the speaker. This was tremendously intriguing, he would have stopped to see if he could tumble to what it all was but remembered immediately that he had no brakes—and the bicycle had already been seized and was being borne on by the incline down into Strath. He did swing up his right foot on to the top of the front wheel which sent dry mud in a grey arc of dust from under the instep, but there was too much way on the machine: it was now shuddering almost continuously; he was too far past . . . and there was the cow . . .

"You know, Ewen . . . what strikes me is the way that everything you say is at variance with the notion of history everyone else carries about with him." They were standing under the trees at the gate end of Mr MacAulay's garden and Mr Macpherson Bain was speaking.

Mr MacRury smiled broadly. "I'm not surprised at that. By the way, where does 'everyone' get this notion of history that he carries about?"

"Oh, well . . ." said Mr Macpherson Bain, sweeping his jacket back and thrusting his hands into the pockets of his trousers. "I suppose it's in things they read . . . the sort of books everyone reads . . . newspapers . . . I suppose really it's the notion everyone brought away from . . . from school."

Mr MacRury ruminated, his hands in the side pockets of his fawn raincoat. "What one tends to carry away from school is a sort of historical mythology, really. There are historical facts embedded in it, although often so distorted as to be falsified; but those are not the chief thing. A historical judgment is built up, it is a thing of the mind; the myth is absorbed directly into the region of feeling and emotion. Look at your notion of 'Progress'. It's a dead cert to become a component of a popular mythology. The idea in it is utterly clear and simple—the course of history is seen as a completely firm, straight line rising continuously—one clean straight course all the way from bottom left to top right. No strain on the mind there: it's plain to the simplest, without effort. But an even greater attraction for, and hold upon, its devotees is in feeling and emotion. The notion of 'up, and up, and up' has an effect positively hypnotic; it is equally uplifting; one falls under a pleasant spell to it. And then of course—most irresistible of all because it allows us to indulge the whole gamut of self-complacency and pride—the conviction, the assurance it carries with it, that *we* and *our* age are the very top of the top, the highest yet, the best ever, the historical cat's pyjamas, in a position to look down on, or alternatively to knock spots off, anything that was ever in the world before. What a surge of pleasurable emotion this is fitted to evoke. And just because the emotion is an emotion of *pride* you won't eradicate it by anything so simple as proving that the idea is totally unhistorical. For most of us the historicity of an idea is a matter of no imaginable consequence, whereas whatever flatters us has a root hold on our acceptance. So far as historical truth is concerned the 'modern' myths were killed stone dead long ago—but they still continue to run as strongly as ever; showing that truth is no part of their vitality."

They were now outside the gates again and standing

on the road in the sunshine. Mr Macpherson Bain's back and the legs of his trousers behind looked not delicate green but altogether white where the sun shone directly on them. He stood planted with a sturdy squareness on the road, his hands in his trouser pockets, looking at Mr MacRury every moment with eyes slightly screwed up behind his glasses, his jaw muscles contracting from time to time, his brows slightly drawn together. Every other moment also his knees gave a little jerk inside the trousers that appeared pale green in front and white all down the backs.

"What's the function of the thing then—the historical mythology—if representing historical truth is no part of it?"

"Well, to boost the victim in his self-regard, of course, making history into a background having the property of throwing into relief his distinguished merits. Chiefly, I should say, to give meaning to his activity—I'd go further, I'd say the function of the myth was to give a desired meaning to a desired sort of activity."

From David Macpherson Bain came the sound of a sharp, indrawn breath ... "You're hitting hard, Ewen." He stood a moment in thought. "You're right, though. You *must* be right, about the thing giving *meaning* to activity, because that's the effect your talk is having on me. I mean if I'm not to be allowed to believe in Progress and the special worthwhileness of our specifically 'modern' activities ... it's going to take the meaning out of most of my personal activity. It ... it opens a chasm. And not for me only—for most people who try to relate their activities to something bigger than themselves, to give their activities some kind of general or supra-personal reference. What in the world are we going to do with these discarded notions? If what you say is true—and I'm not admitting it mind you; I can't afford to *yet* anyway—we haven't a clue *where* we are, or where we're going—or where we should be *trying* to go. That's what it does, you're quite right; it takes the meaning out of all our activity. It's . . . it's . . . it makes you dizzy. I see your point there well enough. If you take away from us the belief in the intrinsic superiority of 'modern' values or however you like to put it—the Myth of 'Progress'—we're not going to know what to relate our activities to, so as to give them some meaning. We're not going to know what activity we should give ourselves up to so as to have value."

Mr MacRury raised his eyes to the deep blue scarcely yet occupied by more than a few slow, opulent clouds moving above the earth, the thin fringes of atmosphere. "I don't see why that should be, Davie. Especially for *you*, or should I say *us*. It seems to me that if a man knows his duty to God and his neighbour he has all he needs to be going on with, he has got his feet morally on the ground and is really getting somewhere—instead of abdicating his moral autonomy in delivering himself up to be a mere agent of impersonal historical Powers—largely conjured out of his own inclination to evade the irksomeness of his immediate duty."

"Are you referring that to me? . . . that last bit?"

"No, not in particular." A faraway look came with a smile into the young face turned up to the sky's light . . . "Everybody's inclinations bend that way. The temptation is to lose the real value of difficult acts that are morally good for the sake of the illusory value of acting on the easy assumption that our inclinations put us in accord with the Purpose of the Age, or whatever highfalutin title you care to give to your supra-personal sanction for your feelings of personal importance and private unction."

Mr MacRury's heels came down a little sharply on the road, his hands with the same movement thrust a little more deeply down in the side pockets of his fawn raincoat.

14

Mr MacRury was just putting his foot on the pedal, after a glance at Mr Macpherson Bain's receding vehicle, which he saw leave the gate of Mr MacAulay's drive and crawl away with a decrepit, forlorn air in the direction of Kinloch-Melfort, when a cold sense of dissatisfaction with the whole afternoon's proceedings flowed over him. Mounting, he felt that he had been mumbling a tasteless husk, without noticing till now that it was tasteless . . . After all, what a man had made his leading idea he leant upon to give meaning to his life, to make sense of his activities: to insinuate radical doubt of its validity was to risk knocking away the prop of his self-respect and courage. He knew how seriously Davie regarded the issue of the various arguments by the note, the defensive note of facetiousness or flippancy that had been from time to time in his voice. He was defending his notions from too radical injury by that flippant tone—Davie had not really a high sense of humour; he had a sense of fun, a sort of rollicking sense; he would mostly miss a joke, but if he once saw a thing as funny he would continue to see it funny, and funnier every time he thought about it. The facetious tone therefore was a sort of half-hearted defence mechanism: he had his decent pride; did not want to admit too publicly that his leading ideas, the great conceptions on which he had nourished his somewhat fussy but well-intentioned activity, had no objective foundation. He feared however that in reality Davie had gone away home without some of the unction of his good deeds and uplifting, laudable activity. Which, he thought—spinning down the slight brae into Strath—was perhaps a bad thing, a pity, even if it had been a fatuous idea: Davie was a man of such goodwill, and to have taken away or lessened the spring of his good action . . .

Yet, he thought—running out on to the level—Mr MacAulay none the less with his dry penetration had gone "*sip-sip*" to the root of the contradiction in him, fingered the dislocation on the joint of his action, which was a following after good without reference to God . . . Here he braked up a little as he came down to the houses in the one street of Strath, with on his left hand now the wash of the loch-edge slapping uneasily among the black boulders; a chill dampness from it drifted across his face. (He knew what that uneasiness in the loch portended: some motion was alive in the deeps, far out, coming all this way: he even cast a speculative glance into the still serene and open sky.) The only person in the street was a tall woman with a dirty apron hanging in front of her bloated-looking body, coming towards him on thin legs. As she came on she seemed to be pillowing a too abundant drooping bosom on her folded forearms. She was looking at the ground, but as he came abreast she heard him, raised her somewhat untidy head quickly and gave a sudden, bright smile in return for the young minister's. The smile, with dazzling teeth, lifted a score of years from her on the instant; so that for a moment he glimpsed the young and charming girl improbably buried in the sallow, untidy, middle-aged woman. Something hit him in the heart when he remembered the hair of worry that had been in her forehead while as yet she was unconscious of him, walking along the street wrapped in preoccupation.

Immediately the consideration became solid in him that, when all was said and done, Davie's leading delusions were of a dangerous sort . . . "Progress"—continuous, irreversible, unilinear Progress, swinging along with the tide, looking down on the past—a psychological mechanism to justify self-admiration and the easy way of taking our inclinations as objective duties. The associated notion or feeling was that all men and women who lived in past ages were, as compared with us, deficient in mind-power, in real-knowledge and insight, in rational measure, in either macrocosmic or microcosmic "know-how" and sheer sense: the practically universal impression among us and our contemporaries being that all men and women of the past were either slow-moving, bovine creatures without minds and with hair hanging in their eyes, or else frenetic zealots with hair standing straight on end—but in either case utterly fogged in the unenlightened notions they hadn't *mature* intelligence enough to see past or through—but of course *we* can, with scarcely a glance! . . . Very dangerous, all that . . . And then that other typical associated notion or universal delusion of the day, that the whole of life consists in a number of questions to which simple answers exist and are accessible—so that manifestly if things are not perfect for everybody it can only be because of the wicked malice (or too-stupid incompetence) of "somebody"—with the obvious push towards criticism and violence in social action, whereas societies thrive and grow and maintain themselves only on affirmative kinds of thinking and acting. But that was the extreme danger of the whole contemporary frame of mind tainted with the notion or climate of "Progress", for by excessive simplification it relaxed the effort to understand, at the very moment it imparted a formidable push towards activity; it set people acting too violently in situations only partially understood, or completely misunderstood. Time—human time—is not a medium through which an impersonal force of "Progress" draws or drives its puppets for their ever greater good or advantage, but a continuous "present" in which history is shaped irrevocably in the totality of human wills. What everybody thought and felt and aimed at was not only therefore no matter of indifference, but a matter of the utmost importance in every instant of time—only, what is important is the inner quality given to acts by the Will, not their gross material quantity. Gross bulk of material activity was in itself more likely to be injurious than otherwise; joint-loosening to the structure of society. No harm therefore if someone suffers a little in his personal feelings and his sense of direction in being arrested, or slowed down, on a wrong course.

After all, it may be pretty late in the day; this sun is warm, and the air balmy, the smell of spring comes across the moors, but it would be folly to be blinded by the pleasantness of the prospect spread before the senses to the existence of an invisible, inaudible, and much more real set of forces in continuous tension of opposed pressures, and the outcome of whose opposition is the final issue of life and the signature written and to be written by time in eternity. In spite of the dust raised by the multitudinous trivial scuffling in the dead-level plains, all that was of real and ultimate moment was taking place invisibly "in the high places", in the heights of *being*. All that ultimately mattered concerned *that*—not this brightly-tinted, sweetly-smelling, envelope of material things—real indeed, but, relatively, far too real-appearing . . . He was aware himself by this time that his reflections seemed to be growing bodiless, his thoughts were getting transparent;

some other more lively or personal consideration was pushing itself to the front in his consciousness. With it a still greater feeling of emptiness and dejection—desolation even. What was it? But of course; how could it have slipped so long from his mind? What a waste of time—speech and conversation, every word of which brought one up towards the surface of oneself, arrested the deeper operations of the meditative or questing spirit and rendered the objects of profounder contemplation vaguer and more inapprehensible. Every word spoken was in some measure an abandonment of the depths, the whole of customary life with its incessant conversation is an assault upon the depths, a device to keep the soul inarticulate, silent.

He dismounted, to walk up the long slope towards Aultnaharrie. The sun was more definitely in the West. He couldn't look up now without seeing the great hills holding up their heads away in the north-by-east. Suddenly from beside one of the group of houses at the foot of the slope, behind him, a woman's too-shrill laughter burst out. It sounded like "*turree, turreee, turreeee . . . tuck-tuck-tuck-tuck* . . ." The warm saddle was in his right hand, in his left the left handle of the handlebar, the sun all bright on the road below and in front, as he paced up the slope, bent slightly forward. From the foot of the hill the laughter followed him, diminishing—"*tureee . . . tuck-tuck-tuck* . . ." Some unknown person, out of sight: it had nothing to do with him, he knew that; he was but passing through an arc of the orbit of another microcosm: a moment, trivial or pregnant with what he had no means of knowing, in another life was just then touching his own and passing through and mingling with his experience of walking up that long slope, filled, that spring afternoon of sunshine, with an inward desolation (though a coldness or emptiness, not an abjection). What he carried mostly was the sense of loss. The loss of whatever contemplations might have brought him to augmented consciousness, the affirmation, the enhancement of being, that he might have attained had he but preserved stillness in his own depths all afternoon instead of fleeing upwards and forth into the shallow chaffer of wordy notions. He regretted the forfeiture even of the contemplations of no more than historical, temporal sweep and reference, the effect of which imaginings was to give a dimension to the moments of present living: present feeling and fact alike were given particular depth, when experienced consciously against the sweep of time, felt as in motion, experienced simultaneously with the recollection or the "sense" of countless lives in more uncountable situations in the "now" as in the past and vanished. The spirit burgeons in the sense of Man; in as it were the shadow of that sense the virtues are a natural flower; out of the sense of Man judgments tend to be tempered with understanding, even as informed with knowledge. One is oneself more real, and all one's acts . . . every act and event standing clear because multi-shadowed . . .

He had walked past the houses of Aultnaharrie without noticing them and come to the top of the slope. When the changing tilt of the ground under his feet caused him to raise his head he saw his grey manse and church right ahead and just a little below him, standing clear with the immense sweep of live water and white sky above and behind.

He raised his left foot to the pedal but saw that the chain was about to come off. He stooped to adjust it and as he was doing so the air over the sea, having scarcely swayed for so long, moved forward, then came in a solid mass towards and over the land. He was stooping and adjusting his bicycle chain and the air in a large movement was rolling over him, pushing with quite senseless weight on his left side, at the very instant he was rather flinching back from the sensation of oil and grit soiling the thumb and two first fingers of his right hand. He straightened, and was pushed in the chest, had to brace himself, while the hat on his head shifted slightly. He stooped again to work his finger-tips together in the white shell dust that had ridged up along the centre and at the verges of the road; then he fingered the long grass on the raised ditch bank, and when he straightened himself again he had to put his left hand quickly to the top of his hat and press it down with a roundabout pressure. The sky seemed all at once to have suffered a whitish suffusion like albumen, the light was duller, and harder, the measurelessly wide, hitherto shining surface of the running sea was swept by broad, twiching swathes of dark roughness, like fur . . . He knew the signs.

He mounted, was held a moment as if poised, then with fluttering coat sailed on into the wind. There was in him still only a desolation of yearning towards those contemplations lost and forfeited, the feeling of emptiness lingering after the "normal" use of time, unfilled with consciousness or more conspective thought . . . But when he had to brake at his gate it was like a burden to him: to open it he seemed to have to call upon himself; and again in closing it. On the crashing gravel his footsteps seemed to falter once or twice going towards his house: he appeared under some constraint or impulse to fall motionless, his eyes bent on the bright gravel a little before his feet, while his whole person stilled, his features were as if brushed with serenity. It could be seen that it was more than spatial images, temporal contemplations, that he was missing now. He had visibly to pull himself towards himself, in order, sighing, to drag rather than push the skidding bike through the screaming gravel.

15

The trouble was that Bando, where he stood, was effectively blocking egress, without seeming to do so: he had the minister at his mercy, for he could not get out without pushing his way out—and no minister, certainly no young minister, was strong enough to take the risk of offending Bando by so obvious a brushing aside of him and his conversation. He was standing more inside than outside the door—in fact in exactly the farthest-in spot that allowed him to keep his cap on without too grossly and obviously violating the code of respect which even he was not yet confident enough to set at naught. One step farther in and he would have had to take it off, which he would have done with reluctance for any man: where he was he was just, by stretching the point, technically outside, and could retain the cap because of considerations of the draughty wind, his bald head, and so on.

They were in the shed, the tool-shed at the back of the house where the minister kept his bicycle. Mr MacRury was very uncomfortable, kept standing there. He was never in that shed without experiencing irritating little tickling sensations in the palms of his hands and soles of his feet because snails abounded in it and in their season one could scarcely move without crushing a shell: they would be everywhere, over the floor, on the walls, crashing through the spiders' webs near the window, even on the work-bench, on the tools. The shed smelt of oil. Most of all he was irritated by

Bando's failure to come to the point: he wanted to make it, of course; all his palaver was to prepare the way for its effective release; yet he was unable to overcome his reluctance to part with it. He stood there with his back to the opened door, chewing and looking alertly this way and that—but not at the minister, to whom he presented only his profile, a dry dirty-white curtain of eyebrow overhanging an unresting little eye, and under a thin, rather finely shaped if somewhat reddened nose, a drooping curtain of wet and stained moustache through which every now and then came—*ploop!*—an amber squirt of juice descending upon the cemented walk outside. He had known there was a point from the very moment he came round the corner of the house and found Bando hanging about the door of the shed—having no doubt heard the splashing noise of the gravel carried by the wind.

"Well, a Bhando," he had said, "the wind is rising again"—assuming a light tone that far from corresponded with his feeling, and feeling partly emptied at once. Bando had stood back to let him into the shed with his bicycle.

"The wind is rising again, Mr MacRury," he said at his leisure, and contrived to make it sound like, "You are weighed in the balances and found wanting!"

He stood there in the doorway moving his shoulders and hands, loooking this way and that, the wind turning and folding his trousers about below the knees, inwards and out.

The minister stooped to slip the cycle-clips from his trousers at the ankles, and straightening looked again at Bando. He was a dirty little man. Dirt lay thick in the convolutions of his upper ear above the dirty-white tufts that protruded from its centre. It was black too in the folds or deep-cut wrinkles on his collarless neck above the grey flannel shirt. An amber globule hung tenaciously from half a dozen long hairs of his stained moustache which it held wetly glued.

He said—and he was aware himself that irritation was making him outrun discretion, that he was pushing matters too fast and too crudely—"Well, but, a Bhando . . . what proof have you got of this? You're telling me that young Mr Balneaves the teacher is drinking. If that is so it's a pity. But you haven't said what proof you've got of such an accusation." All the time he spoke he felt how trivial and nasty this was.

Bando jumped. He leant his back against the ridge of the open door, looking out at the world as if surprised to see it so open and so windy.

"Proof is it?" he squealed, moving his arms and hands, and moving his body against the door as if there was an itch between his shoulder-blades. He turned his head away and there was the sound of a discharge of spittle. Without turning back towards the interior of the shed he said, and his voice screamed and trembled with self-righteousness, "Them that will be on the road between here and the Duaray Hotel will be able to speak of proof!" Averting his head even farther he flourished with his hand—"At hours in the morning . . . hours in the morning!"

Again came the flourish of his hand. As if he had abundance of proof at disposal . . . proof and to spare.

Mr MacRury looked at the back of his head, set above his narrow, sharp shoulders, and wondered what he could do to make himself stop his nervous twiddling with the cycle-clips in the right hand pocket of his raincoat. To get out of this snail-paradise with its smell of oil. Although every few minutes, without interruption of the seething sound of the air outside, that smell was dispersed towards the back of the shed by a fresh healthful gust, glorious with scents of the sea and the moor, turning aside and blustering in through the door.

"How many times has Mr Balneaves been seen coming home from the Duaray Hotel at hours in the morning, a Bhando?"—the note, he felt, was unintentionally far too magisterial.

Bando was shocked. Turned round and looked at Mr MacRury with reproach, his cheek muscles for the moment resting from their rhythmic bulging, and his jaw seeming to have fallen, his mouth to be open behind the curtain of dirty-white moustache.

"Oh, plenty of times, plenty of times!" he screamed through its damp fringes.

"But how many times, a Bhando? That's important, you know."

A pained look disturbed Bando's always rather rigid expression. He turned his narrow back and looked this way and that outside, as if to see they were not being overheard.

"Three times at any rate," came his voice . . . "And mind you, all in the last week. No doubt he'll always have been tippling at it. You can't be getting proof of that so easy . . . who can tell what he will be bringing in a suitcase? And he takes care nobody will be knowing what he has, for they tell me he carries the keys of everything about at the end of a chain that he fastens to a button under his braces. He knows best himself why he would be needing to be so careful . . . But it's coming to the front now." Turning again his profile to the minister, its expression seemingly indifferent, or simply empty and rigid . . . "Yes, it's coming to the front now. This is a bout he seems to have taken." The air, swiftly and massively passing over, moaned occasionally. His trousers below his knees folded and unfolded vigorously against his legs. "And if he takes this one he will be taking others."

"You know, a Bhando, it's a serious matter to take away a man's character. We ought to be very sure it is true before believing anything against a man, much more before spreading it abroad among others."

"*Ptchawch!*" Bando exploded with a squeal of contempt. "A young foreigner like that one is! Not a drop's blood to anybody in the district!" He shuddered with disgust.

"Mr Balneaves is no foreigner, a Bhando. His name is better Gaelic than . . . many hereabouts." (He had been about to say "than your own", but realised he had again forgotten Bando's legal name. Easy to do, since one never heard it.)

"Do you tell me that now?" squealed Bando in questionably genuine surprise. "Well, his behaviour is not good Gaelic nor good anything else!"

"If he is guilty of what you say, perhaps. But you have done nothing to prove your statement. And mark you, a Bhando, that Mr Balneaves doesn't come from this neighbourhood is no excuse for our treating him with less consideration than we'd give to our own. It should rather be the other way. The mere fact that he is a stranger, without friends or relatives here, ought to plead with us for *more* consideration, for more strict and careful justice." I'm managing this situation badly, he was saying to himself; too impatient, too impetuous.

Bando's expression, turned to him along his right shoulder, was confirmation. Bando affected to be outraged.

"You put surprise on me, Mr MacRury! You put surprise on me! To think that I have lived . . .! And the man a drunkard!"

Mr MacRury was annoyed to feel himself blushing

slightly, even forced to feel a little guilty in spite of himself, and of the absurdity of the insinuation.

"You're quite wrong if you're suggesting that I am making little of drunkenness, a Bhando. Quite wrong. But we are supposed . . . Justice is a virtue, you know. Charity a still greater one." He was thinking, I'm wasting my time: no one will ever convince Bando of anything.

From a continuous seething sound the wind rose in a sudden pipe, and on the roof of the house slates could be heard to rattle. In the shed they were deluged with free-flowing air drenched with mildness and scented freshness, and again deluged with it.

What seemed to be causing Bando to register the utmost amazement—his tufty eyebrows pushed up till they almost seemed attached to the underside of the snout of his old grey cap—was what he was standing contemplating, his extremely long, spidery spittle which the wind had seized, shredded apart and printed on the concrete path before him.

His narrow shoulders jerked, then crept up towards his ears as if defensively, when the minister said, "I have myself been twice in the Duaray Hotel this week."

But when the voice behind him went on to say: "You may have heard that Finlay MacAskill, the proprietor, is ill," he pulled down his eyebrows, gave a very private, significant glance at a spot on the house wall, and recommenced comfortably moving his jaws, waiting . . .

The minister's voice behind him had a certain thrust and insistence none the less. He said, "There is a man staying at the Duaray Hotel, a guest. What do you think his name is, a Bhando?"

Bando swung round so that his shoulders were against the door jamb and looked up at the minister with his head thrown high, pointing straight at him his chin dabbled in tobacco juice.

"I wouldn't be knowing, Mr MacRury," he squealed, suffering with dignity, even some hauteur, proclaiming himself patiently ready for martyrdom.

"His name is Balneaves, a Bhando." The minister paused to let that statement make its impression. "I know because I distinctly heard a servant call him by it. Has Mr Balneaves an older brother do you know?"

"A brother, Mr MacRury?" Bando enquired airily. "He is a very secret man that . . . he tells nothing about himself . . . Who would be knowing?"

"Well, I put it to you that he has. A brother or some other near relative, who is on holiday just now in the Duaray Hotel. And I suggest that *that* is the quite innocent explanation of Mr Balneaves being seen late on the road several times this week. After all by the time he had his tea after school and got the length of Duaray he wouldn't have long with his brother before it would be already late."

Bando's raised eyes summoned and commanded patience and more patience for himself and enlightenment for the poor minister from a spot high above the latter's head. He was impressed none the less.

"That was very clever of them to arrange!" he squealed, with real admiration. "Would you not be seeing that, minister! They could be drinking to all hours and saying it was only the meeting of brothers." He turned aside . . . "*Pssst!* Who indeed would be having more to say to each other than brothers?" He sent the back of his left hand sharply across his stubbly, wet chin and tossed his head in appreciation.

Mr MacRury was feeling slightly sick. He seemed to have become more conscious again of the smell of oil and the crawling everywhere of the ghosts of snails—

even in his hands, closed in the side pockets of his raincoat, and under the soles of his feet, in spite of his shoes. But chiefly he was conscious of being cut off, enclosed . . . a serious thing when one felt oneself inhaling the stench from Bando's mind. Not that the effect of that was to make him feel himself superior or conscious that his own was more lily-flavoured, but there was a hopelessness . . . there was a malice that seemed ineradicable, utterly impervious . . . He had begun to feel that he was suffocating: probably that was excessive nervous sensibility, a weakness in him, which he ought to conquer. There could be no doubt at any rate about the smell of unwashed body that came from Bando—a whiff from time to time. And—he could not be sure, but—he seemed to have felt something in his face the last time Bando sent his stream of tobacco-spittle into the wind . . . It was simply intolerable, this.

He could not keep a note of some sharpness out of his voice when he said, suppressing the feeling of nausea and slight suffocation . . . "Have you any proof that Mr Balneaves has been drinking at all? Did anyone *see* him drinking?"

Bando's look was commiserating again.

"*Oooh!*" passing utterly light-footed across the point, "that would be done in private rooms!"

He turned to the out-of-doors again looking speculatively up into the wind-filled sky. His shoulders and hands began swinging again. "And what the policeman is thinking about I don't know . . . never there when there's anything . . . I think he's sold his boots, that fellow . . . *Huh—psst!* . . . Or else he's in it himself, if the truth could be told." He considered the ground. "Yes . . . probably that."

Mr MacRury had withdrawn his left hand from his pocket and was dabbing a handkerchief against his cheek, under his eye. This time there had been no doubt about it. And there was more than a suggestion of heat or "feeling" in his voice.

"Just tell me this, will you? Was Mr Balneaves *seen* to be drunk . . . on *any* occasion . . . by anybody?"

He felt the round collar under his chin. Disgraceful everything seemed, vulgar, out of joint with propriety; hopelessly, disastrously "not as it ought to be" and not to be twisted into focus. Bando's thin, small figure seemed at home at any rate. He even seemed to have begun to purr. He was certainly—since the minister's voice betrayed rising feeling?—oozing complacency.

"Oh!" he screamed, surveying the sky with utmost apparent self-satisfaction, the sky which had now become overcast with white flying cloud, so that the light was harder on the house wall, and there were no long, dark shadows. "Oh!"—his shoulders and hands were swinging more than ever; he gave the impression that he felt everything was going as he would have wanted it—"He can carry it well! There's no doubt he can carry it. You would have to grant him that . . . He must have been at it a lot, to be such a young man, and carry it so well."

Bando might have seemed to be grinning, such was the self-satisfaction he distilled—had he ever been known to grin. His air said everything was in his hands, just as he wanted it: he had only to stand still and wait for it. Mr MacRury felt his face flaming. But it was the two brown globules relinquishing almost simultaneously their attachment to the moustache that finally caused his nausea and angry disgust to overflow upon tact and discretion. The globules fell on the chin and immediately spread out, seeking their way among the stubble.

Mr MacRury sharply pulled his hat down by the

brim with his right hand, pressing down the top with his left, and stepped out past Bando with his arms swinging too free.

"Don't worry yourself further!" he was saying as he went crushing past. "You can depend on my warning Mr Balneaves on the dangers he is running."

Bando drew himself up against the door more than was necessary and with exaggerated alacrity as the minister went past him through the doorway. Then, "Nobody could blame you for that!" he said, screaming.

Mr MacRury, hot with humiliation, was half-way along the side of the house, buffeted by the wind, when Bando's voice rose again. And to his exasperated nerves it sounded like a scream of triumph. "It's only your duty when all is said!"

PART II

I

Right among the houses of the small township of Garrynamonie a south-bound green car was forced to draw up because of a flock of sheep occupying the roadway. Just at that spot a crofter in his shirt sleeves, slightly over middle height, about forty, had been shouting and waving his muscular arms, burned mahogany-dark with the sun, helping to clear the sheep along. Now he stood still for a moment and watched how they were moving, sturdy calves showing under his baggy plus-fours—or rather one sturdy calf since his trouser-legs were at different elevations, one thick grey stocking in wrinkles. Satisfied, he turned and nodded to the driver, but peering past him the while to see who was in the car.

Leaning back inconspicuously in the corner of the back seat, not stirring even to see what was afoot outside, with an air of disinteresting himself in the whole affair and in everything, was a figure in the black clothes and round white collar of a minister, a grey cloth cap drawn rather far forward on his head over a long impassive face, and the crofter at once started in recognition, then came energetically forward. Leaning his elbow on the window, which was wide open on account of the heat, he stooped his head to look inside, and meanwhile a great change had come over his expression, which from being rather placid and vacant had in an instant become charged with some over-mastering emotion.

"I hope you'll see to him, Mr MacAulay," he said loudly and brusquely, with a hint of admonition or threat in his voice, which was shaking with the sudden intensity of his feeling.

The minister took his time before raising his greenish eyes to give one flashing glance from under the snout of his cap. The face he saw at the window was red under its brown, the eyes, as with short-sighted people, diminished behind the thick lenses of the rimless spectacles on the short broad nose which was uptilted somewhat so as to bring the lenses to bear; two rows of regular but large and yellowish teeth were exposed, and the opened thickish lips were visibly quivering with an emotion which—one had the impression—was in control of the whole burly body outside.

"See to yourself, Donald," said Mr MacAulay without movement and with withering dryness. "And if you don't take your elbow off the window you'll get a tumble when the car starts."

The crofter jumped back from the window. He threw a glance back over his shoulder at the two women standing in the doorway behind him, then stepped back and stood just in front of them. He gave them over his shoulder another wide, open-mouthed stare which might have meant anything, eloquently impassive, then all three were looking after the green car moving away southward along the road.

Before they had time to relax their rigid attitudes, which were as if they had been transfixed by some emotion like anticipation, something caused them to stiffen to an even greater rigidity, except their eyes. Another car, black, had appeared from the north and went at an easy rate, sand rattling underneath it, past the house. In the back seat were sitting together two black-clad clerical forms, one noticeably grey-faced and old, abstracted and solemn-looking, the other with a round red face, smiling affably.

"Maclennan and MacKenzie of Aarayvruich," announced one woman, only just aloud.

"That's the whole lot," commented the man a little above his breath.

The black car seemed to drag their fascinated eyes with it as it passed, and after it away along the road, the crofter's muscular brown forearms hanging stiffly by the seams of his grey tweed trousers, one of the women grasping her throat and seeming thereby to make her eyes bulge outward slightly.

2

The Reverend David Macpherson Bain was subtly a different person in his shining collar and black clerical clothes. Some air that he ordinarily carried with him or cultivated, something not irresponsible altogether, but of the boy, had been put off along with his sporty or natty tweeds; there was a dignity and tension in his chubby form standing in the tight-fitting clerical black, as if not only his plump body but his mood also were more buttoned-up and alert. He gave the impression of being braced to meet some situation. A gravity, unaffected and unstrained, hung upon his kind, frank, chubby, snub-nosed face, his glasses looking steadily and solemnly under the short yellowish hair brushed straight upwards and back. Yellowish, but a good deal darker today because of some oil or brilliantine put on for the occasion.

He looked this way and that.

"It is true that this is my church of Kinloch-Melfort," he was saying, with even a suggestion of hauteur. "But I don't choose to preside here none the less." The grave set of face and mouth, with perhaps some quality in the acoustics of the place, or an unconscious "pitching" of the voice because of the associations of the place, imparted a flute-like quality to his pleasant tenor.

A voice said, reasonably, "I understand this is all to be perfectly informal, Mr Bain."

Mr Macpherson Bain let his knuckles rap lightly on the long yellow table before him . . . "I know. But I don't choose to preside none the less."

He paused, with the same looking this way and that, and drawing his brows together. "I must say here"—a flush seemed to start to his cheeks—"that both my regard and personal affection are deeply engaged on the side of the . . . the 'accused'."

There were some sounds of deprecation, even *tut-tutting*, and a voice that seemed to have a bitter twist somewhere in it observed only half audibly, "The whole thing's ridiculous anyway."

Mr Macpherson Bain's colour deepened further with a rush. It was certain now that there was a touch of "feeling" in him, which might have been simple impatience or might have been, deep-down, indignation. His thickish lips when he spoke had that look of snapping the air.

"I can't even pretend to *want* to be impartial," he threw down with a flash of defiance. Then with a brisk movement and a settling of his plump shoulders he calmed himself, going on . . . "But I agree that 'all things should be done decently and in order'', or else we'll be at sixes and sevens before we know where we are. And I therefore ask my nearest senior colleague, Mr Aulay MacAulay of Strath, to preside."

There was a confused low intoning of male voices of different pitch, resonance and quality, in the midst of which David Macpherson Bain could be heard saying very quietly, lightly, almost in a formal falsetto, "Will you take my place, Mr MacAulay?"

The sound of the voices had been of agreement. Mr Macpherson Bain's short chubby figure moving energetically met and passed Mr MacAulay's slightly over-middle-size, medium-built one moving more leisurely.

Now Mr Macpherson Bain was sitting on the chair Mr MacAulay had vacated. In front of him was the end of the long table; close to his left hand the door into the church. This door was a bright yellow colour, glossy, as were all the plain chairs the ministers were sitting on in a row. As also were the long table in front of them and the panelling of the walls all round and behind them. The fact is they had rather let themselves go on the stonework and exterior of Kinloch-Melfort church—intending it to be symbolic and adequate to the hoped-for industrial being of this corner in the hills—and had therefore had in the end to "cut down" drastically on the interior woodwork. The result was that the lining and furnishing of the vestry here, especially, yelled its cheapness—when the staring, plain-varnished boards were not actually creaking or giving off banging reports.

Mr MacAulay's long face was more than usually equine and solemn. He too looked somehow different in the dark black, in his best suit, not a rusty or dusty-looking one today: his bald skull a shining span between the reddish tufts above his ears. He sat all by himself on his side of the table. He raised his greenish eyes as if with reluctance and passed them slowly under their red brows almost as if with distaste from face to face of the six ministers in a row facing him, their black-clad chests above and beyond the warped yellow top of the vestry table. There was no sound for the moment—in the silence the screaming of the yellow woodwork was all the louder.

All of them, in fact, facing Mr MacAulay, looked slightly troubled, or not quite at ease. Away on his left, far enough to his left to be beyond the end of the table, was sitting the Rev. Murdo MacKenzie of the northern, boundary parish of Aarayvruich. His face and head seemed round, like a cannon-ball covered with ruddy skin, his slightly staring blue eyes fixed on him with a sort of docile attentiveness, his bright red cheeks bursting with health. His sixty-five years were showing, though, in his nearly grey hair and the expanding bald patch on the top of his head. Murdo MacKenzie was a *round* man altogether, born not many miles away at Sand. From here the table top cut off the view of his round paunch, although even so his body, with sloping shoulders, gave the impression of roundness. Then too he always had his trousers heavily bagged at the knees. And they always looked too short in the legs: at this minute if one were to bend down and glance under the table the tops of his boots and his worsted stockings would be showing—and probably a good "cut" of his (in spite of the summer weather) long, thick, blue-grey woollen underpants as well. He had the idiosyncrasy of always wearing thick rubber heels on his boots. He put them on himself when the boots were new, always without removing the original top layer of leather. The result was that, the heels being too high, he was thrown forward and walked heavily on the forward edge of them, with a sort of bent-kneed "clump", the round toes of his boots always remaining—even when the weight was off his feet—somewhat turned upwards.

A figure more bucolic one could not easily think of—or one less military; yet Murdo had been a chaplain in the First World War—the war to end War; on a cane-topped occasional table in his drawing-room at Aarayvruich stood a photograph of him in uniform, gathering dust: a quite slim, slope-shouldered young figure with a round face, somewhat prominent eyes looking out with an innocently bright expression. In that photograph the knees and boots were in the shadow of what looked like a heavy mahogany table bearing a pot with an ornamental fern whose fronds rose between breast and shoulder high to the unmilitary figure that stood there, the tips of the fingers of his right hand resting on the table-top with an air of formal yet self-conscious pride. One could imagine him none the less, his knees slightly bent inside his tartan trews, clumping along with the troops on the route of march, his bonnet sloping over his young, round, innocent face . . .

Murdo had never married. He had an aged housekeeper who had looked after him all his years at Aarayvruich (he had never been anywhere else). Also his parish was declining, even more rapidly than it was ageing. Almost certainly he would be the last minister. A parish of scattered crofts now, the young people flying the nest as soon as fledged, never returning, at any rate never to settle, and the crofts in consequence one by one going back to the heather. He had under a hundred of a congregation now, and the Free Church had little more. Up to the time of that First War both the schools in his parish, the one at Ault and the other at Aarayvruich, had three or four teachers. The children had seemed to swarm; and when they were all inside and the doors shut you almost expected to see head or legs come protruding through the windows, forced out by the press inside. Now there was but a solitary lady teacher in each, and the handful of children were like unfledged pelicans sitting lonely in the wilderness of vacant benches . . . Yes, things were running down altogether in his parish . . . Murdo MacKenzie, sitting facing Aulay MacAulay with that docile, expectant look, was the rustiest man present in his blacks.

Next to Murdo MacKenzie was sitting the Rev. Norman Maclennan. It was appropriate that he should be sitting next to him since their parishes adjoined and since they were lifelong friends in an unexpressed, taken-for-granted sort of way, like two plants that had naturally grown up near each other. They were natives of the same place—Sand—and bachelors living each with an old housekeeper. Norman Maclennan was the oldest of them all, at something past seventy. He kept going, at his life-long leisurely pace, but his hands had begun to tremble, his expression had taken on a somewhat "dead" cast, his complexion was noticeably turning the hue of ashes. Those grey features—they were in such contrast to the round red ones near them, a little below their level—were remarkably fine, square-set and sculpturesque. The brown eyes looked at you out of well- and wide-cut eye sockets, under a square, spacious brow above which the grey, almost white hair was still thick and abundant; the jaw was strong, the chin generous and firm. The total impression of the whole countenance was one of equal gentleness and strength—if only some of the strength was not illusory.

Norman, with his strong, firm look and something trim and well-set about his bearing, and well-knit, tallish figure, carried a definite suggestion of the soldier. And that was curious because, unlike his unmilitary-looking neighbour, Murdo MacKenzie, he had never been in the army, in any capacity. Nevertheless, to epitomise the impression he bore about, one would have said he resembled a kindly, military man. One knew, however, that he was far more kindly than military. All his life he had been an extremely "mild", gentle man, an apparently complete stranger to any sort of resentment or malice. He was one who never sought anyone out, yet welcomed everyone with every evidence of pleasure and was ready at any time to accord his indulgent attention to no matter who asked for it. He had the liking and respect of everyone who knew him. All the same he made a faintly negative impression, conveyed a slight suggestion of a lack of something—was it simply of life? There were times when one felt more certain he was kindly disposed than that he knew to whom he was speaking. That doubt, as to how far he could be taken to be "on the spot", lessened his influence. He was just slightly liable to be overlooked. One readily accorded him the respect due to one who would never be associated with anything in the least degree questionable, but scarcely the respect one gives to those capable of going crusading after righteousness. There was ever so slightly the feeling that he was one of those who are good by temperament rather than by moral ardour or the pursuit of virtue. As if he were not capable of being touched by evil, rather than having grappled with or overcome it. As if, having been given by kind favour of Providence all ordinary virtues in perfection, he would have been too much favoured in being given extraordinary ones in any degree whatever. So that he was in the end the loser. However that might be, he was a really good man, of a clear and candid temperament, and of an altruistic conscience . . .

He had ministered for over forty years at Drum, a better, more solid parish than most in the West: a whole long southward-looking ridge of pretty good crofts, with an arm of the sea in front, more or less protected from the depredations of marauding English trawlers. Here he had spent his whole life in attending to his professional cares and in fishing, and raising the yield of his garden, and if his voice resounded on Sundays in his large, square, roomy, solid church, it was not for the usual reason—echoing, empty spaces. Unless for an occasional visit to Edinburgh for the Church's General Assembly, never would he be away from his parish or his avocations. He was sitting there, and through and as it were behind the nobly shaped head—the deep-set brown eyes of which were looking at him with a soft, slightly tentative expression—Aulay MacAulay could see a sort of ghost of a large bowl full of tobacco-pipes, and he could smell as it were a distant and disembodied odour of strong pipe tobacco. Norman's study or personal sitting-room at the back of his house used to be heavily saturated with it, and that floating shape was of a bowl that still—or had till recently—sat on the mantelpiece there, filled with a large assortment of well-used pipes. But dusty pipes: Norman had not smoked for years; he would again explain that he simply got so that he could not stir himself to the labour of preparing and filling a pipe, and so became a non-smoker almost without realising it, through laziness.

But the eyes moved, and fell—and it was as if they had fallen on a stone—on an entirely different face. Next to the Rev. Norman Maclennan, but, again, lower. The face of the Rev. Roderick MacAskill—he had to be here, of course. Ah well . . . that was "Ar-Jai" as he was invariably known, from his initials: the minister of the small, still Gaelic-speaking charge of Melfort-South, three miles away; he too was looking at him, with little muddy-brown eyes, and Mr MacAulay was conscious as always of the inevitable twinge on seeing him, disagreeable fascination and slight nausea. "Ar-Jai" with his short but very thick and strong arms and legs, his barrel body like an animal's, seeming to be broader from chest to back than from side to side, his thick short neck which looked, in so far as it existed, scarcely at all narrower than his narrow, sharp shoulders—he gave an impression of something slightly misshapen. And yet did that impression not come even more from what one detected inside him, from his nature and disposition, the inner man? As usual he was wearing his massive or rather more than massive chin drawn in tightly back, his heavy cheeks and neck being forced out sideways so that the top of his cramped-looking skull was the apex of a triangle. This face, especially the large, heavy, immobile lower part, was of an unhealthy mud-colour, with a wrinkle of permanent unease in the small perspiring forehead. And muddy too were the whites of those small, dark-brown eyes when he lifted them up to you (they were more usually lowered or kept turned aside) with an expression of mingled wariness and resentment . . . But resentment—he was quite clearly conscious of the fact—was a strong element in his own antipathetic feeling about the man.

He *resented* Ar-Jai MacAskill: because he saw in him a threat to the ministry of the Church, the threat of dilution by lowering the standards of education and personal worth in those permitted to occupy the pulpit. What respect could anyone have for a church that sat under the ministrations of an "Ar-Jai"?

What *was* Ar-Jai? An able-seaman from the township of Valtabost in the remotenesses of the island of Lewis. That is to say, he had come from Valtabost in a bodily sense, but in the sphere of moral or metaphysical or any other concepts he had never left it. He had entered the ministry by an educational short-cut, a back-door, by a ladder out of the fo'c'sle. The pity was that he was not alone, in these days when the right young men were simply not coming forward, or not in anything like the necessary numbers. The policy was gravely disquieting even if not actually mistaken: if carried too far the filling of the pulpits would only end in still further emptying the pews, through loss of respect for the ministry among those who were still church-going.

Ar-Jai one felt uncomfortably should be kept out of sight, lest his braying and antics frighten off persons of decent refinement who had unsuspectingly and in good faith approached. His clerical collar was not sufficiently hidden by his sideways-spreading chin and chaps, or dewlaps. Not that there could be the least objection to him on the score of his humble beginnings—nearly all of them present were of similar origins, sons of crofters and crofter-fishermen—nor yet to a workman-looking figure in the pulpit. The man was *personally* unacceptable, disagreeable to the taste, low in mental endowment, inadequate in education, and wanting in dignity. Yet, no, the irritated antipathy he aroused was not entirely from that. An element in it was simply the nervous uneasiness awakened in others by his own unease and unsureness in company. Ar-Jai one never knew at ease or accepting of himself: always tense. Always, even when silent, he seemed somehow at once hesitating and crudely self-assertive; one thought of him as aggressively rushing forward at the same time as he was shamefacedly, even abjectly retiring. One felt that he was always insisting on being despised, claiming it as a sort of right, even while, and as much as, he furiously resented it. With all this, and his blaring self-righteousness, he invariably struck a wrong note . . . Then his profound uneasiness if there was laughter—a look almost of fear . . . Taken over all, with his muddy hue and skin, his discomfort, his eyes averted or else heavily, uneasily raised upon you, his iron-hard though ill-assembled frame, which you would almost have expected to give out a clanging noise had anything hit against it, his hangdog, almost threatening air—and his voice!—he affected one with a little surprise, as something slightly freakish and improbable, like a caricature of something . . . not, let it be hoped, of a "Highland minister" . . .

Of course, there could be no doubt the man himself was far too conscious of his shortcomings and limitations. Probably he was not at all as stupid as he seemed, or as he felt he was, and consequently acted: circumstances had prevented his trying out his faculties along with his fellows in a normal educational course of preparation for the ministry, and doubtless with an uneducated man's sensitiveness he tended to exaggerate both the amount and the value of what he had missed and its accessibility to normal brains, and in the bitterness of exclusion from that supposedly unattainable excellence felt he wanted to call down a curse on it . . .

And what a voice the man had for cursing and Biblicating! Ar-Jai's voice was a ministerial period-piece, and at that almost a masterpiece—a high-pitched dulcet scream with declamatory echoes. The stopper normally to some extent modulating the voice was removed in the pulpit, and the screaming filled the church. Never a screeching; it was a remarkable, even amazing, but not intolerable noise. It was what used to be called in other parts of Scotland a "guid pulpit souch". Much admired and appreciated it was by the generation of the old, who formed the bulk of his congregation and were nostalgically responsive or sentimentally addicted to the sounds that they recognised as having echoed through the spaces of their childhood. So Ar-Jai did not lack backing in the country round about, since by his voice, the antique splendour of his more exalted intonations, by his faithfully exact and studied reproduction both of the manner and the matter of the pulpit of Valtabost in his young days, he carried the bulk of his people back to their own more distant childhood, to hallowed recollections that soothed and comforted them in a world becoming more unfriendly towards their way of life and outlook. They would not have had him different—for that he made safe noises. And as he reproduced with the greatest fidelity not only the time-honoured forms of theological discourse and definition but even the pulpit noises with ancient and time-hallowed intonations, everything *direach mar a b'abhaist ann an la nan seanairean*, just as it used to be in the days of the grandfathers, many regarded him as in the doctrinal sense and in the moral and every other sense "the *soundest* minister in the countryside", and the whole of the generation in his district, regardless of all visible and outward shortcomings, stood round about Ar-Jai and with their moral approval held him up . . .

He himself now, Aulay MacAulay, had always felt he could afford to dispense with such adventitious aids to piety as the ancient ministerial howl, to say nothing of the one-man brawl in the pulpit, and to draw the people with the accents of reasonableness, to encourage them without hortatory exuberance, to instruct without startling or stunning their senses. But perhaps some of his antipathetic feelings towards Ar-Jai were a sort of unadmitted envy, came from a persistent sense that he "hit the mark" with the people in a way that the moderate, the serene, the reasonable, in a true sense the pious, never had and never would; from resentment of the knowledge, pushing up for recognition, that his own congregation *tolerated* what he gave them, while their real predilection in religion was still for spice—when they were not getting butter. He shut off the disgusted and horrified thought of an immediate wholehearted response of his congregation should he revert to the pulpit accents and antics of the past; the deplorable possibility that the sweet incense they really craved for was the smell of brimstone . . . aye—*sip*—and those they supposed to be their enemies sizzling in it . . . But this was morbid: he was not himself. It was looking at Ar-Jai MacAskill's figure and expression that was imparting this something nightmarish and distorted to his thinking.

One habit from his seafaring days Ar-Jai had retained, Aulay MacAulay knew, and his muddy or clay-coloured complexion was no doubt in part the sign of it; it was the smoking in quantity of strong black tobacco. Not in the house: his wife, a genteel person and very much the lady of the manse, would not tolerate it in the house, or in the presence of their three very young children, who were to be "well-brought-up", to look down on their father no doubt. But in his own room, in his "stuttee", in the heart of a dense cloud of choking fumes a squat iron-hard figure, jacketless and without a collar, with sleeves rolled up over knotted, short forearms, anguished and at the height of the ordeal of sermon-making, writhed with groans many and audible.

Colin Gunn was next, on Ar-Jai's left hand and

directly across the table top from himself—"young Colin" as he always thought of him, a contemporary of Ewen MacRury and Davie Macpherson Bain, therefore not yet forty: the son of his old colleague Gilbert Gunn, long dead, but once minister of Ar-Jai MacAskill's parish of Melfort-South—a much larger parish then. Little Colin—how well one could see in him, or through and behind him, this thin, vital little mother, whose managing will, it was credibly believed, extended from South Melfort where she still lived, as far as the manse of Sand where lived Colin and his buxom, good-natured wife (she would make two of Colin) and their five lively children. There was an element of unease or discontent swimming in Colin's eyes too at the moment, but unlike Ar-Jai's unease it was peevish instead of anxious. There always seemed to be something "working" in Colin. The idea came that perhaps he kept that heavy lock of soft black hair tumbling over his right eye in order to provide himself with something to be perpetually irritated about, since he was constantly tossing it back impatiently. It was a question whether his actual irritability might not be due to his smoking in such quantity the cigarettes, or whether the smoking to excess was the result of his irritability—there could be no doubt surely that tobacco put that sallow, almost yellow colour in his skin, even if it did not make the cheeks sunken and cadaverous, in his small thin face of a small thin man. There was something soft and expressive all the same about the dark brown eyes—a most exceptional thing to see that in Scotland, three pairs of brown eyes side by side and not belonging to the same family, Norman Maclennan, Ar-Jai and Colin Gunn, although different browns—and there was something appealing and soft too about the sensitive mouth from which dropped few phrases that were not acid and sharp. One had the mental picture of him going through the world swaying purposefully from side to side above his thin little legs which the too-long skirts of his black raincoat flapped around and threatened to entangle, looking briskly and irritatedly hither and yont, the sleeves of his coat coming down to his swinging knuckles, as if he would have liked to wield a thin whip on this side and that.

Yet in general he did not give offence, perhaps because it was felt that his malice was general more than personal, superficial rather than radical; it was a spice that he dispensed—malice without ill-will. Then . . . he was known, he belonged to the place, and therefore what in a stranger might have given rise to resentment was in him overlooked as no more than a characteristic, nothing to be taken seriously . . . "just his way". He was well-thought-of, rather.

That could not be said of his neighbour, who was a contrast to him in every way. Little Colin Gunn should not have sat beside him; he could not have more accentuated or marked the fact of his smallness; his head scarcely reached to the other man's shoulder. This giant was the Rev. Norbert Legge, and he looked half asleep as usual. Or half alive. At any rate—the only one in the row—he was not looking at Mr MacAulay, had his eyes lowered. The large head—though only large in proportion to the rest of him—was completely bald. The skull was magnificent considered as a box made of bone: every bony convolution and ridge in head and brow and face clear and massive and strong under the white, taut skin. It really deserved, that skull, to come to rest finally in the museum of a medical school, or in an anthropological museum, an impressive bony box labelled "Cranium of Nordic Man". At this moment highlights from the two narrow windows behind the ministers were wavering this way and that over the polished dome as it swayed scarcely perceptibly. The lowered eyes were perhaps actually closed in their wide, deep sockets under the strong bold ridge of hairless brow.

Those eyes when one saw them—this was one of the facts that made an impression of something "not quite right" about Norbert Legge—his eyes were grey and seemed made to be alert and eagle-sweeping, instead of which they showed themselves heavy and as if turned inward. There was that vague unpleasant impression, as of something "all wrong" about the man. His slow, formal movements, especially with his large, heavy, perfectly-formed, but also stiff, dry-skinned hands, the "too-largeness" and at the same time shining hairlessness of his total effect. Also that disconcerting "deadness", the sense that he was miles off the spot—and much too inertly large to be pushed back on to it. One had a sensation like physical cold in his presence, as if he were by some degrees colder blooded than a normal man. Then his "*tth, tth*"—a mannerism guaranteed in the end to reach the quick of the toughest nerve: that was his habit of every few minutes dreamily sucking his excellent, indeed perfect, but again just too large and massive teeth, with too large and massive a "*tth, tth*".

But over and above any physical or outward things, there was an indefinable something spiritual—as if he carried about with him a slight odour of taint: one could not have said what it was . . . To be fair, the fact that he was an incomer, a stranger to the district, probably accounted for some part of the dislike he engendered, and that was a pure injustice. Such an attitude—liking or disliking a person according as he belonged or did not belong to your own part of the world—when you were away from the place seemed utterly unreasonable, the more that you would not then have cared to have it applied to yourself, but when you were back in the native atmosphere there was a pressure of accepted attitudes on you to fall back into it again: many made no attempt to resist such pressure and indulged the impulse or inclination to persecute the outsider to the extent of feeling morally commendable for doing so. But even making allowance for that, he still thought he felt that faint odour . . . Also there was the still unclear question of the circumstances in which he—from so far away to the east or south—had come into the district at all, ten years ago. Nothing was definitely known, yet the impression lingered that there had been "something" . . . Of course that was nobody's business. And why had his wife left him, or at any rate gone away and not come back? Or was the loneliness of the place really the explanation?

The place, yes . . . one tends to dislike people who are associated in one's mind with unpleasant things: that was another probable cause of the unpleasant feelings the man occasioned. The sight of Norbert Legge naturally conjured up the thought of his parish, and the thought of Slaggan was a harrowing one. Slaggan was one of those Gaelic communities which had been as utterly ruined by the First World War as if they had been bombed and sacked outright . . . the state of those townships was as Rachel weeping for her children and not to be comforted, because they were not. Nearly a score of men had gone from Slaggan to the War—the entire able-bodied young manhood—and when the whole thing was over not one was left to come back. As it was so far out of the way, away out in the West above the waters of the Minch, there could be no question in the circumstances—all the adjacent districts having been likewise decimated—of fresh settlers. The community lingered on, but the spring of life was broken in it. Most of the young women, naturally, who in the ordinary course would have become the wives of those whose bones rested in France or Palestine, or, less easily, at the bottom of the sea, and so the mothers of the succeeding generation—that is, of the present generation that might have been and is not—found their way, no long time after the War, into the outer world, into employment and positions of one kind or another, formed ties outside that grew stronger as those with Slaggan grew weaker, and ere very long belonged to it no more, and finally came no more . . . There had been fewer than thirty people, all aged, when Legge came ten years ago, and now it was a question if there were a dozen. There would of course have been no minister at all in Slaggan if it had not been for that eccentric American endowment—the money was to revert to a Cats' Home or something should there at any time cease to be a minister in residence . . . So, what would be the situation when the people were all gone? Was that what Legge was thinking about—the dereliction and imminent disappearance off the earth of his parish and community? As he sat there towering and hairless with his eyes looking closed in the sockets of that white, imposing skull, the highlights on it faintly stirring, or swimming slowly to and fro.

Last of the line was David Macpherson Bain, on his right, somewhat beyond the end of the cheap whitewood table top. Looking at *him*, he saw, his plump round body rigid inside the unusual constricting blacks. Very upset, he knew Davie was. Nothing in him for the present of that large laughter of his, the genuine portion of which was very genuine indeed. Noticing that the discs of Davie's glasses turned on him held a severe, expectant gleam, he realised that quite some time—

perhaps half a minute—had slipped by as he looked at the faces and bodies opposite him and allowed to pass through his mind the thoughts or reflections each conjured or engendered. He pulled himself up.

3

"Well, gentlemen," he heard himself saying, "this . . . *eh, um* . . ."

He looked this way and that among the ministers, suddenly and as if unexpectedly finding himself somewhat put out, at a loss. Davie Macpherson Bain got up and pushed a sheaf of papers over in front of him. He reached out his long, dry hands and fiddled with them.

"This peculiar business . . ." he said, and *h'm*-ed again, and again threw that perplexed look down the line of those sitting opposite. There was silence for a little, an uncomfortable movement among the ministers.

Mr MacAulay's dry, quiet voice was heard again. "Of course, it's all quite irregular," he said as if doubtfully, looking down at his hands half-clasped on the table edge. "Still . . . *sip*—our intentions . . ." From someone there came a vocal sound of impatience.

Ar-Jai MacAskill's chair creaked under his hard body: his breathing, nervous and tense, became audible.

"The whoal country will be reenging tomorrow," he squealed, his voice a sort of brass falsetto, much too loud. He conveyed the impression that he was labouring under a grievance.

Mr MacAulay raised his eyes and gave him a short nod compounded of what looked like uncertain proportions of acknowledgment and acquiescence; then lowered them again.

"Yes, I agree there's no doubt about the quantity and violence of the emotion that's being liberated . . ." He sighed. "*Sip*—I wish I could be more convinced than I am that it's all sanctified unction"—he sighed again—"and not just—*h'm*—bolshevistic emotion—*h'm* . . ." He started in the midst of the half-reverie he had been sinking into, his eyes lowered, and looking over said, "Begging your pardon, Mr Macpherson Bain."

David Macpherson Bain shrugged the thing past, without emerging out of his expectant gravity, settled more deeply into it in fact, and seemed still urging Mr MacAulay onwards by his air to the main matter in hand, frowning concentratedly behind his spectacles.

Mr MacAulay said, "Yes . . . *h'm*," and for a moment sought his cue here and there. He flicked at the papers in front of him with a long forefinger. "You know all this, of course." He hesitated again. There was the same uneasy shifting among the ministers. There actually seemed to be some faint stirring of colour in Mr MacAulay's long, flat cheeks. It was warm; in the silence there was only a very faint buzz, as of flies, apparently from the adjacent church, and in the vestry the cheap woodwork preparing to creak.

"Well . . ." Mr MacAulay's greenish eyes flowed down the line of ministers opposite him again. All, except the Rev. Norbert Legge, were looking at him expectantly. "Well . . . I propose we have him in. We've no right to keep him sitting waiting."

There were sounds of agreement.

"Yes," a little voice said acidly—Colin Gunn's: he tossed his soft forelock back, "for heaven's sake let's get on with it!"

Mr MacAulay then set his reddish brows formally and turning his eyes on Mr Macpherson Bain seemed to give an almost imperceptible nod.

The latter started, gave a look round through his spectacles, then jumped up with a bouncing, purposeful spring, opened the door beside him on his left and went brisk and willing through into the church.

They relaxed in the vestry waiting.

But a moment or two later they were expectant again, becoming tense. Nothing had come from the church, no sound or movement. Davie Macpherson Bain had disappeared into a yawning emptiness, containing nothing save a distant droning of flies, louder now that the door was standing open. All the side-faces were turned. Except Norbert Legge's; but even he shortly raised his head as if to gather where the situation was moving.

The interval was becoming more inexplicable and awkward, the impression of emptiness more solid from the church. Then Davie Macpherson Bain's voice was suddenly heard—there was no mistaking his tenor—but confused, half-swallowed, half-smothered in the emptiness of the building. Only a few words, seemingly in question, but even the distortion of the many hollownesses did not quite account for a something almost startlingly unanticipated in the tone or the voice—something or other that did not seem to belong to the situation as it was understood.

Almost immediately a deeper replying voice had chimed in, the few words also distorted by echoes, half-swallowed, unintelligible. Then came the renewal of the former silence. This was unexpected: all the heads were turned, eyes fixed on the door. They waited for the voices to speak again in the church, or for sounds of motion.

Instead, Mr Macpherson Bain startled them all by suddenly appearing again at the vestry door, almost in their midst, tiptoeing. Like an apparition. He must have come on tiptoe through the church. Nor did he look at anyone, but after a quick glance over his shoulder into the church behind him, slipped back on to his chair, and with a short flourish of his left hand and a wide double flourish of his right took off his spectacles and withdrawing a white silk handkerchief from his breast pocket began ostentatiously polishing the glasses. The others looked in some surprise at his determinedly lowered eyelids, and at the colour which, now that they could see him closely and at leisure, undoubtedly was flooding his face. It even seemed to deepen.

But their attention was immediately drawn elsewhere. Sounds had started up again in the church. At first a dragging sound, but mixed with another, a peculiar sound that did not seem to belong to the same order of things. One would almost have said it had been a sigh. Dead silence succeeded. Then the dramatic and mysterious quality of this was suddenly shattered, loudly and blatantly shattered, by a shrill and profane trumpeting which rolled all through the church. Those in the vestry started, and there was some looking aside at one another as if each was afraid the others might have noticed he had been waiting for something entirely different to happen. What *had* happened was that someone in the church had, without compromise or subterfuge, blown his nose. The extremely flat, commonplace echo of that matter-of-fact sound still hung about when footsteps started up, and somehow, following Mr Macpherson Bain's recent apparitional entry, and his present industrious and red-faced polishing of his glasses, they were all looking towards the vestry door with mounting anticipation.

There was nothing subdued or disguised about these footsteps. Smartly, purposefully, vigorously, somehow relentlessly, and again somehow commonsensically, matter-of-factly, they came from a good way down the church, alarming its protesting silences which became every instant more vocal. All at once, swiftly, the footfalls turned echoless and hard in the doorway of the vestry; and they were all, with the exception of him who was polishing his spectacles, looking there.

At last, "Good God!" said the Rev. Colin Gunn in a whisper, with a withering effect. "*Tth, tth*," went Norbert Legge loudly in his large teeth, though probably with no reference to anything. Eventually Ar-Jai MacAskill, not the quickest among them, sat suddenly forward on his chair, looked across, very sharp and narrow-eyed, protruding his broad mud-coloured jaw sideways consideringly. His chair protested when he sat back as if with satisfaction and flashed a rather crude look, like cheap sneering triumph, about, finally directing a sort of unexpressed smile upon Mr Aulay MacAulay opposite him. (He had in fact grunted when Mr MacAulay was proposed to take the chair, looked dismayed, and pushed out his lower lip dubiously.) He was all triumphant satisfaction now apparently.

Mr MacAulay was aware of the look, without seeming to have raised his eyes, and perhaps it deepened the colour that was already in his long cheeks, made him press his thinnish lips together. He got up, back turned to the vestry door, and, stooping and with his left hand pushing his chair under the table, making room, "Sit down there, Mr MacRury," he said as naturally as he could: and was aware of a person passing him gladly—that was the only word for the impression he had—and going to sit down on yet another plain yellow chair that had been sitting empty all the time some distance to his left, the only other chair on the same side of the table as himself. Then he drew his own chair out again and reseated himself and that silence fell again. Mr

Macpherson Bain was finishing polishing his glasses, but the rest of them rather gave the impression that they were waiting for the table top, straining anxiously at its nails, to warp and curl itself still more, under their eyes.

4

Mr MacAulay's dry voice stopped. He turned his head round and his greenish eyes rested with a look both considerate and considering on Mr MacRury.

"Well, there it is, Mr MacRury," he said, the long dry fingers of his right hand twitching among the papers on the table in front of him. "I don't know what you think of it . . . Of course you recognise the possibilities . . . in certain hands, that is . . . and we have to be so careful nowadays on account of the Enemy. We are as it were a city besieged." The papers rustled as he put them together then laid them flat on the table top. "If it were only ourselves, but the push is from certain laymen . . ."

"For heaven's sake keep the laymen out of it," interrupted the Rev. Colin Gunn, "keep the laymen out of it."

"That is what we want to do," said Mr MacAulay in his direction, then to Mr MacRury again, "You see at any rate what our motives were . . . and since we were all in Kinloch-Melfort today in any case, we thought . . . We really ought, I think, to see if something couldn't be concerted. I don't know whether you will consider we have presumed, and whether you will care to . . . *sip*—you're perfectly free, of course . . ."

Mr MacAulay's voice dwindled away into silence and Mr Ewen MacRury, who was smiling, allowed it to become quite clear that he was not to resume, before he said, "I quite understand." His voice was—could it be called?—a Hebridean baritone, a baritone lightened as it were by the wind that will be blowing forever this way and that above the face of the Atlantic: its free, expressive quality was more noticeable in the roofed-over space of the vestry.

He himself seated on the chair a good way along from Mr MacAulay's left hand, looked about with the most natural air in the world, friendliness like a gleam in his face rather than a smile upon it. His wholesome, well-groomed look, his meticulously shaven face with its slight broadness at the jaws, his grey eyes, his short yet wavy dark-brown hair, his free bearing even when seated, all shouted of health and normality, and should have made for attraction. Yet he could not have known that while there had been, during Mr MacAulay's recital, some weakening of the first impression of a radiance only just faded about him, there still seemed to be in him, now, a *realness* beyond the natural. No one could have more strongly appeared to be present, to be there . . . yet curiously only by dint of carrying the impression of being still more really present somewhere else, in some other region, some other place. So a man might look who had come from the arms of his beloved, and one would know that he was only smilingly, with great good will and in every faculty, present because he was really still "one with" another, an invisible, an incomparably dearer presence. A man who appeared like that, invulnerable, inviolable—above all, indifferent—might unconsciously arouse deep antipathy. To say nothing of the affront he might cause by reason of the sensed or supposed nature of the other term of his two-some.

The Rev. Mr MacAulay on his right was not looking

at him now but, slightly crouched over, was looking at the floor straight down between his thighs while plucking at a rusty tuft, on the edge of his shining dome, with the long fingers of his left hand. Further away, out beyond the end of the yellow table David Macpherson Bain was rigid, looking straight down the wooden surface at him with a fixed expression that might have been either reproach or question. The Rev. Colin Gunn at the moment he looked at him was tossing back his forelock, looking down his nose disdainfully at the nails of his left hand. Ar-Jai's little muddy brown eyes were narrowed on him in a manner sideways and shrewd, and there was a something secret and knowing too about the smile that seemed to be playing about the mouth above the drawn-back chin and mud-coloured spreading jowls. Ar-Jai gave the impression that he had definitely something in reserve—"up his sleeve". The two at the end, Norman Maclennan almost opposite him and Murdo MacKenzie somewhat to his left, were quite obviously all prepared to be his friends notwithstanding—Murdo MacKenzie with bouncing goodwill in his scarlet face almost nodding at him, and his bulging china-blue eyes.

Mr MacRury was saying, "I think your motives have been most praiseworthy, and I thank you all for your friendship in assembling here. I'll do my very best to clarify the issue, to clear up the cause of this"—his mouth twitched—"and co-operate with your suggestions in every way I can."

He had all their eyes at once, however, when he said, "There are several things in that"—he nodded at the papers in front of Mr MacAulay—"that are not related to each other, some of them not at all connected with the main ... *eh* ... matter. I think these would be better cleared away first."

He had a sensitive, even mobile mouth and this began twitching at the corners again and with his head aside he passed the palm of his hand upwards over his brow and his tight-waved dark-brown hair, saying . . . "First of all the question of my late hour-keeping"—he seemed, smiling a little, to shake his head slowly from side to side in incredulity—"based, I think, on the solitary recorded instance of my having come home one morning with my bicycle about four o'clock."

"Information laid by Kenneth John MacAulay, merchant, of Mellonudrigill, commonly known as Smootch,' confirmed Mr MacAulay with a withering, expressionless effect of dryness.

(He could still hardly believe it. Smootch was massive and corporeal in his mind's vision on the instant, in his characteristic place and posture. Standing inside the window of his general merchant's shop, which had in front nothing but the highroad and then the beach, looking out, dreamily, with the suspicion of a complacent quirk about the corners of the mouth under the full and slightly straggly moustache, looking out at where the tide lazily lifted, held and lowered again a crowded assemblage of empty tins, boxes, cartons, sheets of packing paper and a wide area of packing straw. The broad nails of one large, plump, pampered-looking hand—his shirt sleeves always being rolled above the elbows—caressingly scratching among the abundant fair hair on the other massive forearm crossed over his drum-tight paunch. His rather washed-out grey eyes dreamily, complacently, resting on his acre of private flotsam, as Nebuchadnezzar would have said, "Is not this great Babylon that I have built?" Yet never conveying an impression of duplicity, of treachery, even when quite unnecessarily protesting the point of his personal devotion to the church and to the ministry and the extent to which he had been trusted with the confidence of previous and other ministers. No, he had never thought of treachery in connection with Smootch . . . although . . . yes, here came back to mind the occasion on which he had overheard Smootch quietly, ruminatively, his eyes resting with a speculative caress on the retreating form of a plus-foured "veesitor" who had just gone from the shop, almost whisper . . . "We'll see . . . maybe we'll take a pound or two off him yet . . ." He had been shocked and confused, incredulous, and when Smootch at that moment catching sight of him standing in the shop turned round towards him his distended belly with all customary dignity and deliberation and greeted him with complete normality and composure, he felt happy to conclude he must have been mistaken, and had put the matter out of mind. Now he felt not so sure.

It occurred to him that perhaps Smootch had been undisquieted simply because he was so much inside another code altogether—a code which made planning to "take pounds off" people permissible, even meritorious—that he had had no consciousness of any need to be disquieted on finding he'd been overheard by a minister of the Gospel. Perhaps so; and that raised the very large question of what he after all, Ewen MacRury, knew of Smootch . . . "the real" Smootch if there was such a person. The idea which in his mind represented Smootch might be of a quite different colour from Smootch's consciousness of himself, whereby was raised the very much larger question of what after all he knew of anybody. Perhaps he had only assumed he knew the people round about him. To what extent was what he "knew" of others only a picture he had built up in his own mind and bearing little correspondence or none with the persons concerned as they actually or really were, in themselves ... assuming there was such an actuality? Did it not more and more seem to emerge from the contemporary study of man that personal consciousness was at varying degrees of non-correspondence with personal "being" in act and reality, from wild hallucination to the useful or provisional structures we are accustomed to build up as a means of carrying on the business of actual living ... Anyway there was enough in all this to make him see he might have been radically wrong in his conception or estimate of Smootch's character, and that what was now alleged against him might very well be true to it and in accordance with it.)

He was saying: "It is perfectly true that I returned home about ... I daresay it must have been ... about four o'clock one morning. I had been by the deathbed of a parishioner ..."

"Till *that* time?" Rev. Colin Gunn and Ar-Jai almost echoed.

"What doing at aal?"

"I ..."—young Mr MacRury crossed his legs and lightly entwined his fingers in his lap: he smiled, a slight but serious smile, consideringly at his two questioners—"I agree with you ... I remained with the dying man at his insistent asking, of course ... but I am bound to agree with you if you suggest there was nothing I could actually *do* in these circumstances. That was what troubled me. I had somehow never realised it before, that there is nothing, simply nothing at all that we, ministers of the Gospel, can actually *do* to a parishioner, a fellow-man and a brother, to aid him ..."

A squeal or bray interrupted him. "We can do aal that iss nee-tit. There is the reading of the Wurrt and prèher." Something seemed to have stung Ar-Jai; a faint flush went through his clay.

"There are times," said Mr MacRury gently, "such may be the patient's state of weakness, when the mere voice of another man might well in itself be enough to send him into the other world."

Mr Aulay MacAulay half-coughed suddenly and leaning forward passed his finger-tips along his mouth. The Rev. Colin Gunn also instantly glanced at Mr MacRury brightly, with expectation, but Mr MacRury had obviously had no intention beyond the plain statement of the fact and a look of impatience at once passed over Mr Gunn's thin face.

"The reading of the Word to a patient in the throes of death is likely to be a doubtful help, might in fact do great harm. And similarly vocal prayer . . . if the patient isn't able to follow what is said, it is merely a noise in his ears, which he may find insupportable. Silent prayer made *for* a person we can of course all engage in at any time and with benefit. But a man in the very portals of death, between the two worlds—you know the Gaelic expression—waiting each moment the summons that will call him away for ever out of this world . . . he is likely to be too weak, or too much in pain to follow discourse . . . even to form ideas. What can we do for a man in such a case? There's only one thing he can do in so far as he retains consciousness."

"What's that, Mr MacRury?"

"He can move his will . . . he can make affirmative or negativising motions of his will. That's all. What his situation seems to call for therefore is something I can bring to him, that to do him good needs only the adherence of his will. I never realised until that night, when I had to support the look in the eyes of a man conscious of his plight which will be the plight of all of us some day, and, I felt, wanting help . . . desperately . . . and from me . . . the look in the eyes of a man who was already some way passed into the other world and passing away every moment further, but still capable of benefiting from help given to him in this, provided there was any that could reach him . . . that I had in fact no help that could reach him, nothing I could do *to* him suited and fitted to his need . . ."

It was the silence that stopped him. He had been talking more and more as if conscious of his thought rather than of his audience, in a pondering abstraction, until he became aware of a silence within the silence. The air stood up motionless all through the church and vestry, and in it, in its stillness, had fallen a nearer, a more local stillness. He saw that they were all looking at him—except Mr MacAulay who was gazing at the table in front of him as in a dream.

After a moment—"What would you suggest?" said the Rev. Colin Gunn in what might only be described as a dangerous whisper.

But, beside him, Ar-Jai could not let it alone. "Whaht would the maan be wanting?" he burst in squealing, seemingly in a state of touchy irritation. "He had the Wurrt! Aal his life he had the Wurrt . . . and p-preaching." He may have thought that Mr MacRury was about to break in with his reply, but he cried even louder—he would have none of it—"No, no! If he is sayvt he iss sayvt, if he is dammt he iss dammt. And if he iss dammt there is nawthing you or me can do to-to-to to paatch his condeetion." His short nod across at Mr MacRury, as he drew his sharp narrow shoulders together and sat a little forward, was like the putting of a very full stop after the last word on the matter.

Mr MacRury was looking at him as if seeing him for

the first time—and with some surprise and speculation. Then when Mr MacAulay said only just audibly, as if to the table top, "It's to be supposed you don't see the trend of your ideas, Mr MacRury," he looked round them all, as if seeing all of them for the first time. To his right, beyond the far end of the table, David Macpherson Bain remained rigid as if trying to see *him*, to "tumble to" him. Next to Davie the Rev. Norbert Legge had his grey eyes in his fine, massive bare skull fixed on some indeterminate point away in the distance: at that instant he went "*tth* . . ." drawing back his cheeks as if in a broad unamused smile—"*tth* . . ." the upper row of his too large, formally perfect teeth appearing in view—"*tth*". Little Colin Gunn and Ar-Jai beside him gave the impression of lightning sitting beside a thunder-cloud. Mr Maclennan and Mr MacKenzie, opposite, were looking at him too, from close by, but with the kind, encouraging expressions they had worn from the beginning, red-faced Mr MacKenzie even nodding every time he caught his eye. In circumaffluent yellow, black clad, they all sat white-collared.

"*Eh* . . . had Mr MacRury something to tell us?" asked Colin Gunn in his softest, most cutting voice. A black sleeve was twitched on a swept up arm, while he consulted the watch revealed on the slender wrist.

"Oh, yes," Mr MacRury said, immediately recalling himself from his solemn-reflective and at the same time slightly surprised or "awakened" scrutiny of the line of them opposite and at once reappearing—as if it had fallen about him—under that strange aspect or bearing which had struck some of them at the first when he came in from the church, as if he had reached a point of the real which was both solemnity and a gladness and was both final maturity and never ending youth:

that something about him and in him that had seemed to embarrass Mr Aulay MacAulay, to stupefy and bemuse plump David Macpherson Bain, to irritate little Colin Gunn, to infuriate yet arouse a sense of some crude triumphing emotion in Roderick John MacAskill, and as far as Mr Maclennan and Mr Murdo MacKenzie were concerned simply made him seem a more than ever attractive young man, so that they went on feeling ever more friendly and affirmative towards him—enjoying feeling it, and, especially since it was a good emotion, not having it in their nature or inclination to isolate and turn about and scrutinise its cause.

Mr MacRury was saying, sitting behind the table, "The second thing that appears here"—with a nod towards the papers—"and has no relation, or at any rate no direct relation, to the main matter . . ."—he stopped abruptly and leaning back recrossed his legs and put his hands into his trouser pockets; his half-smile was indulgent and patient: it was Mr Colin Gunn who the moment he started to speak had jumped up and whisked round behind Norbert Legge's chair and stretching up his thin black arms begun to work energetically with and pull two long thin cords hanging down from somewhere aloft in the narrow pencil-shaped window between Norbert Legge and Davie Macpherson Bain. Mr MacRury's eyes crinkled and involuntarily contracted as if an optician's frame had been set momentarily on his nose and his eyes required to adjust themselves to two unaccustomed lenses when "*turr-rrur*" loudly went some mechanism high above the cords and a small square trap-door of glass opened in spasmodic jerks high up in the narrow window, just under the pointed top.

He resumed, "The second thing that has no direct

bearing . . ." "*Turr-rrur*" went Colin, now at the other pencil-shaped window of greenish opaque glass, behind and between Mr Maclennan and Mr MacKenzie. There was nothing to do but wait. Mr MacAulay lifted up notably expressionless eyes on what was going forward.

5

When Mr Colin Gunn returned, and sat down with his eyes lowered and a very unconscious expression on his thin, yellow face, "Thank you!" said Mr MacRury and Mr MacAulay at the same instant, then glanced with an unformed smile at each other. (It had indeed been getting stuffy in the vestry, the smell of varnish rising.)

Mr MacAulay raised his eyebrows on Mr MacRury. "Yes?"

"Oh, yes," said Mr MacRury, drawing his hands from his pockets and clasping one over the other on his lap . . . "the statement that I am in the habit"—he moved in the chair—"of spending hours looking at obscene pictures which I keep in a locked drawer in the desk in my study. Is that more or less it, Mr MacAulay?"

"Yes . . . that's it more or less . . . and the informers . . ."—he said "informers", and the rustling he made in checking the facts among the papers was no drier than his voice—"were Williamina MacGillivray —*h'm*—your housekeeper, and Margaret MacMillan, housemaid. They claim to have discovered the pictures together"—his voice changed—"or should it be—*sip*—while acting in concert!" (Whatever the facts of the business he was not going to let it be thought that any of his sympathy lay with certain parties.)

He stiffened, however, and his eyes moved sideways, to his left, then turning his head he looked squarely, enquiringly at Mr MacRury. As they all did, except Norbert Legge. It was true! Surprisingly . . . inappropriately . . . what Mr MacRury was struggling with, striving to stifle, was laughter.

He was imagining those two "informers", the moral censors—he had laughed inwardly at first to recognise them under their high-sounding legal names—in the act of making the awesome discovery: Peigi Snoovie with a thin trembling all through her with excitement, her pathetic little mouth a pinhead of contraction, Mina Bhando with her eyes drawn in to suspicious, sideways-looking pinheads, her teeth and pale gums exposed.

(What he imagined was in fact very close to the actual event—except that he had not, as he supposed, one day left the middle drawer under the top of his study desk, as he had found it on coming back, unlocked. It was Peigi Snoovie who in a spasm of exasperation had irritatedly thrust into the lock the end of the hairpin with which she had been scratching her head, then found the hairpin had stuck, and in her panic rattling to free it had released the catch by accident and found the drawer come smoothly towards her.

"Oh, oh, oh! *trobhad a Mhaina, trobhad!*" "Come Mina, come!" she shrieked in accents of fright or danger, and for an instant, looking down on the veritable broad books—bright colours on them—lying in the drawer, felt a swimming lightness in her topmost portions, and her large-boned knees with the raw skin, gone weak, leant a moment tremblingly together under the brown, coarse dress.

"*Aw!*" cried Mina in a profound nasal, pausing in

the doorway to press her hand flat above her heaving bosom, having come in a ponderous rush upstairs from the kitchen, seeing Peigi standing there, "There you are and you're all right . . . and me thinking something terrible might have happened to you!"

Her indifference or disappointment went, however, when she noticed the beauty that irradiated Peigi's face, her thin face, and how her light-grey eyes, always fine and with a kind-looking expression under their soot-black lashes, first trembled on her with a lovely light, then moved away from her caressingly to the violated desk, drawing her with voluptuous invitation.

Now they were standing side by side at the desk. They even both had a hand in throwing the album open, in haste, at random.

Peigi cried: "Oh, oh, oh! Oh! a nèhkit wumman, without her clothes . . . and look, she's dancing!" With a pouncing movement she turned over pages . . . "Oh! and here's another one! What a ——! Did you ever see such a ——! What's she doing? And a hairbrush of hers on the table! Look, she's washing herself in a tin, the filthy cree-ture!"

The excitement was really too much for her; her weak lips and her little breasts were trembling. Mina Bhando became all long, yellow teeth, her narrowed eyes moving points. As they worked through the pages she gave an occasional contralto croak or groan.)

From the first Mr Murdo MacKenzie had formed no idea of what the matter really was; for him it was simply "one of the young chaps been getting into a scrape: must go along and help get him out of it": hence the smile in his bulging blue eyes all along, the continual nodding of his round head in encouragement. He and his neighbour, Mr Maclennan, who was also somewhat in a mist, and Mr MacAulay who was not quite so much so, all looked at Mr MacRury with indulgence, indeed some reassurance: such innocent amused laughter could hardly go along with anything very lethal. However, Ar-Jai opened on him one muddy, magisterial eye, not altogether free from incomprehension, which for him was not far from apprehension; Mr Colin Gunn looked speculative but derisive.

"Please forgive me, gentlemen . . ."—Mr MacRury flashed out a white handkerchief from his breast pocket with which he enveloped his nose and gave a dab in passing to the corner of his right eye before returning it to its place. "I must confess . . . there doesn't seem to be any point in trying to keep it hidden any longer, does there? I have been indulging a secret vice. I don't know what sort of view you'll take of it." He looked round them, certainly with no sign of an apologetic frame of mind; still as if suppressing amusement, rather. "It came upon me . . . That's the strange thing . . ." He propped his right ankle on his left knee, taking the right knee in his clasped hands. "I had always thought a vice had to be acquired, but this came upon me fully developed, sprang upon me as it were fully armed, and overcame me in the instant. I have been an addict ever since. It happened . . . in an art gallery." It seemed more than ever certain that his laughter was not yet far away, if it was not on the way back. "I had gone in . . . What is it that takes a Scotsman of the authentic tradition into an art gallery? Perhaps the rain had come on . . . I can't in the least remember.

"Well, gentlemen, you may believe me . . ."—he had become serious again and sat up, placing both feet on the floor—"while I was standing in front of a picture there suddenly descended on me . . . like a flash of light . . . an intuition, an apparition, call it what you will . . .

anyhow—it seemed to me—the fullest realisation, not involving the knowledge of and acquaintance with technical means and merits, of what the whole business of art and painting is about. A matter which had till then remained quite hidden—in fact, had never seriously occupied my attention. It was like a revelation, like being suddenly endowed with an extra sense, and a new faculty to correspond. It was—could I say?—a thunderous illumination, yet as quiet as a dawn. And like a dawn it brought light. It was essentially a dawn of *vision* . . ." He drew himself up a little, sighed, and went on with less of himself in it: "At any rate, that was what happened. I became enamoured, if that is the word, of painting, perhaps especially of French painting of what are called the Impressionist and Post-Impressionist schools. And as, up here, I had no means of indulging my vice, I brought back with me some albums of reproductions of paintings. These I kept in the long middle drawer of my desk in my study and from time to time I would retire there and spend—too long, I fear you would have thought—bathing my sight and refreshing my spirit in the contemplation of them. I kept that drawer locked, because I was well aware of the danger of misunderstanding and . . . yes, scandal—should those albums be turned over by anyone who was likely to be in the study casually."

"May one ask"—Mr Colin Gunn's tone was innocent, as was the look from the soulful brown eyes, but there was acid in the words dropping sweetly from the mouth with its soft lips—"in what did the scandal lurking in your albums precisely consist?"

"The possible scandal lay in this, Mr Gunn, that some of those paintings—not many, I hasten to say, but some—displayed the unclothed female figure."

"Tisgrèhsful, tisgrèhsful!" uttered the Rev. Ar-Jai

MacAskill in heartfelt, natural, unsquealing tones, and there was a general sense of movement and as it were of disapproval about the room.

The Rev. Murdo MacKenzie's voice was reminiscent, though not in any unpleasant sense, of the tumbling of stone cubes. He had been shaking his head admonitorily at Mr MacRury, but in a personally detached way, as if it had been automatic and from an objective duty—and still indulgently, without radical disapproval, having brightened with some apparent light of understanding. His stone-cornered words tumbled out now, though with the effect of a spoken reflection.

"Can't say I was effer very much bathered with it myself. Though I believe some folks have a great deal of bather with it."

He was shaking his round head slightly, looking at Mr MacRury, but from the benevolent smile in the bulging blue eyes it was plain that he did not consider the case hopeless.

Mr MacRury might have given a slight smile. He answered the feeling in the room rather than any statement. "I should say here that I recognise a good deal of force in the objection to that particular subject for works of art. The force I see in the objection is this . . ."

His eyes were on the black, red and white butterfly which, coming in no doubt by the glass trap-door Colin Gunn had opened in the greenish window, was obstinately fluttering just an inch away from Mr MacAulay's gleaming pate.

"It's not that I think the unclothed female figure is in principle or in itself illicit as an object of contemplation or artistic representation. But the emotion proper to artistic appreciation is aesthetic emotion, and—with human beings as they are—this particular object has a tendency to arouse emotions of a different order, other than aesthetic, thus defeating the end of aesthetic creation by clouding the aesthetic perception."

"This iss a fery strèhnsh discussion," opined the Rev. Ar-Jai MacAskill, with heart-felt complaint, looking up at the ceiling as if in hopeless search of discovering a single familiar spot in it.

"You mean"—the Rev. Colin Gunn ignored him, spoke pointedly past him—" you mean it's not the pictures, it's the nasty minds of those that look at them."

His air hinted the provocative. Mr MacRury ignored it, smiled slightly rather.

"Yes, I think that's more or less what I mean. An expression or two might perhaps be . . ."

He turned sharply to Mr MacAulay in the corner of his right eye, who seemed to be making some energetic signals, but saw he was only flicking his long fingers in front of his face to drive off the black, white and red butterfly which after a swoop or two round the room had returned to flutter about his head. So the two created objects, a black, red and white butterfly and a gleaming ample head housing a largely Gaelic, Presbyterian, male, twentieth-century—considerably flavoured with nineteenth-century—consciousness, of the north-eastern Atlantic littoral, had for this moment of time become juxtaposed and after their fashion conscious of each other.

"Could Mr MacRury tell us . . ."—small Mr Gunn had had the impulse to try again—"in what precisely this pleasure consists that he gets from looking at pictures . . . in other words the content of this . . . this revelation he had in the art gallery?"

"To me, Mr Gunn," Mr MacRury said, "art seems

to be, in brief—I believe the expression has been used—significant representation. Representation of an object or objects isn't enough in itself to constitute art; there must be the admixture of an element of human sensibility, an element of . . ."—he looked about, seeking the word—"of human *vision.*"

"This *significance* you speak of, then . . ." Mr Gunn's brown eyes lay on Mr MacRury, deceptively, with a hurt and begging expression. "This significance you speak of, the imparting of which to the material constitutes the *art*, and of which you own yourself a humble devotee and worshipper, is a purely subjective element, something of purely human sensibility or imagination."

Though cast as a question it was meant to have the force and effect of a leading statement. On the last words Mr Ar-Jai MacAskill gave a start and looking at Mr Gunn for the first time, with a look of having just discovered him sitting at his left hand, gave a sharp, sideways nod of deep approval. A profound if silent Amen. Of which Mr Gunn again ostentatiously took no notice, though he was plainly conscious of it.

"No, no," Mr MacRury had said, "no, no, Mr Gunn. I wouldn't admit that: indeed I feel it very important *not* to admit it. I feel quite certain that in some sense—which I am not yet prepared to define in close terms; I merely say, in a real sense—the beauty is *in the thing*. Of course I understand the whole ground of aesthetic speculation is bog-infested with controversy. I wouldn't venture on it. But this much I claim to discern from a distance, looking across the disputed territory: that the *thing* in a work of art, that which gives the perceiver the pleasure properly to be experienced on seeing it, is something *out there*, something in a strict sense independent of us . . . something real on its own account, something which existed first and of which the work of art is a representation."

"Of course you have the advantage of all of us here," interrupted Mr Colin Gunn looking round at the others as if silently waiting their attention, with acid in the sweet preciseness of his words—the sallow skin seemed a little flushed—"in that you have spent a great deal of time in considering those questions, while the rest of us were occupied with—*eh*—other matters . . ."—he gave a thin little shrug and a twist of his sensitive mouth—"parish affairs and things of that sort. But I hope you don't think even so that you'll leave us altogether behind and out of sight while you disappear over the hills in pursuit of your theory of aesthetic . . ." He tossed back his forelock. "*Eh* . . . when you spoke just now about what the perceiver perceives in a work of art being *out there*, independent of us—in a strict sense and so forth—were you referring to what the artist has in his mind before he begins the work, or to what is to be seen in it after he has completed it?"

"To both," said Mr MacRury. "Ideally, of course, they ought to be identical . . . As I see it, the artist by virtue of his sensibility and artistic perception attains the vision of the beauty, which he then by means of his artistic talent *represents*. Thereby he enables us, according to the measure of our capacity, to share his original vision and perceive the beauty in turn."

"Isn't that representation, then . . . which you said art was not?"

"It's representation of a sort if you will. Not, however, representation of the material objects that occupy the space of the picture, but of the immaterial or ideal form which all the material objects together, in the character and arrangement given to them, compose. It's that immaterial 'form' which is the original vision of the artist; in it the beauty of the created object resides, the perception or contemplation of which is the pleasure or end of art.

"But the important point is that the ideal forms were there to be perceived before they ever *were* perceived—and would have been just as much there supposing nobody ever perceived them; only in that case they wouldn't be given representation. The sensibility and artistic activity of the artist are the means whereby the beauty of those ideal forms and immaterial harmonies become accessible to the many: the important point is that not only the artist's primary vision but our appreciation of the work of art once made are *objective* experiences, and essentially so. If I may put it this way, the experience of art—any art—is not a shared illusion but a participated vision.

"That is very important. The contrary view, that art is purely or essentially a subjective matter, would make the experience of art something like—and little more than—taking a sniff of the artist's personal cocaine, to induce in us a similar intoxication to his or a corresponding disturbance or excitement in our sensibility. Something like that . . . at any rate an experience, whether licit or not, of no more significance or solid consequence than any other event rooted in the nervous system and reacting on the emotions."

"You say this is important and that is important . . . I am sure I speak for my colleagues when I say we don't see where the importance comes in."

"But surely Mr Gunn it's important whether what we nourish our souls on is truth or illusion. If the experience of art is objective then what we have apprehended is an aspect of truth; if art is subjective then all we have experienced is a phase of illusion. Illusion is thin food for the soul, indeed it's certain to be deleterious, whereas truth is the soul's true food, whereby it cannot help but grow."

"Are you justifying art now as being to our moral advantage?"

"No. That's another quagmire of disputation . . . Art and Morals . . . I don't care to venture into it. I wouldn't admit there was any direct connection between them in any case, or should be. Had you said art is to our *metaphysical* advantage I'd have agreed with you."

He waited—only to notice that everyone, all in the yellow room, appeared to be waiting on *him*. There was a sound of fluttering wings. He said—two black, red and white butterflies there were now, in an intricate, circling dance together over the table, slightly above the level of all their heads, with a quite definite sound of their fluttering wings surprisingly hard and solid at moments—he said, "That, I must repeat, is only so far as I have been able, or felt inclined to reason the thing out, just far enough to satisfy myself of the objective nature of aesthetic experience, and of its metaphysical value therefore. For anything else . . . there are some questions that seem to get more obscure the deeper you go into them. But about the experience of looking at distances I have no unclearness. It is absolutely . . . net, *sui generis* . . ."—he failed for words, had a welcome expectancy for the right word, which however failed to come—"I don't remember whether I mentioned being particularly attracted to French painting, especially of those called the Impressionists and Post-Impressionists. That was because they seemed to have a wonderful sense or perception of, or addiction to, or at-home-ness with the 'realness' of the things in the world, the world *as seen*. Things seemed to present themselves to them with an unexpected force and freshness . . . as if there was something dramatic in the light . . . Yes, there does seem to be something in the sky of France . . ." For a moment he let himself be occupied by that thought, half-smiling into some immaterial distance, unconscious of them facing him, and Mr MacAulay near his right hand. There was a slight impression of a leaning towards him, with scrutiny of his state of mind: something was felt that Ar-Jai had given expression to earlier—that there was something very strange, incongruous, bizarre even, about a man in *his* clothes sitting there talking on such matters.

"In any case"—his grey eyes returned to their kindly, lively scrutiny of them—"the effect these French painters had on me was like an extraordinary opening of my eyes. An opening of my eyes not to a distant beauty of far-off things, but to a sort of glory in things of everyday, and unconsidered objects round about. It was like a quality added to all visible things. Anything at all—an old chair with a broken seat, an old man in his shirt sleeves and with his waistcoat open, his cheeks unshaven, and untidy hair appearing under his cap, a pile of dishes and coloured dishcloth, a pair of old boots obviously 'set down' by a hand no longer seen—all these now assumed under my vision a reality or striking or forceful quality I have never detected before, appeared as if endowed with a nimbus, or more correctly an inner light, of significance."

Mr Ar-Jai MacAskill could contain himself no longer. "Not deeficult to s-see the signeeficance of a nèhkit wumman-ah!" he burst in with a braying squeal. "Sure we can aal s-see the signeeficance of a nèhkit wumman!" He was drawing back his broadened grey chin so strongly that he might have been trying by the pressure on it to shoot the back stud of his collar into the yellow panelling of the wall behind him. His look of severe reproach and reprobation had to be bent on Mr MacRury from under his brows, which were so coarse that they resembled thin black wire.

Mr MacRury halted.

Mr Norbert Legge stirred and suddenly said, "Yes," and Mr Gunn beside him instantly turned round head and shoulders fixing a bright and lively question on his face, looking up. But Mr Legge merely added "*tth*, *tth*", and his eyes were withdrawn and distant, while his too large frame and head swayed slightly backwards and forwards.

Mr MacRury's grey eyes passed in question from one to another—was he intended to continue? Mr MacAskill gave no sign. He had closed his eyes as if in pain. Mr Gunn was stroking and restroking the back of his head and his eye was evasive, not to be caught. His black silky hair would have been the better of cutting. And still the butterflies were flittering up and down, above the heads.

6

Mr Aulay MacAulay whose should have been the guiding hand and voice in the proceedings had been strangely silent for some time. He looked pale, abstracted from the discussion he should have been pulling together—the eyelids drawn down over the greenish eyes. The air was coming ever more warm to the nostrils, with the odour of cheap wood varnished.

Old Mr Norman Maclennan, directly across the table, leaned forward. He was about to put a question, judging by the intelligent lighting up of his aged brown eyes, the courteous enquiring smile that began to stir his lips. He had drawn a visible deep breath and tilted his handsome white head in order to do so, the eyes soft with a personal tenderness, when he started as another's voice broke in, looked round to his left, then relaxed, leaning gently, self-effacingly, back in his chair.

It was Mr Ar-Jai MacAskill, beside him, who having beenloweringly pregnant for the last few moments, suddenly brought forth, unable to contain himself for another single minute:

"I must possiteevely ask the Reverent Mr MacRury *too* state-ah"—his eyes narrowed in a peering, inward look of extreme concentration—"where duss he s-see his nèhkit forms, whether of weemen or old poots, standing with respect to Gòht?" He continued awhile to travail visibly with words that would not be brought forth. Then like the breaking in of another drone on his bagpipes the squeal came augmented in power and volume, "settling down" to its best . . . "After aal we are only here to p-pass theolotchical tchutchment." The words were leaving his well-opened mouth with vigour and roundness.

Mr Aulay MacAulay immediately broke in with his normal dry tone, "I must point out to Mr MacAskill that we are not here to pass any sort of a judgment at all—*sip*. We are here to listen to a statement if it is given to us." His voice was as ever reassuringly cool, if matter-of-fact beyond the point of deflation. "After that we may consider a course of action, if any is open to us—*sip*—but we are in no sense whatever empowered to pass a judgment. This is no sort of a court. A party of friends, simply . . . met . . . well, *you* know for what purpose, Mr MacAskill."

Mr Ar-Jai MacAskill had been taken aback. He was blinking at Mr MacAulay out of his clay-coloured face.

"Well," he said, after a second or two, "let him answer the question, then."

He folded his arms to show he was at his ease. He had to raise them well forward to cross them above the barrel of his chest, the muscles could be discerned bulging inside his sleeves: they looked hard like iron. It was meant to be a gesture with dignity, his folding his arms; Mr MacAulay observing it reflected sardonically that he looked rather as if "setting" himself to break into a few steps of a hornpipe. The nostrils of his long nose quivering, in rôle of chairman of the company he turned to Mr MacRury.

Mr MacRury said gravely, politely . . . "I'm not sure if I've quite understood the question . . . There can't be any *direct* relationship, as far as I can see, between art and theology. If you mean is either the practice or enjoyment of art ethical or permissible at all, I think yes. To be a creator is natural to man. It's one of his functions. Of course, like any other faculty it can be abused, put to bad use. But in itself . . . it's all right. It's simply that man was created to be a creator."

"No, s-surr, noah! This iss not whaht I haff learnt at the coallege . . . aye, surr, and at my m-mother's kneece. N-nor wass it for this toctrine that our P-protestant forefaathers kave their podies to be purnt for a sweet-smelling sacrifice to Gòht. Not for this toctrine-ah, but for the c-contrary toctrine!"

The feeling seemed to be that "Protestant forefathers" was high-pitching things a little.

"The contrary doctrine?" very softly said Mr Colin Gunn raising his eyebrows and turning his right cheek slightly, interrogatively, towards Mr Ar-Jai MacAskill beside him.

"Yess, surr . . . the contrary toctrine-ah."

Ar-Jai gave the impression of wallowing towards his point, a broad-bottomed craft making port in a choppy sea. His inner agitation was tremendous and incommensurate. Sweat was not only standing on his small contorted forehead and temples but drops of it detached themselves and trickled down his clay-coloured cheeks and disappeared into the folds of his chin. His travail was painful to watch. But he would concede nothing to his limitations or weakness.

He pointed the first finger of his smallish, well-haired hand as if it had been a small gun at Mr MacRury's smiling face across the table from him.

"Y-you could not tell *me* what wass the connection between your art and painting and our theolotchy. Putt *I* can tell *you* what iss the connection." He jabbed his finger, making his eyes small by pulling up the lower lids from below. "The connection iss *sin.* You haff contemned your art and your painting of picturss out of your own mouth when you haff said they come out of the nèhture of maan. Pecause the nèhture of maan iss eefil . . . ant aal thaht giffs pleshure eefil from the craytle to the krayfe. Eefil, eefil is maan ant aal his works. Were you in the coallege where *you* were traint, not tolt about the Faal?"

"The what?" came insinuatingly from Colin Gunn.

"The Faal of Maan," said Mr MacAskill scarcely moving his head in his direction but letting his eyes turn for the moment everywhere in the room about him as if perceiving the echoes of that rolling phrase, which his mouth formed roundly and widely . . . "The Faal of Maan . . . since which the nèhture of maan iss altogether faalen, ant aal he can do iss eefil . . . Eefil, eefil iss maan, ant aal his works, eefil from his m-mother's pelly. Peholt the krate toctrine-ah, the krate toctrine veendicatit by our P-protestant faathers in their plutt!" The additional drone had broken in long ago; every pulpit instant the squeal rose in pitch and carrying power. All the same for the others there was something slightly painful in the spectacle of so much straining, so enormous an expenditure of uneasy energy. It was too obvious his wrestling was not with flesh and blood—had it been so his bull-neck and barrel-shaped body and thick limbs would have made him formidable, despite his rather narrow shoulders. "You haff contemned yourself," he cried, "out of your own mouth, in that you haff tenied the krate toctrine, the klawrious toctrine, the fery, the fery foundèhtion of our P-protestant releegion, that since the Faal aal iss eefil, eefil iss aal that proceeteth forth out of the heart of maan ant aal his works aal the tays of his life. Woe to you that you haff tenied the toctrine! Pefore that you would pee tenying the toctrine it were petter that you would pee caast into the midst of the s-sea!" At the word he actually shuddered.

There was a silence, a silence and a waiting, in which the echoes of the pulpit voice with its effects of declamation died away, but in a dead or blunted manner, without the evoking of answering vibrations; Ar-Jai could be heard breathing. But Mr Aulay MacAulay, who received the looks of most of the others, was again strangely immobile, seeming pale, his eyelids lowered, his fingers holding the edge of the table. He made no sign of returning to exercise of his duty.

"Perhaps it may help," Mr MacRury said, since Mr MacAulay made no move—his voice startlingly quiet after Ar-Jai's: in his aspect not at all affected by the near spectacle of an excited, an angry man—"perhaps it may help if I remind Mr MacAskill of my earlier statement that in my view the 'forms' created by the artist are forms that he has in strict speaking *perceived*, that is, that they are in some real sense *outside* him, 'out there', in existence therefore *prior to* his perception of them. Therefore, to that extent *not* coming from, not attributable to human nature which you hold to be radically evil."

"Whaht *I* holt to pee radically eefil!" Ar-Jai was flabbergasted. "It iss not *I* that holts it, it iss the P-protestant toctrine that aal of human nèhture iss eefil. It iss an heresy to say otherwyss . . ."

Colin Gunn spluttered at his side. "You can't have a heresy unless you first have an orthodoxy!"

"Orthodoxy?" said Ar-Jai turning round on him his eyes opened to their fullest extent.

"Yes. An agreed doctrine."

"Oh, I know whaht an orthodoxy iss. Ant thiss *iss* our P-protestant orthodoxy, Mister Kunn, thiss *iss* our akreet toctrine"—Ar-Jai was jabbing with his right forefinger, violently tamping down the tobacco in an invisible pipe with a stem a foot long—"thaht the nèhture of maan iss aaltogesser eefil ant aal his works corrupt ant fèhn."

Mr Colin Gunn threw a look at him.

"You wouldn't get another two ministers in Scotland to hold that doctrine with you today!"

Ar-Jai gasped sharply, stabbed between the ribs. But he rolled backwards, turning his face over his opposite shoulder with bewilderment and stupefaction when as it were clubbed over the head from that direction by the Rev. Norman Maclennan's old man's, whispering voice saying, as if unconsciously speaking a thought, "It's a little bit strong . . ."

One instant Ar-Jai lay against the back of his chair looking twistedly up at Norman Maclennan's fine, ashen-tinted face floating slightly above him, looking away from him, straight in front, with pensiveness, so that the doctrine of the radical corruption of human nature might already—actually—no longer be occupying his mind. Ar-Jai's jaw sagged with horror.

But he sat up and forward on his iron buttocks, clasped a smallish, clasping hand on each knee, shook his clay-coloured jowls to right then to left, and finally fixing his attention on Mr Colin Gunn, and blinking his eyes very rapidly, at last brought out, in a higher squeal than any yet, what seemed to be only just on this side of control . . .

"Putt . . . putt . . . then you are Popishes one ant aal!"

"Oh, I wouldn't say that," said Mr Gunn, with irritating lightness.

"Oh, yess, inteet, Mr Kunn," insisted Ar-Jai, still turned towards him. "At the klawrious Reformèhtion there were putt the two toctrines. There wass the toctrine that maan wass utterly eefil ant corrupt ant kon astray from Gòht, ant that aal the works of maan are eefil ant an offence to Gòht ant meriting His Tchutchments. Ant thaht wass the P-protestant toctrine. Ant there wass the toctrine"—the hands clasping each knee became two quite small fists pressed down on top of them—"that there iss yet koot in maan tespite the Faal, ant that therefore he can yet too koot works ant works pleasing to Gòht. Ant thaht wass the Cassolic toctrine." The fists pounded softly on the knees. "And if now ass you sèh the whole potie of P-protestants to-dèh, save a few, haff kiven up the toctrine of Maan's t-total tepravitèh, ant haff faalen akain to pelieving there iss yet kootness in maan ant that he can by his koot teets pleass Gòht, then lèht me tell you, Mr Kunn, surr . . . lèht me tell you the whole potie of P-protestants of to-dèh, whether they will atmit it or will not atmit it, haff tèhken sites akainst the P-protestants of the Reformèhtion. They are sèhing, *ipsa facte* ant py eemplicèhtion, thaht aht the Reformèhtion the Cassolics were right ant the P-protestants were ronk. Will you now therefore ko ant tchoin yourselfs to-to-to the System of Popery?"

His agitation was painful. Lifting up his right hand he drew the back of it downwards along his jowl, holding his head aside, then looking round as if sensing himself threatened.

"Oh, I don't see that that follows at all," hissed Mr Colin Gunn, with a watchful sideways look at him.

"Inteet!!" Ar-Jai seemed to explode on to his feet. With his left hand he seemed to draw their attention to a wide countryside—Mr Aulay MacAulay at the other side of the table gazed upward with mild surprise at the hand extended almost over his head. "Peholt," said Ar-Jai in a high squeal and in highest excitement, "here iss P-popish Cassolic toctrine! Whaht tuss hinter you, Mr Kunn, ant"—whisking round so that he had his back to the table looking down on the two who had till then been sitting on either side of him—"ant you, Mr Maclennan, whaht tuss hinter you that you should not pecome P-popishes yourselfs?"

The whole air vibrated with the Rev. Mr MacAskill who, it could be told, was sweating profusely.

"I shall have . . ."—Mr Aulay MacAulay's voice at its coolest and driest addressed itself to breaking down the tension and movement, everyone looking at Ar-Jai standing there, even Mr MacKenzie at one end of the row and Mr Macpherson Bain at the other, who had not heretofore ceased to regard closely Mr MacRury, with their different expressions—"I shall have . . ." said Mr MacAulay at Mr Ar-Jai MacAskill's back, "*sip*—I shall have to adjourn this meeting if you don't refrain—*sip*—from discussing theology."

Ar-Jai turned his sweating face swifty towards him over his shoulder, then at once turned himself round and sat down on his chair again.

"*Hah*," he exclaimed quietly, subsiding, making again that motion of drawing the back of the fingers of his right hand down along his jowl, holding his head aside . . . "*Hah*,"—his eyes closing—"it won't pe lot-chic thaht will safe you from Popery now that you are pecome lati-latitudinèhrians!"

He plunged for his large pale blue and white-spotted handkerchief.

"Well then," said Mr MacAulay, contemplating silence again in the room by bringing his own voice down to almost a whisper, "will you continue, Mr MacRury?"

Mr MacRury said, "I'm afraid I can't for the moment recall the precise point . . ."

"You were trying to make out as far as I understood it," said Mr MacAulay, "that art is a licit practice and preoccupation of man because only the representation part is human, the *thing* or 'form' which is represented being something objective, *out there*, existing prior to and therefore independently of man and therefore not involved in the corruption resulting from the Fall."

"Oh, yes . . . and there is a point there." It was the Rev. Colin Gunn. "How and where can these 'forms' which the artist represents exist, how can they be 'out there', even before he has had his 'vision' of them . . . before they have been in his imagination, let alone before he has represented them in his work of art?"

"Would it be like those puzzles . . ." asked Mr Maclennan, "with all the little bits . . . thank you . . . would it be like those jigsaw puzzles? You could say the solution to them, the picture they will make, exists already in a way—it does, you know—before even two of the bits are put together . . ."

"No, that's not it at all," Mr Gunn objected. "The solution to the jigsaw puzzle exists in somebody's mind, in the mind of whoever knows what the picture is going to be when the puzzle is complete. The 'vision' of Mr MacRury's artist, on the other hand—that's just the point—exists, he says, before it is in anybody's mind."

"Wouldn't that point be provided for you if you imagined that everybody who knew the solution to the jigsaw was dead or had forgotten it? Even then you could say the solution existed . . . even while the bits and pieces were lying jumbled up on the table."

"No, it wouldn't at all," insisted Colin Gunn. "Because in that case the solution could only be said to exist in some way or other *potentially*. Mr MacRury makes out that what is to be the subject of the artist's 'vision' exists before he has ever had that vision, let alone before he has represented it for others to perceive—which they very often don't—*he*, *he* . . . Isn't that right, Mr MacRury? The subject of the artist's vision you believe exists in some real or actual—not potential—way before ever the artist has perceived it in his mind? It seems to me you've got your work cut out to prove your point. How, in what sense, can something which doesn't even exist yet in somebody's mind and imagination be said already to be objectively real?"

Mr MacRury leaned forward. "I agree that you seem to have brought the whole thing to an issue. Since you have cornered me I shall have to say that I see only one way in which the harmonies of immaterial 'form' can be real before ever they have been perceived by the artist who is to try to reproduce them, and that is that they exist already, and from before the beginning, in the Mind of God; that they are part of the unsearchable riches of His Infinite Being, which is Reality itself and the ground and substantial base of everything real . . ."

Ar-Jai's wail was agonised . . . "Whaht do I hear! Iss it a meenister of the Gospel likening the Mindt of Gòht to the keetchin of a sluttish wumman . . . full of olt poots sitting under tchairs without seats, ant olt men needing to shave their peards . . . ant . . . deesh-clouts ant dirty deeshes . . . O-o-oh! it's . . . it's plaasphemous! . . . plaasphemous! . . ."

This time no one paid any attention to him. Colin Gunn waited till the noise had died sufficiently for his sweet, insinuating whisper to be heard . . . "I don't suppose Mr MacRury would deny that there are *bad* pictures. Would he go so far as to contend that these with their badness existed also from eternity as part of the Reality of God?"

"It's rather difficult to answer that question," Mr MacRury said slowly. "I would need to know, for instance, in what sense you think of a picture as bad. Aren't you speaking for instance under the unconscious influence of the same outlook as Mr MacAskill's, the idea, the 'feeling' that art itself is somehow bad, naughty, a preoccupation fit for Frenchmen and foreigners whom we suppose to live immoral lives . . . to keep mistresses, and so forth? If you mean simply that the representation is bad, that the work is badly done, that's simply faulty craftsmanship, and has nothing to do with the question, because it has nothing to do with what the artist has *seen*, and only concerns his ability to represent it. If you mean that there are works of art likely to have a bad moral influence I agree that there are or could be such works of art. But here again it seems to me we must make a distinction. There is a *moral* question of *what* it is lawful to represent; I don't deny that it's an important question, but it's a moral question; it only arises when there is a possibility that a specific work of art may move people otherwise than in their aesthetic sensibility, and that in a morally undesirable way. I suppose the possibility that a specific work of art may have a doubtfully desirable moral effect comes from the kind of creature man is—mixed motives, impure vision, wavering intention. But all that is quite aside from my contention, to which you have now driven me . . .

"First I said that the subject-matter of the aesthetic vision and experience is essentially objective, out there, already there to be perceived and experienced—therefore in the first place appertaining to an order of reality unaffected by the corruption or limitation of human nature, on any view of Man. Then you force me on to the further position that such a Reality can be nothing if not the Mind of God. All questions of morality apart—and also the differences of opinion as to what constitutes good art—my general position is that in so far as beauty is in a work of art, in so far as a work of art is a representation of a perception of beauty, it represents a perceiving of the Divine Perfection. God is Beauty just as He is Truth: indeed in a Being who is entirely One and Single, Beauty can only be another aspect of the Divine Truth—real Truth, not a sort of sentimental rhetoric. Therefore, with the reservation already made, one can say that the maker of the work of art—of any kind of work of art, not only the painter of pictures—is privileged as it were to continue or to complete the work of Creation."

"Oh, very well, very well, we accept your explanation about the improper pictures"—Colin Gunn's tone said very plainly, We don't, of course, do anything of the sort. "Can't help approving of your discretion in locking them away . . . It's just unfortunate it should all have come to light." His melting brown eyes looked from his narrow face; his damp mouth rather sweetly forming the spiteful phrases. In general Mr MacRury's last statements had been met with a sort of gasp. Mr David Macpherson Bain had for a moment, however, sat forward with a look of interest. But Mr Ar-Jai MacAskill was wallowing in his chair with a look of having reached his last and with eyes turned up to the ceiling trying to insert his pale blue and white-spotted handkerchief between his neck and collar. He looked terrified, terrified and desperate.

7

"*Ahem*, well, time moves on: is there any other item that you wish to dispose of, Mr MacRury . . . before coming to the main part of the . . . ah—*sip* . . .?"

The broad lights moved on Mr MacAulay's bald pate as it turned. He was as solemn-serious, non-committal as ever and rested his greenish eyes on Mr MacRury.

Mr MacRury clasped his hands round his knee, his legs crossed. A movement as if he would have leant back in an easy posture was frustrated by the yellow chair's straight shape.

"Well, yes, one other matter was . . . unconnected, or if connected, only indirectly. That was the . . . cutting down my food at times . . . and also my standing or holding myself in various postures. I don't quite know how that could have been observed: the standing for a long time—sounds rather silly—with my arms stretched out, and so forth. It was all really quite simple. Simply a little bodily discipline undergone with a view to earning a dividend in greater capacity or grasp of mind, in augmented inner freedom. Just a technique that I found useful for the object I had in view. I seemed to find that not only the somnolent states brought on by repletion, but even the general sensations of well-being induced by habitual eating to the satisfaction of appetite, as well as the pampering of the body in more sleep than was requisite, in much comfortable sitting, and so on; all this, if continued, subtly and insidiously caused a certain degree of sluggishness or heaviness in the spiritual faculties, which kept beyond my reach the attainment of certain mental and moral conditions that I was aiming at. I found that to raise or elevate my spiritual faculties and gain greater power of control over them, to attain a greater grasp and lucidity of thought, a clarity and amplitude of the imagination, an excellent means lay ready to hand in reducing the force or authority of the claims of the physical element of my being by way of a consistent or persistent going-against its inclinations and denial of its satisfactions—by, for instance, to a reasonable degree denying the body food, forcing it to maintain a posture after it had become uncomfortable, even almost intolerable, and so on . . .

"That's all there was in *that* part of the indictment. There wasn't even, in the common use of the word, any *moral* aim involved—I had no feeling that I was 'good' in achieving anything in this way. It was simply a means to an end, a technique. My customary sense of comfort, my condition of ordinarily being fed to the level of bodily inclination—even if that level was never very high in my case (I'd never much interest in food)—seemed to be blurring something in me, and to be a reproach. So this bodily deprivation and discipline was a technique for the acquistion of . . . you might call it spiritual morale: the idea was to achieve a sort of toning-up of the spiritual faculties in general, making them more 'fit', in the athlete's sense, in the sense of being more 'capable'."

"And was the experiment successful?"—the small voice was easily identified—cutting, softly sharp.

"Oh, yes . . ."

Mr David Macpherson Bain's slightly flute-like tenor broke in for the first time since the beginning of the proceedings. "Why Thursdays?" he said, still retaining however his rather rigid, upright posture and stiff, bespectacled scrutiny of Mr MacRury—a severe expression, rather suggesting that he had little hope of finding he had not ground for being gravely disappointed in him.

"I beg your pardon?" said Mr MacRury.

"Your cook or housekeeper," said Mr Macpherson Bain, "Miss MacGillivray, has deponed in the 'information' she laid against you that her orders were for a limitation—pretty drastic, I thought to myself—of food as a regular or standing thing *on Thursdays*. I ask, why Thursdays?"

"Oh, *that*!" Mr MacRury smiled. "Quite arbitrary. Or rather it was for the sake of the working of the house. Out of fairness to—*ah*—Miss MacGillivray it had to be a settled thing in advance, and Thursday was indicated because it happened to be the day rationed goods and household supplies were delivered, in the afternoon, which made it the most convenient—supplies being lowest on that day in any case. Otherwise it might have been any day at all . . . Tuesday . . . or Monday."

"I see"—Mr Macpherson Bain was satisfied.

"You didn't realise, of course"—Mr Colin Gunn broke in again—"that your action had given rise to the strong rumour that you were an adherent or member of some mysterious and secret cult, of unknown origin—though the worst was thought likely—whose initiates went in for fasting on Thursdays and fakir-like postures and dervish-like gymnastics?"

"I had no idea."

One of those silences fell. Only the fluttering of the red, black and white butterflies was heard again, one in each pencil-shaped window. Mr MacRury may have sensed the feeling had fallen against him or become negative in his regard; he said, as if he had to say it: "I know that the only context in which 'going into training' is any longer a familiar idea, an acceptable notion, is when it is strictly for the body's sake—if one is preparing for a boxing match or going to run a race. Yet . . . surely . . . the principle ought to be as sound, and the practice as permissible, when applied for a spiritual end, with the object a gain in mental fitness . . ." His glance passed unheld from one to the other. "At any rate . . . obviously, if there is something to be gained on the spiritual side of human life by the discipline and subordination of the material element in it, that is a something that we are losing for want of that discipline and subordination."

The voice that spoke carried a strange suggestion—as of ice formed over faraway volcanic fires. And there was a sound of teeth.

"I like my meat!"

It was the Rev. Norbert Legge. His eyes already lowered, and with no intention of saying more.

It brought an end and a release however: he had given the only answer possible.

8

Mr MacAulay said . . . "And now?"

"Yes," concurred Mr MacRury, with a sort of willingness, and any suggestion of lightness fell away from him at once. A distant consideration having passed in a moment behind his grey eyes, he got up.

"I am accused . . ." his light baritone voice said very clearly and softly, while he stood at his full medium height, shoulders setting themselves squarely a little, bracing or preparing himself. "I am accused of this, that . . . that . . ." They all saw it—saw his person give a slight appearance of a flicker before their eyes as if just then smitten somewhere in its innermost, and shared that impression of more than common *reality* in their sense of his presence. He had in any case been stopped, and now seemed unequal to what he had been about to say. "No . . ."—he grasped with his right hand the back of the yellow chair, placed his left fist on the cheap, warping table-top, so turning himself half sideways to it, the more directly facing Mr MacAulay and all the other ministers, except Mr Maclennan opposite, who was now facing his left shoulder, and Mr Murdo MacKenzie who was slightly behind it, looking at his left elbow—"no . . ." he said, giving that impression of sudden unequalness to what had been in his mind to say, an impression of burden and hesitation. "Perhaps you would . . . Mr MacAulay . . .?"

"Ah, yes"—Mr MacAulay straightened with rather too jerky a readiness; cleared his throat—"*krm*, *krm* . . . your housekeeper, this Miss Williamina MacGillivray"—his long, dry face was above the papers—"states . . . *sip—krm*"—the long fingers crinkled and rustled the papers, it seemed loudly—"*ah* . . . here, yes, here"—in a reading voice—"states that on one occasion coming up to your study to announce a meal she was unable to make you hear by knocking on the door, and that when she opened it and entered, thinking you might be ill or fallen asleep, you were seated at your desk—'not in this world' she puts it—unconscious, though your eyes were wide open: and that when you came to yourself your look at her—

which she will simply say was 'terrible'—frightened her so much that she suffered a severe nerve shock, accompanied by temporary loss of vision, and followed by prostration—*sip*. She adds that—*krm*—you were *krm*, *krm*—she observed you to be weeping—well, really!—in an unnatural way while you were unconscious, or 'not in this world', continuously and very copiously yet without any signs of distress such as sobbing or contracting of the features—*krm*."

(How well Mr MacRury remembered that occasion. He had come in from the snail-haunted, oil-smelling tool-shed where he left his bicycle, along the side of the house in the wind, splurging through the gravel on the path, angry with Bando for his insolence and for his malicious effort to involve an innocent person in a harmful scandal; full of a familiar hopeless feeling (mixed with anger), because of what people were, and with disappointment with himself because of his—as he felt it—presumptuous entertainment of disgust and bitterness: when he was met inside the door by a mass of woman's talk and laughter: Mina Bhando's nasal alto, the shrill twitter of Peigi Snoovie, and another voice, commanding and brazen, from a major-general of local gossipers. And so he had gone stooping up to his room, hand on banisters, as if exhausted by having fought his way all across the hall through and against the stream of sound. Bowed down now by more than the sense of Bando's malice, or the sense of smallness of mind everywhere; rather by an emotion of generalised abjection, on his own account equally with others, a sense of nothingness that was none the less evil-tainted, and formed a burden bruising in the inmost; almost borne down on to the stairs that smelt of cheap cleanliness. The talk from the kitchen, now again coming, but muffled through the closed door, released a poignancy of some sort of grief, because of the amount, the degree of *being* forfeited by everyone, everywhere—without the least earthly hope of stopping it—by the lack alone of interior stillness, interior silence. The grief of a world dying of thirst for *being* while immersed in the ocean of it became *his* grief then, so much that he retained an impression of groping his way to his chair at his desk, and, sitting down in it—he recollected—feeling himself, in an agony that did not consume, dissolving, and in that compassionate sea being carried away . . .

A sound or some outer impression penetrated at last and he became aware of her. Mina Bhando: well into the room. Standing half-way between his desk and the door. Her white and glistering blouse first reached his awareness, the bold mass of it as an objective fact, tight-filled with her abundant breasts: her white and glistering blouse put on for her guest, above her black, go-to-meeting skirt. He noticed the massy sweep of her throat then—rather fine, though spoiled by the large aggregation of brown, freckle-like spots over her breast-bone, extending with diminishing incidence down almost to the "V" of the shining white blouse. The skin there looked yellowish enclosed in shining white, and there was—rather bold for her—the beginning of a cleft between twin swellings, a narrow valley-line which as it were entered the point of the V in the beginning of a precipitous plunge to the abyss of femininity. Mind, in the statuesque, breathing mass, was elsewhere.

He was in time to see the lips conclude a sliding, sheathing movement over the bulging teeth till they just met thinly, covering their bulkiness. The eyes on either side of the large, narrow, choked-looking nose were in the act of distending until their upper parts showed staring white. He saw the eyebrows raise themselves towards the head of floppy-looking black hair, which made a perceptible movement downwards to meet them. Even through the dash of that purging sea which still blurred his vision, he recognised panic affright in her, in expression and bearing—still more so, and with more incomprehension, when the statue of feminine flesh chirped or croaked out, "Oh! oh!"—as if suddenly affrighted somewhere in her overstrung maidenliness. He was astonished to see her shy away as if spur-touched at some point where she was nervous and overmettled: then step back, with another startled croak, and twirling on her heel plunge from the room. He had known on that occasion, however, a twinge of uneasiness, of something like apprehension, on realising a little later that he was mopping away the signs of copious tears—especially since they had been unconscious. For the first time it occurred to him that he could not go long unobserved, that perhaps he had been already observed . . . that perhaps something was afoot. Now for some time he knew that it had been so.)

"I take it, Mr MacRury"—Mr MacAulay was concluding his recital of remaining accusations, summing up—"I take it that all those matters complained of, chiefly by your man Murdo MacGillivray, your housekeeper Williamina MacGillivray and the housemaid Margaret MacMillan, namely the—*krm*—shall I say? trance-like states in which you were increasingly found or observed when alone, kneeling in the church, or for as long as—it is alleged—hours on end in your bedroom through the night, or seated at the desk in your study and likewise the similar—*krm*—episodes which twice occurred in the pulpit, and for which there are"—scuffing the backs of his fingers upwards over the papers—"all these witnesses and deponents: I take it that all those episodes are connected, in that they are, all of them, the outward manifestations or—*krm*—

symptoms of what you have called—*krm*—the 'main matter'."

Mr MacRury's "yes" was almost inaudible. He was stooping forward, as if looking at his shoe. Raising his head then he gave the impression of being deeply ashamed or embarrassed, his eyes over the heads of his confrères seeking about the yellow walls and pencil-shaped windows, the red in his clear and open face fading. "Yes."

He looked down again, then up—not at anyone:

"I know before I begin that I shall not succeed . . . *can't* succeed. The words of a medical textbook come nearer bringing about a participation in the experience of disease or illness than any terms I know . . . extant . . . could convey . . ."

"You admit, then"—Colin Gunn's small acid voice injected softly. "It is important at the outset to have your assurance that you yourself regard the phenomena as pathological, essentially a . . . a question of disease."

"Oh, no, not at all . . . I make no such assurance . . . On the contrary . . . The effect was altogether an assertion of the personality, a rising over weaknesses . . ."

"Guard against pride!" admonished the Rev. Colin Gunn's voice with a touch of the superior in its tone.

"No, no . . . it had nothing to do with that either. The whole experience was much too real, too objective: 'self' in that sense must always be a casualty . . . there is simply no room for it . . . But, there, as I said . . . I have not yet begun and already I fail to make myself understood."

"Just keep on, Mr MacRury," Mr MacAulay's voice broke in, cool and dry, "and count on our sympathetic efforts to grasp your meaning."

"Well"—Mr MacRury looked a puzzled question into the corner of the room—"the beginning . . .?"

Then he smiled a little very quietly to himself, tolerantly, as at something in recollection—"I believe that really, in a sense, and in an unconscious way, I brought it on myself . . . invited it rather, since there can be no question of commanding in the matter either consciously or unconsciously: it is purely and of its essence something 'given' . . ." The quiet smile intensified as it were inwardly, all sensing the approach to the foreground of consciousness and threshold of speech of what was causing it. "I don't know if any of you have read a novel . . ."

Ar-Jai could not restrain the impulse to cry out at this. "Iss it noffels, now!" rose his dulcet squeal. "Iss this the next off it!" But he subsided again at once, only drawing in his broad chin with such spasmodic emphasis as if, *this* time, he were determined to shoot his back stud into the panelling behind: the collar stood so widely from his neck—so energetically was he pressing in his chin—one could have dropped an eel with ease right down his back.

"No, this is not about novels, Mr MacAskill," Mr MacRury reassured him. "But there is a novel which I happen to have read, called *The House with the Green Shutters*. There is a character in that novel of whom someone says that he could conquer the world '*if he swalled his neck till't*,' which means, I take it, if he put all his energy into the attempt, really strained after it, and it occurred to me . . . I think, yes, I always wanted to try what I could do in the spiritual life, to 'swall my neck till't', if I may put it so. Though not in any sense of seeking a ground of vainglory. Rather it was from a sort of economic sense operating in the spiritual order, as it were"—his brow wrinkling told he was experiencing difficulty in finding the words—"from an instinct to lay hold of reality, to safeguard myself against the irruption of nothingness . . . to make myself safe from the danger of the surrounding sea of non-being breaking in upon and drowning my essence. The point was I had the feeling, the conviction that man's life is not achieving 'the thing' until it is touched by something outside himself; the idea that even goodness is not, ultimately, good enough."

"You mean," enunciated Colin Gunn sweetly, "you wanted to be better than anybody else?"

"No; this is beyond ethical perfection—not that I claim to have achieved that: nor is it necessary, since as the 'something' is outside the bounds of—is other than—ethical perfection it could not be caused or brought into man's life by such perfection.

"So as I say, I *wanted* to make an effort spiritually—and here is the connection, indirect and if any, of my ascetic practices, in that they might have constituted a sort of 'training' or athletic preparation spiritually . . . I am trying to explain what I meant by saying I may have 'brought it on myself'. The whole thing of course is gratuitous and 'given', of its very essence, but . . . I mean . . . how shall I put it?"—he looked with a sort of gentle earnestness up at one of the narrow windows—"I mean . . . *perhaps I may have been taken at my word.*"

A few other eyes were raised when a bee suddenly boomed loud at the open section of one of the windows, but they were lowered, withdrawn, when unexpectedly it passed, the boom swinging widely off and at once dying under the blue sky far away in the distance, smothered under the weight of the sunshine which must have been pouring down on to the soon extinguished sound.

"On the other hand it is so gratuitous, so objective, so 'given', that any prior desire or disposition of mine may have had nothing whatsoever to do with it.

"I never at any time pursued it, or even adopted an attitude of curious wondering what would happen or what would be disclosed next. Because I perfectly understood from the very first that that was the one way to make sure there would be nothing further. I understood that it was altogether something conferred, not attained, that I had been approached from wholly *outside* myself, and that I must wait humbly and without expectation, since it was utterly free to come or not to come, and could not co-exist with such presumption as it would have been on the part of my nothingness to go in pursuit of its plenitude. One such movement in me, I knew, and it would veil itself and depart. So I am not to be thought of as having 'indulged in'. Apart from that initial implicit invitation (the effort to 'swall my neck till't') I did nothing but what I felt the developing reality called for from me, and that was largely an attentiveness and of course some degree of cutting myself off from self-indulgences.

"I used to make use of considerations. That was at first. These might be of any kind, with a starting-place in whatever I chanced to think first about. If my eyes happened to fall on some part of my person, I would take that as my starting-point: fix my mind on it, think about it, let my mind pass then to the whole of my person, the various parts of my body: I would in imagination as it were attentively wander through my whole bodily organism so far as I have knowledge of its structure and working, intending to achieve a consciousness of the whole, in act and simultaneously, even to awareness of the physical event of consciousness at that instant in my brain, so that holding my instant awareness of the bodily universe in all its parts, functioning, holding it strongly, fervently, I might right out of that consciousness-simultaneous send forth my affirmation.

"But that would have been a simple act of the thing. I learned to make it more and more complex and comprehensive . . . I might perhaps, not letting go this newly-conquered consciousness-simultaneous of my bodily person in act of life, place it in the midst of the totality of its spatial-material co-entities, a living point in the total universe of space and matter, in so far as I had knowledge enough and imagination enough to represent that to myself.

"The world itself, a rotating stony sphere with fiery depths. In such and such position in relation to the unimagined multitude of moving spheres. Anything of a physical, ponderable or measurable order, I sought to form a spatial setting for this throbbing, living, affirming being. I might raise my eyes, for instance, and so immediately, seeing them, think of clouds, overhanging, chequering or presiding over the fertile skin of the solar satellite. And so to each zone of different climate and temperature, bearing its proper vegetation. Very fruitful then to pass to the human population of the orb, an innumerable sense of contemporary man, an instantaneous apprehension of his living multitude—colour and race, language, dress and occupation, belief and infinite opinion, all, at this very moment when I am thinking of it, in action.

"That innumerable sense became at once and incomparably more multitudinous when extended into time to take in history. I would cast myself, that is, not into the spatial abyss but into the abyss of time, among not spheres and nebulae but the infinity of wills and of intelligences which I could use, in my knowledge of them, as a deepening, strengthening, extending and meaning-giving element in the ground-base of that affirmation which I desired to send forth from the depths of my soul. In a word, the fruits of a life-long addiction to the pursuit of truth, whether intellectual or moral, I made use of, carrying all along till I should have built up as widely inclusive, as divergent a body of facts as with all my effort I could maintain a sense of *simultaneously*—so that everything I learned, the whole of my experience, might contribute to the affirmation I sent forth then."

Ar-Jai was looking distressed, mopping his face; Colin Gunn on Ar-Jai's left under the tumbled lock of soft black hair had his eyes on the speaker, his mouth set small; Davie Macpherson Bain beyond the far end of the table still had that somewhat rigid and "drawn-back" goggling look, his glasses two grey discs steady and opaque upon his face under a questioning wrinkle; Norbert Legge's towering form, between Davie and Colin Gunn, might have been listening intently, the highlights motionless on the high, bent-forward skull, or might have been occupied with something altogether different and far away. The Rev. Norman Maclennan—and still more Murdo MacKenzie, being across from his left shoulder—were less squarely in Mr MacRury's eye: they gave none the less, simply, a steady, open impression of listening—the former a face of oblong shape and the latter a round one; in front of him Mr Aulay MacAulay's air was entirely non-committal, eyes mostly on the yellow table-top.

"I may put it that what I aimed to achieve was an enlargement of consciousness—through as heightened a sense of *myself* as possible, even to a consciousness of activity in my very body-cells, held simultaneously with as large, as clear, as multiplex a grasp and sense of the universe not-myself as I could by any means attain—and this enlarged consciousness held *steadily* for the necessary space of time. If after an instant it began to elude my grasp, to dissipate, I would recall it by a summoning up again of the flagging faculties and another swift conspective glance through the ranked realities of time and space and of my experiencing self, and so hold the multitudinous consciousness steady once again and for the space of yet another affirmation . . ."

(What a pity those black, yellow and red butterflies could not find egress at last, flitter-flittering: ever ending their swift and hesitating, uncertain sweep up and down through the space peopled by ministerial heads and black shoulders by a gyrating swoop and a bash that battered black or yellow pollen from them against the greenish opaque translucence of narrow glass.)

"You will see that an Amen given in these conditions must have its own certain value—so deep and wide a field so deliberately affirmed must reflect itself in the reality of the affirmer, on whom the effect would be a metaphysical increase simply, a growth of positives in the spirit, *a becoming more real*."

Mr Aulay MacAulay shuffled in his chair, seemed to press his lips together, frowning and closing his eyes.

"I must caution you, however, against the idea that such was my objective. These affirmative, informed acts were merely preparatory: not the thing itself. Dare I put it that the possession of truths is merely a preparation for the advent of Truth? At any rate those reflections, the use to which I put any knowledge I possess, the content of which I made stand up before me by my imagination, so that I could look at it, and take it in, all this was merely a technique of preparing myself for . . . for the thing itself . . . for the type of experience with having had which I am now charged by an uncomprehending and therefore apprehensive countryside. The main thing, the thing itself, was utterly different from all those acts and had nothing to do either with them or with me.

"The time came when there appeared to be no further need for the reflective effort, the preparatory concentric-comprehensive sweep of the imagination, for mental considerations of any kind. They had brought me where they could: I had no hesitation in discarding them. Perhaps they were in some sense implied or embraced by the act I now made without their aid, without any mental preliminary whatsoever. That act seemed to take place entirely in the will, where it was an immensely simple movement. Too simple now to be described as an Amen—an utterly monosyllabic utterance of the soul . . . And in the issue all that had at first been the content of knowledge and focus of imagination, my own physical being, the world, the entire universe and all its facts, floated away, vanished utterly as it were from underneath my feet."

A bang sounded in the church: Mr Macpherson Bain, jumping up with "*Ah-mm!* It's all right; all right!" sat down again, very red and embarrassed about that interior woodwork.

"Later . . . there was no need even for acts of the will . . . Simply . . ."—but Mr MacRury shook his head, put up his hand along his brows as if to hide his eyes and face. Then again he shook his bowed head, slowly; made a negative movement of his waving hand in silence . . . Expression seemed beyond him.

"You still have not told us"—Colin Gunn looked more watchful than ever under his tumbled soft forelock—"what this main thing was, or is, which is, after all, taking up our time here."

Mr MacRury turned on him a large, compassionate look, and was about to answer when Mr MacAskill broke in. Ar-Jai appeared in a terrible state, his colour jaundiced and sickly, sweat glistening as it ran down his temples out of his indeterminate black-grey hair.

"*Too* you," he now squealed at his least dulcet and most agitated, holding the blue, white-spotted handkerchief against his barrel chest, "*too* you . . . *too* you conceive you haff to do with Gòht?"

Mr MacRury said, "I could answer that question very easily, but I hesitate to commit myself to terms which vary greatly in their meaning from person to person. This I can say however in perfect accuracy, that it has to do with an experience of *love*."

"Yes, yes," said the Rev. Colin Gunn in a kind of hiss, "but love of *what*? That's the whole point. How you beat about the bush! You can't simply experience 'love', by itself, without an object of love."

"You have yourself supplied the term," said Mr MacRury. "It is an experience of love, poured out in, and drawn forth from, simply, the Object of Love . . . Love looking at the Object of Love, and unable to see anything else, and not wanting to see anything else ever."

9

"Do you know what I think?" (It was the Rev. Norman Maclennan in his rather quavering, old-man's voice. Mr MacRury had departed, having completely broken down in his effort to convey what he wanted to convey; he had however conveyed enough—and they had now to consider what he had said.) "Do you know what I think? I think our young friend has been having some of those—what do you call them?—ecstasies." He looked around him with an expansive, helpful smile.

"You know when my brother James was in Italy on his holidays—oh, a great lot of years ago—he was in one of those churches. It was in the middle of the day. There was nobody there but a man sweeping, and another one away up at the front. This one was saying his prayers, all by himself, as you see them doing yonder at any time of the day. But what my brother noticed was that he was very high up. In fact when he looked he wasn't on the ground at all: James could see the light of some candles shining on the floor clean through under his feet. He tapped the old sweeping-man on the shoulder and asked, "Look, what's the matter with *him*?" nodding towards the other. The old fellow looked round, said—as if he was a bit annoyed at being disturbed for anything so obvious—'The holy man is in an ecstasy', then with one of these continental shrugs went back to his sweeping."

He looked round them amusedly as if expecting to receive from them answering smiles. But recoiled sensitively with altered expression on encountering looks of disquietude and alarm.

"Disgusting!" Colin Gunn broke forth, a redness in his sallow face, and almost hissing with his intensity screamed out: "perfectly disgusting!"

"Supersteetion!" squealed Ar-Jai by his left side, his muddy eyes at close range resting with repugnance on him. "Supersteetion of teemons!"

A calmer—though no less concerned—voice oiled the floods: Davie Macpherson Bain's tenor saying, "I'm sorry Mr Maclennan should have thought fit to make that suggestion." His hardish-looking lips placed themselves together in grave precision. The wrinkle of anxiety had deepened in his brow above the twin grey discs still immobile in opaque attentiveness.

"The suggestion . . ." Mr Aulay MacAulay facing

them, seated all alone on his side of the table, the yellow chair lately occupied by Mr MacRury empty by his left side, seemed to speak abruptly and unexpectedly loudly, like when one is struck in the wind at the instant of speech. He then bowed his bald head and when he lifted up his face a moment later it was drained of colour. And he spoke next as if some tension were muting his breath, his eyelids drawn down over his eyes. "The suggestion of continental ecstasies is not acceptable to the meeting," he said, and none could say if there was a cutting edge under his dry speech and whether the spasm which seemed to overcome his lips was simply a variant of his "*sipping*" movement. Another moment and he lifted up his greenish eyes in normal fashion and let them flow, one would have thought sardonically, under the sandy brows in the long face, along the line of those facing him. "What *is* acceptable, then? You all saw Mr MacRury when he was here. I take it no one wishes to press the suggestion that his mind is disturbed."

"I make the suggestion that he is possessed by a teemon!" cried out Ar-Jai MacAskill with a swift dash of his blue and white-spotted handkerchief at his narrow brow, seeming to have been driven frantic by Mr MacAulay's sardonic note. "I *too* not accept what he offers in explanation of his unmentionable pictures. Tuss he think we are children? A nèhkit wumman is a nèhkit wumman and always will be."

"Until she puts on her clothes, presumably," muttered Aulay MacAulay.

"What wass that, Mr MacAulay?"

"Nothing, Mr MacAskill. Proceed."

"Our young colleague inteet cannot tell us anything about *that* that we do not know . . . Yess, yes," he shrieked above the disagreement that he sensed around, "I sèh he hass been given up to secret lechery, devouring in secret the forms of forbidden beauty with impure eyes!" (One or two glanced at the narrow windows behind him as if to gauge whether anything could be heard outside.) "To lay the eyes impurely on what is forbidden is an invitèshon to the Teffil. He sèhs he brought it on himself! I will believe him that he brought it on himself. He wass tèhken at his word by *Hell*!"

The "*tut-tutting*"—a hard, strong mouth-noise—came from the Rev. David Macpherson Bain. The others moved in disapproval.

The Rev. Colin Gunn was looking round and up at Ar-Jai witheringly: "Of course," he said at his most softly cutting, the words from his rather sweetly held mouth falling like blistering drops on the air, "as to knowing all about 'that', Mr MacAskill will not forget that the rest of us have not had his exceptional opportunities—for observation, I mean. He has very much the advantage of us in having travelled so widely all over the world."

Mr MacAskill might not have heard or at any rate understood the reference—viciously intended—to his former trade of seafarer. After a pouncing movement to loosen with an athletic jerk the clerical collar under his folds of jowl he had looked here and there, casting sombre supplications into the upper distance and, seeming to sway, steadied himself by clasping firmly either knee with a set of strong fingers some of which were somewhat begrimed with ash of "thick-black". His face was a greenish putty-colour and beads of sweat broke away from above on his small skull and trickled down his temples, over the cheek-bone and down into his spreading jowls. His eyelids had dropped and when he sighed he gave the impression of having shut himself away with his private distress.

"The thing is perfectly plain," said the Rev. Colin Gunn magisterially, judicially, with a hint of disdain, throwing himself back as far as that was possible on the hard, upright yellow chair. "You don't need to have read much of the modern psychology to tumble to a case of this sort."

"What is your diagnosis, then, Mr Gunn?" said Mr Aulay MacAulay, and Mr Maclennan looked, and Mr MacKenzie.

"It couldn't be plainer . . . a case of erotic hysteria. You've only to look at him. What would a man in his obvious condition of rude health want staying up half the night on his knees praying? Notice that he himself says he was having 'an experience of Love'! That's no accidental expression. These 'experiences of Love' are merely a transference—a substitute-experience for the experience of a more natural form of love . . . a form which would have relieved the dangerously high inner tensions whose presence is indicated by those copious tears. In the same way he is certainly quite mistaken in thinking his suddenly-developed addiction to picture-looking is not connected with what he called 'the main thing', these trance states. Notice that, as far as he gave us to understand, they both started about the same time—that ought to be significant! I don't of course subscribe to a certain word that has been used here, the word 'lechery', though it is probably rather more than a coincidence that so many of those pictures 'happen' to display the unclothed female form. The attraction, the connection is no doubt unconscious, but . . . in short . . . the picture-looking represents a means of satisfaction of the frustrated and inhibited impulses by an aesthetic substitution just as the 'main' experiences, trances and tears, represents a—shall we say?—mystical or neurotic substitution. The process of subconscious transference whereby suppressed sexuality becomes aesthetic or mystical trance has been well studied of recent decades and now holds no secrets for us. We now know far more about the hermit in ecstasies in his cave in the desert, the monk seeing visions at night in his cell, than those persons knew themselves. It is understood now, not only that those experiences were delusions, hallucinations, but also precisely how and why those delusions arose, those hallucinations appeared. Those languors and deadly sweats . . . and all the paraphernalia of primitive mediaeval mystical religiosity! We know all about what caused them . . . and we also know what would have cured them. It's notorious that the extreme temptations these people are given to commonly take the form of sexual hallucinations. Whereas they always talk of what they have experience of as 'the Lover' and so forth . . . I don't see how there can be any doubt about it. It's a clear case. Our esteemed young colleage is in a state of hysteria brought on by unnatural deprivations."

"Is it your suggestion then—*sip*—Mr Gunn, that—*krm*—to put it crudely, what is wrong with our colleague is that he requires to be married?"

"That's exactly my suggestion, Mr MacAulay."

Aulay MacAulay raised his eyes to Colin Gunn. "You really suggest that if Mr MacRury were to get married all those—*sip*—symptoms would automatically cease?"

"I really thought I had laboured to make that plain."

"Well, of course, there are a number of objections I could make . . . and will make—*sip*." Mr MacAulay was perfectly his normal self again before their eyes. "In the first place it doesn't seem to have occurred to you that the majority of us in this room are—*sip*—

celibates. And therefore if your theory is sound we ought to have been having visions too. You would have to explain therefore why only Mr MacRury should have these experiences while the rest of us do not. That is, unless you are to suggest that Mr MacKenzie and Mr Maclennan, Mr Macpherson Bain and myself—and Mr Legge—have been hiding the light of our mystical experiences, nocturnal tears and trances and the rest, even from our housekeepers." He lifted his green eyes on Mr Gunn whose brown ones avoided them while he mumbled, "Of course I don't suggest anything of the kind. People are of different degrees of sexuality, obviously."

"You mean that Mr MacRury has these experiences while we do not because he is of a higher degree of sexuality! I don't know whether you intend that as a compliment to my celibate colleagues and myself or the reverse, but anyway . . . I can see another objection to your theory in this, that many of the historical persons who notoriously had experiences of the kind you explain as transference of sexuality equally notoriously exhibited in the remaining area of their lives a quite exceptional grasp of, and capacity to deal with, external reality, including, conspicuously, practical affairs, whereas your true hallucinations and delusions, as far as I have heard, represent a retreat from reality and are accompanied by a corresponding inability to deal with it or come to terms with it. I don't think that—*sip*—even in the world of modern psychology, the same cause is credited with producing exactly opposite effects, on the one hand integration of the personality in harmony with the external world of realities, on the other hand disintegration of the personality in disharmony with it. And finally you still have to explain—*sip*—how Mr Maclennan's brother James saw light shining on the floor under the man's feet that he saw in that church. He must have been suppressing a most exceptional degree of sexuality, that fellow, to be lifted right off the ground. Unless you ask us to believe that Mr Maclennan's brother was in his turn hallucinated."

"Really, Mr MacAulay," said Colin Gunn acidly, "I had no idea you were such a mediaevalist!"

"I'm no sort of what you call a mediaevalist at all, Mr Gunn. I never suggested for a moment that I thought Mr MacRury was having that kind of experience. It was you that brought the thing in. But once it's suggested as an explanation of the thing we are discussing we have to look at it on its merits as giving an account of the facts. Facts, that's our business, and I can see where your theory either ignores them or completely fails to fit them.

"It's not mediaevalism that's in question, simply. You'll remember the Apostle Paul had an experience of the kind, when he says he was caught up to the third heaven, and heard words it is not lawful for a man to utter. You would make no question, I take it, of Paul suffering hallucinations arising from suppressed sexuality, or would you? *He* at least was quite convinced of their reality: he claimed he had received at the time a physical or tangible indication of their reality in the form of a thorn or sting in his bodily flesh which he carried with him thenceforward so that he should never get puffed up with pride. He would not have been in danger of pride if his experience had been imaginary and not real: a man isn't puffed up with pride of imaginary experiences unless he's, as you say, a neurotic, or something more abnormal still. Paul wasn't a man, I would think, that you would say showed signs of that. He always seemed to me of all men to have his personality securely rooted in what was real. If you are going to maintain that every experience of that kind is nothing but hysteria, then you will have on your hands the case of the Apostle of the Gentiles, to say nothing of course of the phenomena of Pentecost, when we are told the Holy Ghost descended and 'sat on' the Apostles with an appearance of tongues of flame—collective hysteria that would have to be with collective hallucination; and I know that some would try to make that out, although of course *we* couldn't accept it . . . or could we?" He expelled a deep breath. "So that it would seem you would either have to admit that *some* unusual experiences of the kind at any rate are not neuroses or else commit yourself to the position that the Christian religion was founded by hysterics suffering from transferred sexuality. I know, again, that such an attitude *is* adopted in some quarters but I don't imagine that it is so here. I merely mention these as objections to the hysteria theory that would have to be borne in mind . . ."

"I'm not going to let this pass . . ." It was Colin Gunn's voice interrupting. There was a flush on his sallow face and he gave the impression of almost dancing on his seat. One might have gathered that he had originally spoken out of an emotional urge more than consideration, and was furious to have laid himself open to objections he couldn't possibly, in *his* position, resent or deny force to. "I'm not going to let this pass," he spluttered. "Do *you* think Mr MacAulay"—his black forelock of soft hair nodding emphatically—"that those experiences of Mr MacRury's—*whatever they are*—are of such a kind as can find any room in our theology or practice, or discipline or ethos, or anywhere at all in our Presbyterian Church and tradition? Wherever they come from, these experiences, whether they are objective-real or subjective-imaginary, do you think there is room, or ever has been or could be room for them *among us*?" He finished almost at a stutter, leaning slightly forward, his hands thrust under his thighs, between them and the chair-seat.

Mr MacAulay's greenish eyes bent on him were sombrely steady and the thin lips in his long grave face pressed together a portentous moment before he replied.

"Frankly, Mr Gunn, I do not."

10

"Very well then! You observe, gentlemen?" Mr Gunn's black forelock wagged pendulum-like as he turned his head quickly from side to side, sitting still further forward in order to see past the bigger men on either side of him. "Mr MacAulay believes that Mr MacRury's experiences, with the actions that were their manifestations, are of such a kind that they can't be accommodated in our Church. If that is so it matters not at all of what kind or origin those experiences are . . . I agree with Mr MacAulay, I believe as he does, and it is therefore my judgment that things should be allowed to take their course. Scandal or no scandal, we cannot tolerate in our midst something radically contrary to the spirit and repugnant to the form of our faith and worship." His voice rose. "And we must get rid of it, and cast it forth"—with a drop of froth at the corner of his narrow mouth.

Ar-Jai had all this time been apparently wrapt up in a private distress. At Colin Gunn's sharp, cutting voice raised beside him he seemed to come to himself, opened his muddy eyes sideways and, seeing the point matters had reached, screamed out "Amen! amen!" in a voice that set all their teeth on edge: some even blinked and twitched their faces, starting. He even held out his rather small, prehensile hand across his front towards Colin Gunn who ignored it completely, looking up at him over it with the same furious look in the erstwhile soft brown eyes. The fury was now switched to Ar-Jai MacAskill: he could be seen searching, frantic in haste, for a point to work a dissociation with this unwanted ally.

"I must say," he said, looking straight up at Ar-Jai over that held-forth hand, speaking angrily so that he stuttered a little, "I must say I entirely dissociate myself from the methods that have been made use of throughout . . . The whole affair smacks of disloyalty and has developed in a degrading atmosphere of eavesdropping and keyhole peeping . . . Those detestable women!"

Ar-Jai recoiled in horror, drawing back his hand as if it had touched a needle.

"They were weemen of Gòht, weemen of Gòht," he said in a sort of wail, moving his chin about in his collar and turning his eyes up muddily as if seeking help from on high—"full of *zeal* for the faith!"

Mr Aulay MacAulay's voice fell on the quietening air with a cool effect that made it quiet at once and altogether. "I too think there has been something 'off', something somewhat false about this agitation and the atmosphere in which it has been conducted. If Mr Gunn is looking for hysteria I suggest he'd most easily find it *here*, that is, in the countryside, along with a great deal of the spirit of sheer turbulence and trouble-making and latent if probably unconscious bolshevism, by which last I mean the spirit of No respect for anybody, and Down with anyone in any position of respect or authority . . . However, the trouble has been made now, the situation has arisen. There it is. We have to face it . . . Mr Gunn considers our proper duty is to do nothing to prevent the thing taking its course and going forward as a matter for official enquiry and, if necessary, discipline, and this despite the resulting scandal and publicity which, I'm sure we all agree, the church in these days can ill afford. Mr MacAskill has now indicated his agreement with the course proposed by Mr Gunn."

Ar-Jai was quick to assume the dignity conferred. "And I must sèh"—retracting his chin with wide-jowled judiciality under his small cramped skull—"I must sèh that it comes moast ssuchestively home to me that he should have chosen to organise his refraining from needed food *on parteecular dèhs*, on *parteecular dèhs*. It savours of . . . it savours of . . . ah, I will not sèh whaht it savours of . . ."

"Mr MacAskill has also advanced the theory," Mr Aulay MacAulay continued coolly, "that we have to do with a case of—*krm*—well, of demon possession."

"That I *too* sèh, sir," Ar-Jai burst in, his lids lowered over his eyes . . . leaning aside, not looking at anyone; crossing one short stout leg over the other, "that I *too* sèh."

"Very well," said Mr MacAulay. "Now can some-one else give us his opinion . . . Mr Bain . . .?"

Mr Macpherson Bain had only occasionally through-out the proceedings moved a little in the chair, but without relaxing that shocked immobility that had been on him since he went into the church to fetch Mr MacRury and came out again. He slightly shifted now, forward towards Mr MacAulay and moving his hardish-looking, well-defined lips, said: "I'm afraid I must agree"—very quietly.

"Agree?" echoed Mr MacAulay vaguely.

"With Mr Gunn and Mr MacAskill," explained Mr Macpherson Bain with a stooping movement forward like a bow from his chair, and turning crimson.

"You agree with Mr Gunn and Mr MacAskill," again echoed Mr MacAulay this time in a ghost of his voice. Mr Macpherson Bain crimsoned to the roots of his fair, brushed-back hair.

But Mr MacAulay had not looked at him, and now again turned, as once at least already, extremely pale, seeming this time to move his lips. In a moment he appeared to be changing back to his normal colour, but it was in an extremely small voice that, travelling along the line, he said, "Mr Legge?"

The towering hulk of a man who had hardly once looked up but had carried on various movings and swayings of his own, did not look up here, but stretching out a large, clean, prominent-knuckled hand in front of him, turned the large thumb down.

"Expert opinion is divided," said Mr MacAulay and with asperity, in his ordinary volume of voice, "as to the interpretation of the thumb-sign in the ancient Roman Amphitheatre. I understand the best opinion is that the turning *up* of the thumb meant the victim was to be condemned ... Will you please state plainly, Mr Legge, and in words, what your judgment is!"

"Ah, yes!" An inner movement took place in the mountain. "Down," emerged from him, vaguely, "Out ... yes!" Only then did he raise his lids under the large, strongly modelled, almost hairless brows, and disclose grey eyes still somewhat withdrawn in their expression. "I agree," he said with a noise of teeth, and nodded his large, generous skull to his right at Colin Gunn, to his left at David Macpherson Bain, "with them."

Mr MacAulay was heard to sigh. He put out his hands wide on the table edge, clasping it, pushing his arms straight, and sighed again. His greenish eyes rose to the windows.

"Do I take it that you are all agreed things should take their course for Mr MacRury?"

A loud, emphatic voice said, "No!"

II

"Mr Maclennan?" said Mr Aulay MacAulay in a voice small with amazement, forgetting to withdraw his stiff and wide-spread arms. For once he was shaken out of strict control of his features, which showed simply surprise and the wish for enlightenment.

Mr Maclennan's eyes were amused in his ashen face. He registered enjoyment of the sensation he had created, apparently without intending to.

"I said, no," he said softly but firmly, smiling round at them with his only just faintly weak expression. Mr Murdo MacKenzie beyond his right shoulder, whose expression of mingled concern and puzzlement had deepened and intensified throughout the proceedings, and who had repeatedly whispered protestingly under his breath, "Oh, he'll get over it! he'll get over it," grunted, looking at old Norman on his left, his red, moon-round face becoming over-spread again with its customary rather fixed smile.

Mr MacAulay spoke in a tone of gentle respect. "Do we understand you have an alternative proposal to put before us, Mr Maclennan?"

"Yes, most certainly," said Mr Maclennan matter-of-factly. "There's no need for all this . . . this severity. It's quite simple. Here it is."

Mr MacAulay's hands dropped from the table-edge

to his knees and he sat forward, amid a sound of chairs, movements of turning towards Mr Maclennan . . .

Mr Aulay MacAulay had just said, "Do I take it that Mr Maclennan's suggestion is agreed to?" and the number had said, "yes, yes-yes," when they all of a sudden jumped where they sat and found themselves looking at one another with startled speculation and apprehension and with twistings of their faces with pain: they were suddenly like so many clerical fish at the bottom of a tank, their features distorted in the movements of an aqueous medium.

"Oh . . . it's all right . . . it's the factory," shouted Mr Macpherson Bain, intelligently nodding and mouthing to make himself better understood . . . "You know . . . shift coming off!"

Even the butterflies appeared to have jumped and been set fluttering on the windows by the tremendous dirling that seemed to be going off actually in the room. They could only sit and look helplessly at each other, some of them holding their mouths as if their teeth were being jarred in their jaws, until at length the mad wailing clamour, as if it were dragging their stomachs with it, died away. In the wildly beating silence they sat, feeling emptied out, or like so many large rocks on the shore from which the sea has just receded.

Mr MacAulay sighed. "Let us go hence!" and all got up, with clearing of throats and scraping chairs. Silence again, and the vestry looking cheaper and yellower than ever, the chairs adding to its yellowness, all about the seven perpendicular black figures. "You say the prayer, Mr Macpherson Bain."

Davie Macpherson Bain seeming not to hear, to be still shocked, Mr MacAulay leaned on his knuckles on the yellow table-top. "Oh God, Who hast shown mercy to us, teach us to show mercy to others, as we shall yet answer to Thee again. And may we for no human consideration consent to diminish Thy truth. For Thy glory's sake. Amen."

"'Men-'men-'men-'men—Amen."

12

"What kind of a prayer was that of Aulay MacAulay's?" one minister was heard saying to another on the way out.

On the wide asphalt pavement-approach to the church, white in the sun, the black of the group of ministers standing there mingled with their intensely black shadows. Parts of their clothing, a sleeve or elbow or the breadth of a back, looked white against the part-shadowed cool-grey of the church wall. The Rev. Aulay MacAulay, standing apart from the group, raised his eyes under their reddish eyebrows and, his long face expressionless, studied the wide and generous exterior of the church, up to—his head tilted back under the brim of his hat—the brand new spires and pinnacles of Hydro-Electric Gothic swimming in the blue.

All about the church there was a proliferation of rectangular boxes, in two storeys, the slates of many of them burning, or here and there flashing. In front of each human hutch small squares of thin grass were worn and brown. Between the blocks the backs of other blocks could be seen, and garments, struck dead by heat, fixed on washing lines between boggy earth and windless sky in poignant attitudes, eloquent of hopeless grief, or borne down by immovable thought. Over there too the roofs were burning and flashing: areas of the slates seemed to have run together into a single sheet of burnished copper, which maintained its position a-top the walls, though appearing to be imminently—quivering and glowing—on the point of flowing away. Far away in the distance the top of Beinn Uidhe appeared, raising its brow and looking into the street.

Out of an upper window opposite, a woman was leaning, an enormous woman, immobile as the houses, her bosom overhanging the sill on which rested the elbows of her huge naked arms. As if seeking the secret of release from the burden of materiality she was gazing up fixedly into the deeps of the sky, her face looking disproportionately small tilted back above a staircase of flowing chins. Completely oblivious, apparently, of everything on earth, she gazed up with a steady, wrapt expression—as one might say: "The hungry sheep look up and are not fed!" Not even when three figures appeared away at the north-western end of the street, coming into the village, did she lower her eyes. Not although two of those figures had bright red upon them, one bright blue. Three girls, or very young women apparently, for they scarcely stopped their dancing. Bounce, bounce, bounce, they came—sometimes one, sometimes two, sometimes all three at once—as if made of india-rubber, getting larger as they came nearer, coming further into the town.

Footfalls were in the street. From the opposite direction, from the town, appeared four or five men in a close group, already quite near, covered from head to foot with bright brownish red. They kept together—others too had appeared, coloured similarly, moving briskly in the background—their heavy boots suddenly filling the street with echoes. But not rhythmical echoes: although they moved together as one knot of men, at a rapid, purposeful pace, it was all with different steps—a peculiar walk, too quick and short for anything Mr MacAulay remembered seeing before. Their talk was loud and unceasing as they walked, and they seemed to talk all together while looking straight ahead, but loud as it was he could not make out a single word they said—could not in fact have said what the language was. They appeared to open their mouths and let the sounds roll about in their throats. With strange, alert, rapid, broken walk, their strange steady progress in a compact group, the strange sounds of their incomprehensible speech, and a strange look as of absolute at-homeness, just as if they were not covered from bonnets to heavy boots in dusty red, they made altogether a peculiar impression—as if a party of beings from Mars had commenced walking briskly and talking almost before they had alighted on the Earth's surface.

It was impossible to tell which of them called out in words perfectly distinct though strange and broad—

"Jesus Christ, look at all yon——ing ministers!"

And while he looked all the heads turned; eyes rolling in dark ochreous faces, white like the teeth that broke forth in wide simultaneous grins—pleasant, not unfriendly, quite impersonal grins. It was that perhaps that was disquietlingly strange about them—a something slightly automatic about their total effect—all turning, all grinning at the same moment, while all kept steadily moving forward as a group with uninterrupted clatter of boots.

One of them broke off and turned in at the block opposite.

"Fine day, Mrs (name undistinguishable)!" he called out in a perfectly normal, neighbourly voice—surprising in a bright brown-red man walking towards the end of a house.

For the first time the woman took notice of the

invasion of the street below, removing her eyes languidly, as with reluctance, from the contemplation of infinity. Languidly she turned her face down towards the man below, her chins bulging out in consequence so that she startlingly recalled to Mr MacAulay's mind the upper part of a one-time advertisement for French motor-car tyres. Without altering the expression of a feature she opened her mouth cavernously—one could have sworn the dark of upper dentures was visible from across the street—and gave utterance, as of an impersonal statement, in a strange hollow voice that broke all among the houses:

"Nae bloody rain for yince!"

And turned again in impassive gazing into the sky, her expression unchanged and, still without a single look down at the street where shortly the three red and blue girls meeting the diligently walking group of red-covered men, at an apparent word and amid some effect of laughter, shrieked and vanished behind the houses with the speed and élan of particles chemically repelled.

Mr MacAulay went over to the car that was sitting by the kerb and opening the door went in to the back and sat down. He looked expressionlessly out. There was Davie Bain; where was he chasing off to? Contriving to look slightly "open-air" even in his clerical blacks and collar. His jacket didn't come far enough down . . .

"That's a fine day, Mr MacAulay," came from a broad strong man in a brown suit with faint stripes and with a red, rough neck sticking out of a collarless but white shirt, who had been sitting slouched dovering in the driver's seat. As he spoke he just disturbed his cap on his head and settled it again and slightly moved his shoulders but without turning round.

"A fine day, Roddy," agreed Mr MacAulay. "Just a wee thing on the hot side maybe."

He took his black hat off and laid it on the seat beside him. Then took a grey tweed cap out of his pocket. Wonder why Davie Bain took the side he did today, he pondered, unfolding the cap. Young MacRury and he were old friends of college days. And it must have taken something to range Davie Bain on the same side with Ar-Jai MacAskill! . . . There was Colin Gunn going off now . . . what a small, slight figure, the long skirts of his black showerproof flying and threatening to entwine his legs, his arms swinging to prevent the cuffs from falling down on his hands. The brim of his black hat was rather broad too. Away to get his car no doubt . . . Norman Maclennan and Murdo MacKenzie were drawing out their farewells fearfully . . . Ar-Jai—speaking too loudly as usual—*would* remind one of a piper. He was standing on one spot but because of the way his great flat chin was drawn back, pushing out his collar, and the way the top of his head stuck up, with the hat on it, and because of his aggressive delivery and a sort of echo of a squall or squeal that hung about his speech, he carried the impression of parading among the ministers, with a bagpiperish strut . . . Legge standing there, facing this way, with his hands thrust into the deep pockets of his slightly mud-flecked raincoat, black hat surmounting all—what *was* wrong with Legge?—looked like a half-waked-up statue . . .

He finished unfolding the cloth cap and settled it on his head. Leaning back in the corner he closed his eyes. Then began—little spasms coming in through his cheeks—pressing his lips together. When a little later there was an opening of car doors and he felt the vehicle sway and lurch, and opened his eyes to find

Norman Maclennan, with his ashen-grey face seen so close one could detect a slight trembling, getting in beside him, and red-faced Murdo MacKenzie—his eupeptic presence—climbing in in front beside Roddy, he asked, as if he had been half asleep, "We're away, are we?"

Mr Maclennan said, being conversational, "Funny . . . Not a man of us there that couldn't speak Gaelic better than he could English—except Norbert Legge, and he's just a bit slow; understands it fine—and there we all were speaking English, from beginning to end."

"Yes," said Mr MacAulay, but so shortly that Mr Maclennan, turning round and seeing that his eyes were closed, stopped smiling and didn't speak again, looking out at the spinning countryside.

All the way till they dropped him at the gate of his manse at Strath Mr MacAulay said nothing. From time to time his greenish eyes opened and he looked, under the snout of the grey tweed cap—the Rev. Mr MacKenzie and the driver were having a tremendously long, confidential conversation in the front—looked at the back of the driver's seat as if there was something there he had not seen before, something that made him very thoughtful.

When he had got out the others looked in surprise to see him walking away up the drive to his house, slowly, a grey tweed cap on his head and a black hat held in his left hand, having left the gate open behind him.

13

The Rev. Colin Gunn went off home in a fiendish mood. In the car he felt like grinding his teeth. All the way along he felt himself growing smaller, felt like a schoolboy in the driver's seat, behind an increasingly large driving wheel, and sent out wave upon wave of small-mouthed silent spite sideways against the giant Rev. Norbert Legge: seated on his left hand, like a sleeping tower, one formidable large dry white hand resting on a long black-clad thigh. He could at times have twitched the wheel and sent them both over the edge of the road, he was so irritated. Though had Legge said anything he could not have stood it and must have flown out at him. The brown eyes he glimpsed once or twice in the driving mirror had a spark of fury in them, and his driving was visibly erratic along that narrow road, pot-holed and sand-heaped, so that he had to pull his sense of realities towards him, get a grip on himself. That made him feel ill: with no outlet to it. He had had a trying afternoon.

That Ewen MacRury and the whole stupid business. Metaphysical stite and stumph! Lazy fellow needed his wings clipped. Too much time on his hands. "Idleness is a potent necromancer!" he spluttered at the pitch of his voice. "Eh, Legge?"—flying down the little quirky brae to Alltan-dubh for the moment wide-arcing his hands in a sort of seed-sowing movement on the wheel this way and that like a master. What Legge said he heard not for Legge's large hand had for the moment flown up to hold his hat down on his head and he himself wanted all his attention for the car which bounced and plunged like a horse on the pitted surface at the bridge; the next instant its nose was pointing up and he had crashed into lowest gear going up the Cadha-beag. He sat straight now with an appearance of waiting, his small hands wide spread on the wheel seeming—his arms straight—to push him back into an attitude of expectant dignity, while the thing roared out and dirled slowly and more slowly. And that dry old *sip-sipping* Aulay MacAulay—what cause had he to rise in defence with the judicial highlights sliding on his bald skull? His bald skull and Legge's had been smiling on each other all afternoon in that offensively new-smelling vestry—what call had the old fellow to butt in: gave him a showing up too!

Not only Ewen MacRury with his grave sweet courtesy, and Aulay MacAulay with his sardonic dry rustling voice, but even in a sense that feckless Norman Maclennan, by means of the obviously superior reasonableness of his counter-proposal, and the calmness of its putting forward, had, he thought, shown him up that afternoon. He felt himself standing before them, felt he was in short trousers, and the cold wind round his thin knees. The car bounced over the top on to the level road and with a barely perceptible pause for gear-change surged on. The Kinloch-Melfort Co-operative Society's huge green grocery van going majestically home, dipping and heaving on the pot-holed and sandy or else rocky and soft-boggy road like a laden galleon in a westerly swell, drew promptly in and halted at the nearest passing-place on observing the bounding vehicle hurling itself onwards in a spreading halo of sun-bright dust.

"Ruddy sky-pilots on the razzle!" said an amazed employee to a fellow-employee, looking down from his high driving-seat at the black car that shot past almost scraping their underguards, and—"Hell!" he exclaimed and flicked shut the window at his elbow as a cloud of dust streamed singing into the driving-cabin, and then, excluded, continued for a time to fall diminishingly sideways, toppling into the heather along the road edge, which it made more dusty and gritty than before.

The Rev. Colin Gunn, thirty-six and an M.A. of

Glasgow, was of those who make the great obstacle to the work in the world of outstandingly gifted people. Those are the "halves"—half-gifted, half-learned, from the ethical point of view often externally immaculate though wanting a spark of the fire of generosity which alone would give value to their acts, which are in consequence half-dead in spite of their profession of high moral principles, half-alive only in faith lacking the good works, only half-desirous of mounting to a higher level.

Colin Gunn never for a moment thought that his old friend Ewen MacRury was "putting on an act" for anybody's benefit. That was the trouble. That was what was between his foot and the accelerator. His realisation that what they were dealing with, where their friend had been wandering, was an authentic area of experience, which was not for the rest of them, more than anything because they were simply not prepared to pay the price. He had always been the same, Ewen MacRury; went about breathing a more magnanimous air, you could never get him to take part in umbrage, and what made it a matter of more utter and intense resentment was precisely that you felt it was *not* put on, you could make shift to put up with a pose (isn't life for most of us the maintenance of a chosen pose?) but this Ewen MacRury, all dewy and misty from his Hebrides, was not even conscious as a student of a difference continually arousing resentment round about him. He had "invited" the experience indeed! He had "asked for it", he had been heading straight for it for years. What else could he expect but to run into something of the kind, when for years he had been getting his feet more and more off the ground. What gave the bite to resentment of him was that he was a *reproach*—him and his airy directness and superior floating acceptance! What right had *he*, then and now, always, insultingly to fail to resent an injury—even if it was done with open intention to his very face! That motion for Ewen MacRury's condemnation was really out of him before he noticed. All the same he was not certain he didn't regret that Maclennan's alternative had been settled for.

"Aren't you perhaps"—Legge's voice came down to him with a noise of teeth—"driving a little fast?"

The hulk had woken up! Legge was the biggest thing he knew, physically—he would give him driving! Jiggle some life into him! And there he would be in a few minutes distributing shillings to the children with remote, insensible snow-capped solemnity! He'd better take more care, however—although he would have liked to break his Legge! Serve him right for these impressive proportions. A really fine looking man—a toppling tower of ivory that asked to be pulled down. He was the sort of thing that got into the papers for being discovered in a bog: "magnificent specimen—hundreds of years old."

By now he recognised himself that what was always a spot of latent tension in him had reached near pathological excitation. One of his "bad" spells, in other words. Norbert Legge among others always unwittingly did it by his mere propinquity. The fact was—and there were moments when Colin Gunn came near admitting it to consciousness: he wasn't really too much self-deceived, he was acute and sharp—the fact was, he was in all his feeling and willing conditioned by his dimensions. He had too much of that coenaesthesis, that consciousness of himself in all his members that Ewen MacRury talked about and cultivated for his purpose, and *his* members told him too much, too clearly and all together that they were of a small make and meagre presentment. With his proportions all in order, he was next thing to a miniature. And what struck a blade of unhappiness in him, dividing his consciousness, setting his impulses against each other, was his inability to accept the role of a miniature, even had he been a perfect one. He would rather have been a flawed model so long as it was on a generous scale—even (with a girn) like Legge here. Hopeless. "Which of you by taking thought can add one cubit to his stature?" So the overriding consciousness was of impotence and frustration, colouring all of life. Life then became responsible for the disordered, aggrieved consciousness. Life therefore, circumstances and other persons, became something to be revenged upon; the only weapon available being spite. Spite was in his veins, had been ever since he became conscious of himself over against the external world.

The most frantic thing of all was to feel impotent even in the use of that weapon. He was not to know that he had a wry, quaint charm when he was furious, his melting brown eyes in his thin face became warm with feeling, his rather small, damp mouth forming the venomous phrases with an engaging neatness, so that the easiest thing was to think it was his way of expressing his sense of humour and the malice at the very most not half intended: he did not know this, and he concluded in consequence when he found his malice unresented that this was due to his insignificance rendering it contemptible—so one would reply with patient reason and soothing smiles to the tantrums of a child—which made him more furious, and more wry, quaint and engaging, still. It was not an uncommon experience for him, becoming frenzied with the unsuccess of his attempts to be offensive, to finish with an outrageous, venomous "thrust" stuttered forth with smashing of fist into hand, only to evoke a roar of laughter. Going away he could imagine nodding of heads and remarks to the effect that he was a wag, Mr Gunn. He had earned for himself a name for a sort of waggery and the more he raged in protest against it the more he was taken as giving proof of it. Never could he succeed in getting his rages—that is, himself—taken seriously: or so he felt, being excruciatingly vulnerable on account of his sense of his small, material self.

His wife, motherly Susan Boyd, knew his frenzies to be real and no jest. She knew they made him ill. Therefore she felt concerned when, looking through the window on hearing wheels crunch to a stop outside, she instantly recognised the shadowed and yellow aspect of his face even while he was still sitting in his driver's seat withdrawing his hand from the brake—the special sickly and drawn look that told her he had been under the particular sort of tension he was subject to for a considerable time, perhaps all day. (She had noticed he seemed to be liable to irritation when Mr Legge was present: she couldn't imagine why: Mr Legge was to all appearance, if strange, an inoffensive gentleman.)

At tea Mr Gunn found it impossible to be polite to Mr Legge, who by this time affected him as a top-heavy structure of bone towering on the settee. He got up and left Norbert "wiring-in" to the scones, sucking his teeth, "*tth-tth*", making labouredly polite conversation—his words and phrases were, like himself, of a rather too large and obvious sort, seeming to be dragged up from a great depth—to Susan who as usual was slightly overdoing it in her rôle of hostess, sitting in front of her guest, tea-cup at half-mast, nodding and smiling at every word of his, her eyes bright with a little too much intelligent understanding. Norbert, one too large white hand on one black-clad too large knee, his skull looming like the dome of a mausoleum: buxom

Susan behaving like something hypnotised in front of him with her smile of an automaton: the five sufficient proofs of his virility rocketing with shattering noise about the room and seemingly passing both under and over the tea-table; he left them and went into his study.

There he took great pleasure in the imagined picture of Ewen MacRury married to a buxom, fertile wife, with a wrinkle of care established on his brow, with the sleeves of his shirt rolled up and his collar discarded while he bent over the wash-tub and every now and again held up a baby's napkin and examined the stain on it with more gravity and speculation than he now looked forth upon the billion-trillion-mile spaces between his stellar universes. That would clip his wings. That would knock his affirmations out of his solar systems. All that, he thought he saw wholly convincingly now, was as much a self-indulgence as is a rich man's vice, so that it was meritorious and salutary to place it beyond the devotee's reach. In such cases, ruthlessness may be the greatest kindness and a man's friends ought to do violence to their comradely affections for the victim's good. (A voice whispered: But not afterwards go home to their tea!).

Tea . . . He had this periodic feeling of resentment against Susan, when he could see convincingly how she and the five children stood across his own onward and upward road, and could believe she did it of intention. Susan, all sonsy and rosy, wrapt up in her home and duties and oozing satisfaction when she was left alone to it. He would look at the five children, then at her, all unconscious going about her tasks, and suspect her of having had the children just to keep him "tied down"—the weapon of her sex. At the same time he had to admit it was *he* who had pressed to have the children. The first to demonstrate his virility; the rest took their rise at various times when things were making him feel *small.*

She, while he looked at her with speculative brow, was all oblivious, happily immersed. She didn't need to care in any case what he thought or suspected. She *had* got him tied down. He'd never get anywhere. Nothing was possible in a house full of crawling and hopping brats: neither study nor contemplation nor thought for the future—but what did Susan care! It was infuriating to see her so obtuse, so satisfied with circumstances that at this instant he truly felt meant ruin for him. Hadn't he cause for disappointment? Kinloch-Melfort was where he should have been. His failure there he attributed to the children, the rationalisation being that there was no manse as yet (nor likely to be with Government restrictions on building). And there had only been four at that time. Fact was nobody nowadays would have a man burdened with a family—a distressing spectacle all wanted well out of the way, out of sight. And here he was at Sand where he looked out of the window at two mildewed crofts and a tumbledown barn, a boat rotting by the shore. No doubt but he'd be off as soon as the old lady at Melfort-South was away. But how long would that be? Nor must he forget Susan and the children . . .

He made one blundering effort to get back on the firm ground of what he felt was his "saner" outlook, when he wondered what all this feeling of frustration and protest was about, and things seemed just as they ought to be. And yet he seemed to know he was to some extent "out of it"; the sun shone, but to a certain extent since marriage he felt it did not shine for him any more—for others quite as much as always, but not for him.

Not so much as it did for Ewen MacRury, for

instance. That man was walking about in the sunshine. It was the sight of that glorious free sunshine that he was walking about in that had started up a festering spot in his disposition—which festering spot had at last stung him into his proposal of condemnation. Immediately he had made that proposal another, far worse festering spot had set in—which was the cause of his very great unhappiness in the depths at this minute—and would continue to fester for ever; he could perceive no means of resolving it, since the accumulating festering matter in order to break free must pass out of his moral system precisely where the tissue of his "self" was densest. He had by his action that afternoon caught an infection he would not cure hereafter—until that impossible day when he had cured himself of himself. If it were not so his reflection of duty done ought to have left him reassured and calm—with a conviction of friends "being cruel to be kind"—instead of which . . . There was that here he did not dare to understand—he wanted to understand, and did understand, yet did not—because a censor deputed by himself, and whom something in himself kept him from recalling, was all the time exercising sensitive and concentrated watch, infallibly turning off and diverting the flow of self-knowledge whenever it reached the threshold of the area illumined by the light of recognition.

It all came down to this, that he had acted as he did in order not to feel "small" and the total result was that he now—and permanently, with accompaniment of more bad temper and exasperation for his dependants and all around—felt and would feel "smaller" than ever. His large armchair in which he writhed didn't contain him; it engulfed him.

That contact with Ewen MacRury had corrupted him, and this afternoon's work, that apostate act, had set a seal of unhappiness on his soul from which in foreseeable time he would not recover.

14

Motionless clouds immensely high over him, his tall black figure stepped with long but leisurely steps, straight across moors that stretched away to eye-limit on either hand, their heavy brown only just beginning to show a faint tinge of purple; his shadow like a black fish swam along the track and through the heather behind him, where far away the mountains in a great rugged, blue-hazy pile looked down on him. At Norbert Legge's side the wheels of his tall black bicyle ran on and on along the track, through heather and green area of encroaching reeds. The moors felt dusty and dry, giving out and yet holding a heavy heat of the day-long sun. And the sun with its heavy rays on his face and shoulders might have had the will to retard him, to prevent his forward stepping across the moors.

The Bothan was behind him. A corrugated-iron hut, four miles from his parish at Slaggan, to the locked door of which he among others carried a key. In the hut were deposited goods or material intended for Slaggan, since it was at the furthest point that could be reached by motor transport. And across the moor would come someone with a horse and cart to fetch them. In the Bothan he had left his tall clerical bicycle that morning—the sun had been in his face then too, from the other airt, but there had been a freshness—left his bicycle there on his way to Kinloch-Melfort, and there he had picked it up just a little while ago when the hired car from Sand had put him down, and immediately turned and swept off, back to Sand, driven by that saturnine, black-avid man who barely had respect enough to touch his cap: a member, he thought, of he forgot which of the smaller Presbyterian sects, holding a thin black bitterness against the larger church . . .

Unpleasant . . . It had not been a very happy tea either at Sand. The mistress's scones had been very good, very sweet. He had done more than justice to them; perhaps too much more. A faint sensation brought to mind the man in the Scripture that ate a book that was sweet to his taste but afterwards made his belly bitter. Probably the sensation would pass: perhaps the rattling in that car was responsible . . .

The rest of the tea episode, the whole visit to Sand manse, had left a slightly disagreeable taste: though the cause of the infection of the atmosphere did not come through to him. But before Sand also, all the way along on that car journey that he still thought of and felt as the passage of a stormy sea, there had been an unpleasant impression about him and by his side. That little Colin Gunn moved away from him emotionally, he felt. Not only he. In actual fact—of course he had not looked at the others much—but in fact the only face that had looked into his with genuineness and warmth the whole afternoon was that of young Ewen MacRury . . . That Kinloch-Melfort business! Hazy, most of it . . . abominably hazy. What had it been all about, in actual fact? The very speeches round about him—and made with fire, some of them: somebody seemed to know what the thing was, and what it called for—did not come through to him, his mind kept so slipping away to other concerns and going coldly on its own. Only, just then at the end when he was referred to he had in his nerves and senses a keen intimation given out on either hand that agreement meant a condemnation—something and someone *down*! *down*! . . . smash!

utter catastrophe!—and he would have to throw himself into that, join his weight to that, the condemnation—down!—smash!

Sometimes he had a part perception of his predicament; once or twice saw himself with sails all set for cold and senile nastiness, and pitied himself, and felt coldly afraid for the future, and wished he could have called on some sufficient aid, something in power far above the human, to lift him out of it and set him again at his true centre and in control of his reordered elements, for he felt that power over himself was going, as he slowly froze within. But mostly he simply swung along on the tide and was scarcely aware of it—except that he in part shrank from—even while he looked with anticipation for—occasions of so sharp an incidence that they would be capable of liberating or setting off a spasm of emotions as anaemic and inert as his. In part shrank from: inasmuch as he had a sufficient perception that occasions to be in that way effective would increasingly require to be very recondite and outré indeed by comparison with any norm of human conduct and experience, and might land him . . . where? Of his isolation he was increasingly conscious. His fated course was to walk for ever in utter isolation through a lunar, not human or terrestrial landscape, rock-bare and cold, with occasional eruptions of searing fire from its fervent heart.

At times he had the impression that he was nasty, a sort of putrid smell of himself rose up to him. Something had gone wrong with him certainly; part of the wrongness was that he could not tell how wrong. But he did not know what he could do about it. Where had he gone wrong? Perhaps it was yon queer turn he took as a student—yon terrible time! the strain! and the fear anyone would notice! Yes, perhaps it started with that: it certainly started *after* that. He'd been all right—eager, everything wholesome and clear—up till then. But never after—had he? Since then it had seemed as if some spring were broken in his mechanism.

Now stretched southward on his left the long blue expanse of Loch-na-Beiste, dread of the benighted, and he thought he would ride here for a bit and bent down to put the brown clips round the folded over black trousers at his ankles, the tall bicycle lying sideways, leaning against his buttocks. But when he straightened he had a strange awareness amid the boundless moors and boundless sky of something as it were indescribably ancient and, looking up with a sort of puzzlement in his eye, shouted mentally, What have I done? what have I done?—seeing for the nonce a clear mental image breast high before him of a young man, smiling, wearing a clerical collar, that young Mr MacRury that the business had concerned today—before his consciousness again became sealed with iron walls that touched him at elbows and with an iron ceiling only just over his head; he felt cold again inwardly.

And he felt sorry for himself. Even in the bright, bright sun a desolation came out of the loch. The water was very low in it: long areas of festering and drying water-weed were its shores; well back from the water were the dwarf willows numerous on its true shores, and lines of low scrub with hard-green leaves. Far down its length were two or three tiny islands, their rocky shores grey-pink above, black below: so high above water just now that the trees that crowned them had the effect of high plumes, only not nodding but rigid in the warm air, painted against the brass of the sky. Whence came the desolation? It was not that he was affected by the legend of the "beast" or kelpie that inhabited the loch; he wasn't, even when passing at night. Indeed he felt like that kelpie himself. That's what he was, an old, unloved horse, standing there. As old as the world and unknown to all. Not knowing where to turn . . . What *was* his situation, in any case? Guilt seemed mixed up in it, yet the progression had been involuntary, imperceptible. Things, people, just gradually fell off from him, left him. What had made Ethel go? She could give no cogent or lucid account herself, simply went, looking at him as if she saw in him something horrible and awful. To him the most horrible and awful thing was his inability to *feel* her departure, to *get through* to the situation. No wonder, if he was really the monster of Loch-na-Beiste. He was a sad old monster, standing there out of touch and succour of all. He raised a bewildered, questioning glance at the sky swimming with particles of heat, then looked at the reduced water in his lair this hot, dusty-dry day. He could easily have walked forward, could feel the water up to his knees, his feet slipping on the stones weed-covered in the placid depth as he splashed on steadily, water to his chest now, snorting and trumpeting as he went further in and further. Till at last his head went under and the curving circles widened swiftly, copper and blue. At last as if a hand had smoothed them all out the water lay motionless, silent, betraying nothing that had ever been.

Meanwhile he had lifted his long leg over the seat and leaning slightly forward above straight arms cycled with deliberate movements over the skyline to the west, making for his *empty* house.

15

It was Colin Gunn that got him to drive Ar-Jai home, sputtering aside to him, "For goodness' sake get your car, Davie, and get him away before he gathers a crowd with his shouting and makes an exhibition of us." And indeed Ar-Jai's squeal was all too audible just then, in the group outside the church, and his neck from behind threatened to become as wide as his sharp, narrow shoulders. He saw the danger at once and needed no second urging—outside his own church too.

Coming back he was in time to see the bent-over form of the towering Mr Legge stiffly stepping at one side of Colin Gunn's black car while Colin was a whisk of long coat tails disappearing in at the other. Ar-Jai like a block of granite in clerical attire was standing all alone at the edge of the pavement where a filthy whiff from Colin Gunn's exhaust came and dissipated itself in front of his nose.

He had reason to regret the highly exclamatory decrepitude of his dust-caked, canvas-roofed car. Anything that drew attention to him and his cargo! Ar-Jai immediately set up his squeal when he had got himself seated—with a certain old-maidenish fussiness—inside. He appeared to have a grievance, seemed to imagine that the whole afternoon's business was directed against *him*. "I started from noathing, Mr Pain—we were the poorest of the poor in Valtabost."

As they turned out of Clement Attlee Street into Iain Roy Stewart Street Ar-Jai stopped them by contriving to burst open the car door with his elbow, nearly spilling himself out. Davie Macpherson Bain had to get out and walk round the back of the car and try to get him pushed into small enough space to get the door shut. His face was flaming—he had seen out of the corner of his eye the chin-jerking among the group of loungers at the corner and now was aware of their shuffling approach in a body—but still every time the door burst yet again open the squealing voice burst out with it:

"Yess, surr, the poorest of the poor . . ." At last, with a final bang they were away.

People were turning their heads. He saw one man smile and with his elbow nudge a companion to draw his attention. He was aware that he himself was red with embarrassment, frowning with vexation. They must have looked like a couple of ministers having a squabble, sitting close together in the flying, disreputable little car. That became the worst of it—the man's nearness. He could feel his body moving; little spasms of shivering constantly ran along his left thigh and on his left arm from shoulder to elbow.

In any case he had no time for his complaining; he was very unhappy himself, had a trouble deep in himself which he had not yet had time to look at but which gave warning of formidable dimensions yet to be displayed. He answered once or twice with a snap and at last Ar-Jai held his peace, and sat sighing and groaning, his hands clasped one upon the other over his loins, his muddy-complexioned jowls swelling sideways, his collar sticking out behind his neck, his little black hat set a-top his head—it would have been nearer the decaying canvas had the springs, as he knew, not been collapsed in the green leather covered seat he was sitting on.

He made good time of it, deposited Ar-Jai at the gate of his manse, ran on a furlong till he found a place to turn, then in a moment was rushing past the manse again with a swirl of gravelly sand. The surface was excellent here although the road was very narrow. It was quite new. The old road was under the surface of the loch since they raised its level for the electricity project; and half the old parish of Melfort-South was there too, garlands of water-weed round the chimneys of what had been the crofters' houses.

Ar-Jai's attitude was preposterous. A purely selfish attitude. He seemed to think Ewen had no idea but to hamper *him*, or endanger *him*. Him and his old-fashioned theology! The fact seemed to be that every item in his antiquated Presbyterian theology was linked with a satisfaction of Ar-Jai's in an indissoluble embrace. They were the means by which he, from the poorest family in Valtabost, had risen to a secure position in his society and in man's respect. It was because of them he was in a position to admire himself. And whenever he felt them threatened he felt his position and satisfaction, his security and self-esteem threatened too. The violence of his reaction was simply the most instinctive form of self-defence, but he of course took it as a measure of the depth and fidelity of his attachment to the principles of religion, a sign, in effect, of his zeal in the service of God. And therefore as an additional reason for approving of himself.

Colin Gunn was right about modern psychology telling us a lot about what was going on in our minds unrecognised by ourselves. Ar-Jai was as plain as a pike staff, because he had no reticence and gave himself away all the time if you knew what to look for. For Ar-Jai the Church's theology—theology as he knew it—were the instruments of his will-to-power. So that when he felt the instrument in danger of being broken something warned him his will-to-power was in danger of being baulked, frustrated. So he hit out—in reality in defence of his right to admire himself in security, in defence of his feeling that he was esteemed, had influence, power—while all the time he supposed himself to be defending true religion and earning credit with the Deity. By Jove, it was wonderful how little folk understood about themselves. They needed to have it pointed out to them . . .

Of course Ewen MacRury was just the sort of chap to get on Ar-Jai's sore side anyway. Ewen was such a gentleman, he was bound quite unconsciously to make Ar-Jai feel what a boor he was. And he was so intellectual—although he was modest: you couldn't get a more modest chap—but so intellectual and so unable to hide it; he was bound to make Ar-Jai fearfully conscious of his limitations, which he was already too conscious of anyway. The Ewen MacRurys of the world hadn't a chance with the Ar-Jais: they'd get them down every time they could. And that in spite of the fact that the Ar-Jais were often good men.

Blast . . .!!! He had been unconsciously by force of his thoughts keeping the car at too high a speed, and now some of the caked dust was shaken off in the sudden, desperate stop he had to make to avoid the flopping forms of sheep that appeared it seemed from nowhere right in front of his wheels.

When he resumed he could no longer suppress the thoughts, the unhappiness, he had been trying to smother, partly under his energetic mental "dealing with" Ar-Jai. It crawled out and displayed itself with slow and emphatic clarity before him from the moment he slipped off the brake and the last soiled and towsled tail flopped over on to the side of the road before him and left it clear except for the turds of their scattered excreta. He could not escape these thoughts.

He wondered if the scenery and the sky were quite as they had been, and whether, if they *were* changed for him, they would ever be the same again, and his snub-nosed face burned deep red with embarrassed shame above the driving-wheel.

It was that shock he had got in the church. Seeing Ewen like that. He had known at once that this was a very strange question; and it had exploded at one blow all the patched-up and tentative ideas he had come to the meeting with. He couldn't even remember now what those ideas were that he had been holding about what Ewen's trouble was. Perhaps even he had had no actual ideas at all, only an emotional "set", a determination to be on Ewen's side whatever the fuss was about, and defend him against those . . . those (now, now! no undemocratic stuff!) . . . against those who were against him. But what he had seen in the church—he could still see Ewen's face—had been a revelation to him, a revelation of the existence of an unkenned and unallowed-for element or dimension, and he was not for a long time after able to take it in, to take account of it. He couldn't yet: he'd had too much of a shock. But one thing became clear fairly early, and that was that Ewen—his mere presence in the neighbourhood—was a danger to his objectives. The faintest suggestion that the Church held any dealings with spiritual hanky-panky and goings-on, or was anything but practical, down-to-earth and horse-sensical, was going to counteract the appeal he was straining every nerve to build up. Whatever it was that Ewen was suffering from—and he still couldn't "place" the thing; he hated to think it was something "mystical"; there was something grisly or "spooky" about that (that deplorable unconsidered suggestion of old Maclennan!)—whatever it was, he could hardly avoid sharing Colin Gunn's view that, in spite of his look of robust health, it was some form of hysteria, though he would not follow him—especially knowing Ewen—in the statement that it arose from a base in sexual repression: Ewen was too wise a chap not to have that amount of perception of what was going on in himself.

But whatever it was, the mere breath of it would give

his work, the Church's work, a fatal setback in Kinloch-Melfort. It would probably have done so already had it not been for the fortunate fact of the boundary fixed between the two languages. The Gaelic people kept to themselves; there was a reticence . . . The on-goings of the minister of Mellonudrigill might be the talk of the entire countryside without, for a long time at any rate, coming to any ear in the industrial village. But that could not be counted on to last for ever; and if disciplinary action were taken the whole story could be depended on to come back to the district via the national Press. A horrifying prospect, yet not as horrifying as that it should become public in the other way, by the countryside rumour becoming a village rumour. If it became known only through disciplinary action being taken, the scandal undoubtedly would be there, but it would be very much less, since the business would appear only as something the Church was reacting against, getting rid of . . . Much the best way would be to have it *quietly* suppressed, abstracted from the district without noise and without ever becoming known to his industrial flock . . . But that something had to be done, and drastically and quickly, that he would *have* to side against Ewen, was, from the church episode on, apparent.

It could not be said at any rate that siding against his friend had cost him nothing; he felt the redness deepen again painfully on face and neck . . . If only it had not had to happen at *such* a moment, just when his long, self-denying labours seemed on the point of bearing fruit. It was only yesterday some of the toughest nuts in the parish—oh, excellent fellows, but lacking in the . . . well, lacking—that he had been stalking without their knowing it for half a year, had agreed to join his Young Men's social activities, athletic and discussional. One breath of what they would put down as "religion" and they'd be off like a shot in their unregenerateness and the finer things in them might never be awakened. The opportunity would have been lost. And the worst thing of all—he did hope that a personal element, an element of personal pride, had not entered here into his motivation in going against Ewen—he had been given firm assurances that "Kay-Oh" was on the point of coming in too. "Kay-Oh" Watson, whose fame as an amateur boxer had already reached more than county dimensions, and was likely to expand much further, and soon. If "Kay-Oh" came in he could be sure of the whole youth of the parish. What could he not accomplish in association with a lieutenant of such prodigious popularity and so much "hold" over the youth? He saw the bright future of his usefulness opening out before him . . . and then this business of Ewen's! All through the afternoon, at the meeting, "Kay-Oh's" broad, low brow and crimpy black hair kept floating up before him, and perhaps was more than anything else in the forefront of his mind at the moment he—impulsively when the time came—spoke out in Ewen's condemnation. To lose "Kay-Oh" *now* . . .!

He had driven with better care since the near-collision with the sheep, but even so had only seen the road surface, and hardly at all the grasses and bracken shining and occasionally quivering on either hand. Now rose the factory on his right, the reddened upper walls and roofs redder in the sun against the distant grey frame of the dam, with never a spume of water today quavering and feathering down. And now the streets and people. *His* people, he sincerely hoped. This looked like Mrs Bollington and Mrs Ogsbotham, he thought, two of the engineers' wives: nice people, but strange, attached no doubt to their very different forms of worship and church tradition; it was an emotionally and psychologically foreign country, he sensed . . . still, he hoped that even they . . . perhaps . . .? But just before he came abreast both wheeled, and doubled forward to examine something in the Co-operative shop window and all he suddenly saw as he drew level and passed was their posteriors, and a very dark line of stocking seam running up the exact centre of young Mrs Bollington's white, conspicuously well-turned calves. They had not noticed him, but of course the sunlight on the windscreen would have prevented their seeing who was driving the approaching car . . .

There was another fault there to find with Ewen. That certain "national" something about him. Not that he was aggressive or introduced Scottish things; but if the subjects came up he would speak about national, historical questions—calmly and dispassionately certainly—but as if taking it for granted they were worth talking about, worth taking seriously, worth thinking about at all. Nothing could more inspire ridicule in the people he hoped to attract than a suspicion of any attachment or weight given to historical Scottishness. He had seen the amusement, as at an antediluvian survival, followed by—frequently vocal—contempt and a tendency to intolerant bursting out of anger, when those Nationalists appeared at the time of the election. And he knew the "feeling" was all against it, entirely against it all through his industrial flock . . . And the "feeling" of the Presbyterian church was all against it too. That phrase he had been very much struck by as a student—he now saw the meaning of it—"the movement of Presbyterianism is apocalyptic, not historical . . ." It accretes history, not participates in it, and again, history has the choice of being part of Protestantism, or being "outside" and devoid of meaning. Ewen was a sterling fellow, sterling through and through; he felt eased and pleased at saying he was a much better man than himself, and gifted too, brightly, brightly gifted ... but somehow or other he had managed to put himself in a position where he was a menace to them ... with his thrice-mysterious experiences that could not be given account of in words of the language, and that smacked suspiciously of "religion", and his historical visions and conjurings-up, whereby he claimed—or aimed—to make the stream of history run through his consciousness and thus make himself one with it and perhaps as strong and as wide as it—as if it was laudable or significant or in any sense useful to have one's consciousness cluttered up with ancient headdresses and discarded footgear and extinct notions (down, mark you, to their nuances!) and echoes of faded clamours near and far. And then this new-confessed thing, his picture-gazing ... imagine the effect of *that* on "Kay-Oh" Watson ...! And again, what place had aesthetics in Presbyterianism? No, no: mysterious suspect visions, historical visions, and now aesthetic visions ... the whole added up to something you could *feel* was alien to the ethos of the modern age ... and that was alien also to the pure, incorrupt essence of the Presbyterian "thing".

The last thoughts were going through his mind confusedly, with distortion, by reason of the distraction of the noise in the garage—mysterious noises, which were only echoes of shouts of invisible persons and hammerings proceeding out of sight, passing uncertainly about in the edges of the wide stillness that was the garage itself. He stepped out in firmer, more decisive mind: there was no doubt of it ... Ewen really *couldn't* be accommodated in their ... their preoccupations.

But he had only put his foot on the black, dirty, oil-saturated earthy floor when he felt nauseated with a revulsion of feeling. "Kay-Oh" against Ewen?

At the energetic slam he gave to the old green door of his dusty car a black-oily face popped up in a distant corner where there was a yellow light burning.

"All right, Mr Bain?"—the voice had several hollow echoes.

"All right, Mr Blue," he called over his shoulder with habitual geniality, making for the outside, "give her anything she needs!"

There was no sound for an instant, then—"What about a clean to her body-work, Mr Bain?"

There might have been a laugh in the voice this time. Mr Macpherson Bain merely smiled without looking round, and flourished his hand. Stepping out into the street, immediately falling into his habitual smart step, with bouncing thighs, his colour was slightly heightened. He was rather self-conscious about his little affectations.

His energetic walking kept thoughts at bay for the few minutes till he reached his "digs". But inside they were on him again: reproach and depression could not be kept out. Sitting down in his shining rexine armchair to think things over, he only succeeded in having his accustomed feeling—driven in when his eye travelled over the collapsible dining-table, its turned legs and turned chair-backs, the anaemic-tinted china-basket table, ornaments of unconvincing china flowers, the brown thick-pile rug at his feet, the "bronze" coal container and "bronze" hand-tongs with short wide-spread fingers—that he was sitting in the Co-operative Society's show window on the street.

Then began rising the sounds he knew so well . . . had (as he now realised) expected . . . and, in spite of his conviction of what he ought to do, shrank from and dreaded . . . The man in the flat below—not directly below, but under the next-door house, transversely down—had a difficult "teenage" daughter. He had heard her come in again in the early hours of today—he was lying awake thinking of the afternoon's business, and because of the heat—recognised her because of a deep-seated intermittent cough she had; and now her father, who had been out on his night-shift then—he could see before him his thin sloping shoulders and long stringy neck, the prominent adam's-apple, his way of tucking in his chin and looking down at things over the bridge of his nose—was giving her a "wigging" or "slanging" on her return from her work, opening on her the moment she came in the door. He moved uncomfortably in his polished, slightly sticky, rexine armchair: he was not going to be allowed to collect his thoughts, to come to some sort of terms with this inner disturbance of his concord with himself . . . He sympathised with that poor man downstairs, trying to defend standards of personal decency and respectability on which his own life rested, while knowing—he felt sure he realised it himself—the task was hopeless. And he sympathised too with the daughter, her hair improbably yellowed, her mouth, outlined in wavering scarlet, palpably "posed" with great effort of concentration, her life thin and empty, seeking after what in their extraordinary accent they called "glawmurr", even in the night-long scraping and tingling of the "Shalimar" dance-hall, and after that among smells of frying chips and in furtive doorways, and that sort of thing. The father was getting angrier and seemed to be biting mouthfuls of hard-edged, sharp-cornered syllables out of his grievance, mouthing them in an effort to chew, then dropping them out half-spitting all about his feet . . . He moved tiredly, and felt his sweat-damped blacks sticking slightly to the glossy chair . . . Then the disputation ceased as abruptly as it had begun; someone had walked out. *Now* perhaps he might relax.

But immediately there sounded out in the flat below and simultaneously from a number of windows across the way and about the street—familiar as the climate, as solid a fact in daily life as a feature of the landscape perpetually seen from a window—the wireless time-signal; and immediately one was aware of the whole region sitting attentive. Leaping up out of the chair and exclaiming to himself in an exasperated manner, "The cricket . . .! I'll be late!" he bounded across into his bedroom.

Going along the street shortly after, now in "whites" and a Glasgow University Athletic Association blazer, the air cool on his breastbone just below his throat, the sight of his bouncing figure and spectacled, snub-nosed face confronting him in a window depressed him again instantly. Hang it, he *looked* depressed. He hadn't realised that. He must take himself in hand vigorously; depression wasn't fair to the "chaps".

He was not immediately successful. An association with the large shop-window brought up the vision of Mrs Bollington and Mrs Ogsbotham bending down, and it seemed to him now that there had been something inexpressibly averted and indifferent about those blank posteriors—symbolic, in fact. From that he fell to still bleaker depths, so much so that he realised he would have to take care. He saw again as during the afternoon's meeting the upper portion of "Kay-Oh's" face, the crimpy black hair damp-looking as with sweat; but this time the thought came and shook him that behind that—as he now saw—incredibly low brow with its folds rather than wrinkles; behind those small and watchful close-set eyes, there was in fact a mind no more intelligent than a glooming stot, a kind of minor bull, and that "Kay-Oh" in reality wasn't worth anyone's "getting-in". And it was for this shambling, foot-scraping, shoulder-shaking creature that he would have sacrificed—*had* sacrificed—his old friend Ewen, with his inward flame, on whose unfailing kindness he had rested himself ever since he knew him! This was rank heresy he knew and opened chasms before him deep enough to engulf the whole of Kinloch-Melfort with its red factory and hydro-dam and new-built shops and asphalt streets and box houses peppered about the foot of the hills. Such thoughts if nourished to growth could strike the meaning from his life, and he must take hold till reflection and perhaps sleep resettled the ramparts of his aim and purpose.

But in spite of himself he could not stop seeing in front of him Ewen MacRury's hands holding a knife and fork at the opposite side of the table in their student "digs" . . . and he heard an echo of laughter at some sally of Colin Gunn's who would be in his place at the end of the table, dropping out the remarks with a mixture of sweetness and venom from his sensitive mouth. That he could not get out of his mind—Ewen's hands opposite him holding the knife and fork in a way somewhat expressive of his personality, in a calmly purposeful yet detached way . . . Where was he, poor fellow, at this minute; what was he thinking . . .? But he had to take himself in hand. This would not do. He would have to button up his moods. He was disintegrating into sentiment. This cry of "Judas" inside him as he strode along was purely theatrical, an effect of his constant professional reaching towards rhetoric. He was the more sure of it because the cry, "Judas!" was unmistakably "given" in his own tenor voice, with his own personal note of pulpit unction in which he was accustomed to gain his effects.

By Jove! that was half-past six! He would have to run!

16

She was conscious of his hard barrel-body and her own delicate ladylike person in the kitchen together, but *he* was conscious of something far away, and it was that distant thing he was seeing that was stirring him to a white-heat emotion, something away beyond any entity or relationship in the room. Ar-Jai's spreading lower face with its folds and jowls was a muddy pink, and sweat showed on his tortured temples under the coarse short hair lying different ways on the cramped skull. An animal-looking person, yet in some authentic way he was a man too: underneath the covering weave of coarse responses and insensitivity functioned a fully human if limited range of consciousness. She was concerned about his state: he had the look of one in too much suffering, his strained eyes moving this way and that as for a way out from his torment. There was too much tension there . . .

He was squealing, "Nèhkit weemen! nèhkit weemen!" and because it was for the nth time her brow wrinkled momentarily, a little tingle going through her where a nerve of sensitivity had been rubbed by the repetition . . . "Can you pelieve it . . . nèhkit weemen!" His little eyes sought hers worriedly . . . "In his tesk, Murteena!" But she could see this was not really the upsetting cause deeply at work in him. He stood innerly shaken there, an immense weight upheaved at the core by a veritable earthquake, and she apprehended that he was himself in anxiety, seeking this way and that to identify some external cause. The look about him, and the sweat, were as of fear. She would have steered him off to let the tension lower below danger.

"But if he iss only a baad man, Rottee . . ."

"No, no"—he was this way and that, his agitation and fear (she was sure now it was fear) increased by her suggestion—"No, no, it iss worse, far worse . . . And they let him stand there . . . stand there . . . seeking for wurts to describe his . . . his tieabolical . . . Oh, Murteena, I have no wurts . . ."

He had to be brought to let the thing out; the pressure must be released. "Did they contemn him?"

"Nòh . . . nòh!" He turned away and pointed up his nose which, with his drawn-out way of speaking, and his tone, suggested a barking at the moon. "Not absolutelèh, not absolutelèh. He's still at laartch to wreak mischief among the sheep."

"But, Rottee, tchust tell me . . . what *iss* it?"

"What iss it?" He was more distressed than ever; his squeal approached its thinnest. "What iss it? It iss the Atversary . . . the Grèht Atversary of Gòht and maan, Who goeth about . . . Murteena! if this gets within our church, it will purst our church from the top even to the pàwtom." There was a moving of the suffused whites of his eyes. "It iss the Enemy, come smiling and with soft wurts to beguile even the Elect . . . I saw Him standing there with the aaspect of innocence, so sure, alreatty, so sure . . . but *I* saw the foot that was cloven . . . for this is that abominèhtion of supersteetion that wass putt forth, and now iss returnt alreatty among us and alreatty seated in the highest places . . ."

Thank God, he had found words: it was beginning to pass off in unction. To help it on: "But *you* will defend the truth, Rottee! *You* . . ."

"Yèhss, Murteena . . . yèhss." He seemed to shake his jowls back against his collar, with something like a bitter grimace. "Yèhss, inteet . . . For He hass hid those things from the wise and prudent and revealed them unto babes in learning. Now iss the time that will test us who is faithful, who iss vigilant for truth in an eenfidel and lax tchenerèhtion. Not the prilliant and learnèt, the grèht intellects. These are they that go wrong in time of crisiss, losing sight of the point. Putt the despised dullard, *he* perceives the threat and stands forward in defence, even if he stands all alone . . ."

When, having declaimed himself into a frame of self-approval, he went off partially calmed to his study, Mrs MacAskill heaved a sigh of relief, but immediately felt a reaction in tiredness. She was standing where she had been all along, in her kitchen, her buttocks touching the ridge of a low cupboard, which she rested now more heavily against. It was a trying thing, having a husband. And for some moments there she herself had felt insecure, afraid, exposed to danger like a limited woman, when there was talk of the church endangered. If it was indeed "burst from top to bottom" what would happen to them and their children, their position, her husband down to the lowest fallen—the phrase came singing from somewhere in her associations—like lightning from heaven? But later the danger had seemed less definite. Listening now she heard him "*Ah*"-ing to himself and clearing his throat in a so-familiar way: her apprehension subsided. Shortly afterwards she felt still more reassured, when there came stealing through the house the heavy pungent smell of strong, black tobacco. Lightened, she stood away from the cupboard to resume her occupations.

But immediately heard her name called in a sort of strangled, despairing shout . . .

Only once before had Ar-Jai or Roddy experienced anything as bad as this. That was when there had been a danger they would not ordain him after all. Then too the deck had tilted below his feet, plunged in the swirling trough, then risen, driving his knees upward, and the foc's'le smell hit the back of his throat. And now again . . .

When Mrs MacAskill put her head round the door she saw first the pipe lying on its side on the table with the smoke still spiralling from its bowl, and she rushed over to pick it up and dispose of it for fear of damage to the table's polished top.

Ar-Jai was sitting in a small, low armchair he was partial to. He had thrust his loins forward almost off the chair so that he was lying back in it, and his arms were trailing down by the sides. He turned two unhappy little eyes round on his wife.

"Oh, Mur-tèena," he said, "I'm seeck!" and his face turned green.

She understood. "Oh, no!" she called, protesting, "not in the stut-tee, Rot-tee!"

He could not have helped it. "*Aaow!*" he cried, in misery, the point of the bow swinging against the sky then plunging down, shuddering, into the flashing sea.

"Oh, Rot-tee," she protested, more weakly, standing helpless.

He was rolling his head about on his shoulders trying to get it supported on the back of the small chair, but could never manage it. He stuck his legs more stiffly out in front.

"Oh!" he squealed plaintively when he had a respite. "Sometimes I wonder iss it worth it! Sometimes I coot give it aal up and tchust . . . tchust go to the togs . . . Those men of educèhtion . . .!" he murmured more in sorrow than reproach.

Again, however, the deck swung out from under him—down into the depths, then up, up, while all his innards and his brain itself, and it in water too, were striving still to go down.

"*Aaaow!*" he cried between squeal and groan, the world swivelling and rolling before his misting eyes, and "Oh, Mur-tèena."

While she, aghast at the extent of the tragedy she saw enacted before her, was able to do nothing but draw her fingers continually across the backs of her hands held at her bosom, and say in a whisper of concern from which she could not quite abstract the last accent of housewifely reproach . . .

"Oh, Rot-tee . . . in the stut-tee!"

Another moment of respite with Ar-Jai exhausted, still trying to lie back in the chair which was too short and too low, with scarce strength to hold up his head or his eyelids, the sweat running on his ghastly cheeks.

"To think," he articulated in a voice from which all strength and resonance had vanished, an agonised, almost tearful croak, "to think a man from the Islands would pee putting this on me!"

Then the sloping deck-boards tilted again, up went the bow then and across the sky, down into the flying, green sea, while he cried out in his agony, clutching the arms of his chair that seemed on the point of sliding across the floor, while cold sweat trickled and ran into his chins and the warm sweat of his barrel-body and thick limbs slowly soaked his blacks; and the devastation grew.

At moments there was a respite, then again, ever and again it was—

"*Aaaaow!* Mur-tèena!"

And—

"Oh! Rot-tee!"

17

When he had got out of the car the Rev. Aulay MacAulay was unaware he had not said good afternoon to Norman Maclennan and Murdo MacKenzie, and then most uncharacteristically omitted to close the tall gate at the end of his drive. He had concentrated all on the hope and determination of getting the length of his door. Which he accordingly saw, although somewhat hazy and distorted, slowly nearing him.

This was the worst of all. Worse than any during the meeting, or even than last night . . .

Last night was too much with him—he had reached the door: would the knob turn? It turned and he went in—too much with him as a recollection, and, he feared, an anticipation—would he make it up the stairs? All that afternoon throughout the meeting when it hit, he could hardly keep from groaning or shrieking out loud: they must have thought him very strange at times. Sometimes all he saw of their faces were the coloured shapes. If only he could reach . . .—even his chair: he might make it to his bed later. If only, too, the housekeeper did not come on him!

Last night it had struck him—definitely, fiercely. All night long he had sat upright in the shadows, his bald head gleaming above the pillows and bedclothes; sat through the hours and, when able, looked at his life . . .

And got from it sour consolation, bitter comfort . . .

And here he was in his room: the black hat simply dropped from his fingers on to the floor. Cool in here . . . the sun by now missing the front of the house . . .

And so the whole of the afternoon's business had seemed at once unreal and more sharply real to him. That is, he had noticed it more, every sound and sight and movement as if new to him, yet the whole thing had at the same time seemed remote and empty of meaning. So would anything have seemed—so everything did seem—after the greater reality he had glimpsed last night . . . glimpsed? nay, found himself staring at.

It seemed to have been on an island where he had never been, yet he knew it was on the west-coast as he recognised in recollection the quality of that air: the sea not far away. The light, though it was late at night, was bright over the grassy slope, the lovely sweetness from the grass and clover and meadow plants detectable again and again in the warm, stationary air, which just lapped over the open small window into the room. The room was unfamiliar, low-ceilinged, and with an unfamiliar smell; a smell of strange lives lived in it and the other rooms and round about the house, lives of "big" children and grown-ups and the old, with their incomprehensible activity. He felt the life of those lives hanging real about the room. But he was himself at the window, his eagerness pressing forward to the glass to drink in the intoxicating, magic, sweet-smelling "real". He saw the light on the grass and heard voices talking calmly, lazily somewhere, and he knew that everything was "all right", could not help but be all right, always.

His aim was to reach the telephone, on his desk. He had one thing to do: he had to reach that boy, and tell him—over the telephone would be all right . . . tell him . . . I have seen its Face . . . I am looking at it now . . . and in the light of it everything—*everything*—is changed, while it is still the same, but appears transposed into its true, its final significance. What I saw last night . . . that I had nothing to allege, nothing to show, but a heap of dry commentaries that I had built around me—I cannot deny it: I see in a sense that I knew it all along—as a defence against outside and its claims, a defence behind which I could take my ease and lie protected . . . And now . . . too late . . .

Not that commentaries were unreal, but he had used them for his self-serving purpose—heavens, how comfortable he had been in that chair over there in times how immeasurably many, his body at ease, his mind pleasantly beguiled with ideas, participating in controversy with the authors. He had come to it now—and that was all he had to show. Incredible that a whole life had gone past like that, in nothing more than that. Even his never-broken rule to stand aside from personalities, from involvement in local matters, condemnation and blamings and equally praisings and adulations, how much of that had not been due simply to a disinclination to put himself out, a simple consideration for his private comfort?

He *had* to speak to that boy . . . Could he reach the telephone? Here was the desk-chair . . . he was *so* far . . . if he could get into the chair now he'd only have to stretch his hand. But the getting . . . A little whimpering cry trembled from his lips before he got his teeth clenched together, his hand down on the chair, sweat suddenly falling from his down-turned face—oh! only to be able to *endure and not cry out*! Ah! it passes . . . it passes . . . He sat in the chair, drenched to the ground in icy sweat, recalling to mind what he had to do . . .

To speak to that lad . . . Launch forth, Ewen! Don't listen to *us*, for we can do nothing for another, can do nothing for ourselves. I have just looked beyond the verge, and know that it is all Different, all Different. Only one thing is important therefore . . . Don't hesitate . . . don't wait to listen to dead tongues but launch out—courage—risk! That's it, Ewen, free yourself . . . launch out, don't waste the little moment in the light . . . For the time is going to come for everybody when they will see that everything is really different . . . Now the brittle sheath of body-joined life, the terrestrial mode of consciousness, the very "me" of "me" is cracking apart and Something awaits, about to fly in. Something or Other a universe away from correspondence with every mode of thought and feeling. So don't listen to us, for we can tell you nothing in the least sort useful to you . . . So, although I don't at all know what you've got—risk!—generous courage!—follow through!—

But he realised he was exhausting himself formulating, mentally shouting, what he felt it so important to say, instead of saying it to the person at the end of that line. He stretched towards the telephone. But his hand slipped over the instrument on to the desk top. This time he was unable altogether to quench the cry that came bubbling to his lips. His arm slid forward and off the desk. As he himself with his stiff limbs and bald head and long face was crumpling slowly from the chair to the floor he had one desperately clung-to thought . . . He would never have those arrant medicos presiding over *him*—not while he was animate (and conscious)!

18

He was sitting upstairs between the cream-coloured walls, in a sort of space of bright yellow light, since he had drawn down the yellow blind on the west window where the sun was shining levelly in, a bright yellow space broken by the vivid colours of volumes in the book shelves, variegated strips of blues and greens and reds, and other yellows; sitting, not even really meditating but as it were simply waiting, when he heard the car draw up at the gate, and voices. The verdict, he thought.

And indeed then there was car door slamming, steps sounding clear on the road, the click and musical clang of his small iron gate, a slow deliberate splurging through the screaming gravel out in front.

He was quite pleased this little snarl should be loosened, though indifferent really to any course of events. But it was becoming a distraction, the inconvenience . . . For days before the "trial" no one had come near him. They—Bando and the women, Mina and Peigi—had started simply to indulge their passion for "something", for fuss and panic, for titillation of the nerves, for an occasion of self-righteous feeling, and had ended by frightening themselves. Bando had swung his hands and his shoulders, turning his stubbly amber-dabbled chin about, looking into the sky—until he thought he saw something there! Many times Peigi Snoovie hooked a stray strand of lank hair out of the corner of her mouth with a bent forefinger while her mouth contracted almost to invisibility and her grey eyes, widening, had more and more often a fixed, bewildered look that was new to them. A change was noticeable in her whole disposition. Mina's eyes got narrower, her teeth larger and more root-evident.

Mina and Peigi might have come back after they had had time to realise their precipitation, but by that time they were afraid: then to rationalise their fears they had to tell all over again in more embellished and inflated form: their auditors carried away a part-misheard, part-miscomprehended tale which in retelling they embellished and inflated in turn, as did the next generation of hearers, till the first tellers did not recognise their own story returning to them: the tale-bearers were insensibly drawn on into a competition for the most graphic and telling version, till in the end the whole countryside was afraid—like children who had frightened themselves by stories in the dark. In the end they got to thinking of the minister as a necromancer, a dealer in black arts, sitting up there in his study raising the Devil—when he wasn't (this in broad whispers with a look towards the children) gaping at flesh in his legendary pictures. Ancestral fears stirred and raised their heads again: from down in Mellonudrigill they would look up at the manse, gleaming cream-white in the midst of the brown heather, and see it looming with a sort of grisly aura on its height, and all its shining fence wires and new concrete posts. No one went near; if they had to pass they went purposefully, or scurried, with a nervy sideways look. Once, however, he found a basket packed full with eggs and scones and home-made butter. It must have been delivered in the scanty hours of darkness, lying on the doorstep when he went out in the front to gaze along the transept of the dawn. It was getting difficult, however, distracting . . . better it should be ended.

He had gone down the stairs, through the hall, and opened the inner glass door just as a dark form rose up beyond it and the cascading of the gravel lessened then ceased. Two men were in the porch.

"*A-a-a-ah!*" Mr Norman Maclennan as it were threw over him in a jovial arc, "well, well, now!"

And there was the round face of Mr Murdo MacKenzie redly beaming beyond his shoulder. They hung up their hats without being invited and prepared to come in. Their air was exactly that of two medical men come to do cheerily, cheerily, what had to be done. By their joviality he had the feeling he was regarded as serious, an advanced case . . .

Up in the study Mr Maclennan drew him confidentially near, heads almost touching. "*Ay-ah* . . . where's your bathroom again?"

Mr MacRury showed him where to go, on the landing: had that impression strongly as the white-haired figure walked away from him, of a kindly military man, with his upright carriage and square shoulders, his handsome head so well set. His clothes were a good quality "black", rather thickish for this weather. There were a number of deep creases across the trousers just behind the knees. Either he had a pretty thick leg for a man of his height, or his trousers were well padded within with underpants.

Mr MacKenzie's wide, red-faced grin met him as he went back into the study.

"It's his bladder, you know"—he might have been speaking indulgently of his brother: such a world of old-acquaintance in his air and tone—"He's getting on, Norman."

"Yes," said Mr MacRury—and only to make conversation—"How old is he, Mr MacKenzie?"

Mr MacKenzie did not answer: his mind had passed on. He approached and placed his hand on Mr MacRury's forearm—he happened to have his arms bent, his fingers linked at his breast.

"Listen, Ewen," he said with lowered voice, "I know . . . I know . . ." He pressed the forearm confidentially.

And indeed he did seem to have come to some liberating knowledge. Mr MacRury carried a recollection of a puzzled, an unhappily puzzled look resting on Mr MacKenzie's red face during the latter part of the interrogation in Kinloch-Melfort vestry. Now he wore his happy, comprehending grin: his mind had obviously been in the interval liberated from doubt.

"Man, you must have been going it! How did you manage to keep it so quiet? It's a wonder to me . . ."

Mr MacRury showed he was puzzled. "Keep what quiet, Mr MacKenzie?"

"You know fine! I see the whole thing now. But how did you manage to keep it so dark? That's what I can't understand—the way you must have been going at it!"

Mr MacKenzie's red face was confidentially near, near enough—exactly on the level of Mr MacRury's—for a sort of elderly effluvium to come from him, mingled with a stale breath of tobacco: his rather bulging china-blue eyes were veined and yellowed in the whites, staring. Mr MacRury only looked at him enquiringly, managing a half-hearted "What?"

"Yes . . . You'll need to take a hold of yourself. These turns you were taking! You must have been pretty near the 'dee-tees' . . . You realise that?"

Mr MacRury seemed to sway sideways, looking at Mr MacKenzie. He took a moment to control what looked like inward laughter . . . "Is this the latest?"

"Well, you know, you couldn't expect to keep it dark much longer. You were seen that last time, when you fell that twice getting off your bicycle out there"—Mr MacKenzie made a motion of his head in the direction of the front of the house, holding firmly to Mr MacRury's forearm.

Mr MacRury was at once visibly enlightened, though still, apparently, and even more, amused. He had at once seen in his mind's eye the white road outside two mornings ago, in the small hours after midnight, the moon in the scarcely dark summer sky making the whole intensely silent scene like day, and himself sprawling in awkward fashion under the bicycle, its clatter shattering the silence, because unknown to him the lace of his left shoe had been loose and caught in the chain at the moment he got down, on his return from a run taken through the countryside to quieten and clarify his thoughts: he had just that late evening had Mr MacAulay's letter handed in, informing him of the movement afoot in the countryside and their desire to help find a way out if he'd co-operate—a bit of a jolt to realise how very much things were "out" and that some sort of action was inevitably pending . . . Then when he was getting up from under the bicycle, before he could quite free the lace, he overbalanced and with another clatter that seemed to affright the void flopped down on the road again. Strangely enough he had had the feeling then that there was a spectator near; he even looked all round quite prepared to see someone, but there was nothing but the hills rising up towards the moon, the vast flat area of bright sparkle on the sea, the immense sweep of moors to right and left with a hazy sparkle over them too, all giving out a dewy, aromatic smell . . . Apparently there *had* been someone; perhaps among the trees about the church . . .

"So that is what they're saying!"

He would have explained, smiling, but caught himself up at the first breath. He could see how the new notion freed Mr MacKenzie from troubling perplexity, set his mind at rest. And how could he hope to convince him?

"Is this story everywhere too?" he said. "About my drinking?"

"No, no . . . no, no . . . And I hope it won't be. I've asked him to keep quiet about it. He just told me on the way up."

Mr MacRury only looked a question.

"Roddy . . ." said Mr MacKenzie, in explanation, "*eh*, Tumsh, you know . . ."—with a flick of his hand towards the front window—"the driver."

Mr MacRury raised his eyebrows in surprised illumination.

"But here comes Norman," Mr MacKenzie started up, scarcely above a whisper. "He knows nothing about this. You'd be better to listen to what he says."

The rushing of water gushed out openly, then came distant and muffled. Mr MacKenzie pinched the young minister's forearm again with a warning pressure, giving him a *private* admonitory nod, the look of enlightened knowledge still full on his scarlet face, and stepped back. Mr Maclennan came in quietly.

"Now then, Ewen," he began straight away. "Is this thing under the control of your will? I mean, can ye stop it?"

Close beside him—Mr MacRury had to look slightly up—the ashy colour of his complexion seemed more alarming, unnatural. Under the skin there were large irregular light-brown patches, some blue or purplish blotches in the skin of his lower lip, and over the whole man one could detect or sense an almost imperceptible trembling. His brown eyes too were yellowed in the whites, the brown pupils somewhat overrun and hazy looking.

"I have no doubt that I could," said Mr MacRury with a slight smile as if the statement might have a private meaning.

"Well, then . . . here's what we're proposing. The first thing is that you'll go away, and as soon as you can, the very earliest minute." He looked at Mr MacRury aside, raising his voice suggestively . . . "You'll be feeling the strain of all this, of course? Yes, yes, of course you are. Well, you're seeck. You must look after your health. So you'll go off at once for reasons of your health. Once you're away your health will probably look the likeliest explanation of the whole thing; there'll be not much point in continuing to make out it was anything else—you'll be out of reach"—Mr

MacRury was sure Mr Murdo MacKenzie, who had gone behind Mr Maclennan's shoulder, had winked his protuberant blue eye and given him an encouraging nod: he dared not look—"Anyway, you'll be away, and once you're away it'll all die down. Something else'll come up. They won't think it worth their while to pursue you, you may be sure . . . Then the idea is that once you're away we can see about another place for you. There shouldn't be a great deal of trouble there, with empty pulpits up and down the country. You can count on *us* holding our tongues, and if *you* pull yourself up . . . you need never hear another word about it. You wouldn't be the first that made a false step at the setting out."

"It's very kind of you all to take so much trouble."

"That's nothing . . . For the matter of that I have a place in mind that would suit you down to the ground. My brother Peter is retiring and he'll be very sorry to leave that little parish of his down in Perthshire, among the hills. It might be the very place for you. You could stay quietly there for a year or two. Of course there's one thing, you'd have no use for your Gaelic there. Not nowadays. Not like when my brother went there. We're twins, you know"—looking at Ewen under his eyebrows impressively—"Peter and me. Yes, when Peter went there . . . nearly fifty years ago . . . everybody had the Gaelic. All except the children in the school. They had it when they went in but hadn't it when they came out . . ."

Just then a long blare of a motor car horn came from outside.

"What's that?" said Mr Maclennan with a start turning to Mr MacKenzie who had come out from behind his shoulder and was standing now at his left hand, facing Mr MacRury.

"That's Roddy," said Mr MacKenzie. "He'll be in a hurry."

"The driver?" Mr Maclennan's eyebrows rose upon him. He seemed about to comment, then "Good heavens!" he muttered in private remark and made a shifting with his feet—again with a suggestion of shakiness—preparatory to going out. Mr MacKenzie had already turned and preceded him.

"Oh well," said Mr Maclennan, recalling something and turning back. "Do we understand you agree to all this, Ewen?"

"I will go away," said Mr MacRury, pausing when the other paused, smiling, with the air of pleasantly conceding something: still to an acute observation seeming to have some private thought in mind.

"That's all right then." Mr Maclennan, who was not an acute observer, turned and passed with his kindly, military bearing through the doorway.

"Yes," he said in another tone, looking over his left shoulder just as he prepared to descend the stairs, "Peter and I are twins. When we were young we were very like each other. People had great difficulty . . ."—he gave a sort of giggle—"in fact I believe there is some doubt . . . *I* may be Peter and he may be Norman!" He looked partly over his right shoulder now, half-way down the stairs. "Yes . . ."—with another giggle—"my father used to say, 'Peter! are you Norman?' "

Stout Mr MacKenzie on the bottom step at the foot of the stair rolled his china-blue protruding eyes up towards Mr MacRury coming down at Mr Maclennan's back, expressively, meaningly, and Mr MacRury remembered his voice saying, "He's getting on, you know, Norman." Then they were in the hall, the porch. Mr Maclennan put on his hat with grave dignity and they set off for the gate, Mr MacKenzie settling his rather battered hat—it seemed to be of a small size, and so old as to be almost green—on his head with a casual twitch, Mr MacRury in the middle.

The three of them went towards the gate side by side with slow, skating steps, the gravel screaming and sliding under their feet. Mr MacRury was bare-headed, and the middle one in height as well as position. On his left Mr MacKenzie's knees had the appearance of being more bent forward than usual, indeed he almost looked at times as if he would come down, for, the toes of his boots being directed downwards by his thick superimposed rubber heels, his feet were being checked and held at each step by the gravel.

"Well, then, you'll get away as soon as you can," said Mr Maclennan, on his right. "It can't be too soon . . . Let Aulay MacAulay know where you are. He'll keep you informed about everything . . ."

"You've a good friend there," cried Mr MacKenzie on his left, in his cracked voice, all three skating on . . . "in old Aulay."

Their voices were just a little too clear; pitched above the screeching of the gravel: the driver could be seen hitching himself up alertly in his seat, it may have been merely to get ready to start up and drive off. But the engine didn't start till after they had gone all three through the clicking, iron, breast-high gate and were on the white road—not indeed till they had passed behind the car and Mr Maclennan was opening the door to the back seat. At that time Mr MacKenzie had taken Mr MacRury by the elbow and was saying in a too loud impressive hiss, "Ye'd be better to give it up altogether!"—this with a wink.

"Yes," agreed Mr MacRury, smiling and shaking hands as Mr MacKenzie got in after Mr Maclennan.

He noticed that Roddy the driver was looking at

him. Holding the snout of his bonnet and with an air of willing deference giving him an inexpressibly humane and charming smile, "Good evening, Mr MacRury. A beautiful evening!"

"Beautiful evening, Roddy," he said with a personal kindness melting in his voice, but the latter part of the remark was cut off by a sudden vicious roaring forth of the engine. An uncompromising stench of filthy smoke billowed on the air.

Mr Maclennan's grey, dry hand was extended towards him, without words, out of the interior, and for a fraction of a second he felt its nervous pressure. Then he had barely time to give a gesture of farewell when the two old innocents sitting side by side were jerked past and swept away to his right towards Drum. And he was left standing beside a dark, oily stain on the sandy surface of the road, a smile still on his face.